IMMORTAL PREY

by

DIANA BALLEW

TRIFECTA PUBLISHING HOUSE

To Ariana

Thou wast not born for death, immortal Bird!
No hungry generations tread thee down;
The voice I hear this passing night was heard
In ancient days by emperor and clown:

— John Keats, "Ode to a Nightingale"

A Note From The Author

I began this book with one particular thought in mind: I wanted to write an emotional, fiery tale of eternal love, woven within the fabric of true historic events and legends of the paranormal. *Immortal Prey* is based on documented events.

In 1589, Bedburg, Germany, Peter Stumpp, a wealthy farmer who had made pact with the devil, was tried and found guilty for committing rapes and murders after transforming into the body of a large, bloodthirsty wolf. Under the threat of torture, he confessed to killing and eating fourteen children, one of which was his own son, whose brain he had devoured, two pregnant women and their fetuses, and feasting on a countless number of men.

His execution is one of the most inhumane on record. Immediately following Peter's horrific death, local authorities erected a pole with the torture wheel with the figure of a wolf on it as a warning to others. Peter's head was placed atop the pole. After his trial and death, Peter Strubbe was nicknamed "The Beast of Bedburg".

A sixteen page pamphlet describing the events was translated from German to English in 1590. All that remains now are two copies in London. One is in the British Museum, the other copy, in the Lambeth Palace Library.

In the mountains of south-central France, The Beasts of Gévaudan were first reported in 1764. Known as *Le Loup Garou*, the large, red-furred wolves were believed to have attacked 210 humans. 113 of the victims died, 49 survived their injuries. Of the dead, 98 and been partially eaten. Dispatched by the king, royal huntsman, nobles, the army and civilians, hunted the animals for years. According to records, a particularly large wolf was shot by François Antoine on 21 September 1765 and displayed at the court of King Louis XV.

Enjoy!

Immortal
Prey

PART ONE
THE CHOSEN

Chapter One

"When the Angel of Death calls thy name, do not answer." Those were the last words I spoke before I took her first life.

A hunter's moon sliced through the trees, illuminating the leaves on the damp forest floor. My head filled with the peppery scents of wet pine bark, hemlock, and alder. Adjusting the bow and quiver over my shoulder, I hoisted the heavy sack of pheasant and rabbit and headed for home. Gray vapor curled in front of my face with each breath, vanishing among the low-hanging branches of evergreen.

The moment I stepped into the meadow, moonlight blanketed my house and the gray smoke rising above the stone chimney. Ersule stood at the window. Candlelight wavered above the sill, bathing her face in a seductive glow. Her ebony hair shimmered in the soft light, reminiscent of the gleaming wings of a raven in the bright light of midday. Distracted, my mind set solely upon my lovely wife, I tripped and fell.

The canvas sack and bow flopped to the dirt with a dull thud, and a coppery scent blasted into my nostrils. I jerked my fingers from the dark, sticky substance on the ground. Focusing on the object lying next to me, my heart skipped a beat with recognition. Not more than a hand's breadth from my bearded chin lay a severed human arm.

Scanning the shadows, I scrambled to my feet, recalling it was only a fortnight ago when the wolves had last attacked. I stuffed the spilled carcasses into the bag, seized my bow and quiver, and sprinted for home.

Something unfamiliar lying on the ground ahead made the small hairs at my nape stand on end. Moving closer, my pounding heart suddenly ceased only to resume moments later with an enormous thud against my chest.

"Oh, Lord," I breathed, leaning over the severed human leg, glistening with fresh blood and pearly-white sinew.

An icy howl of wind rushed across the sweeping field. In a blast of feathers, a shrieking owl fled the ghostlike branch of a swaying birch, followed by a sickening scream coming from the dark woodlands to the north.

Listening closely, I spun around, my throat tightening. Again, I heard the screaming. I dropped the brimming sack of freshly-killed game and fled toward the horrifying echoes.

Darting through the lengthening shadows, I readied my bow with the last blunt arrow used for small prey and moved guardedly into the dense woods.

Dense autumn fog surrounded the heavy bottoms of tree trunks, hovering over the trickling creek-bed and swamps. With each advancing step, frosted twigs snapped in my face. Low-lying thickets chewed my ankles, and wiry thorn bushes clawed my trousers, shredding flesh.

A sliver of moonlight angled through the fanning treetops, illuminating the opaque mist surrounding my feet. Something stirred behind me.

I froze.

Ever so slowly, I turned around, and my throat went dry as brittle bone.

A terrifying creature of immense size stood before me. Made

of rippling muscles and fur, the beast hunkered down like a massive dog on all fours. Thick, curled nails gripped the damp earth, and the monster's eyes burned bright as an amber sun. Within its large jaws, a woman's shredded torso hung between gleaming blade-like fangs.

Chilled breath caught in my lungs, and my chest tightened with a vise grip. Moonlight flickered through the bending treetops, bright as a beacon, urging me forward.

From somewhere deep inside my bones, I found the courage to confront the fearsome beast. I pulled the hemp string taut on the bow, held my breath, and pointed the arrow directly at the creature.

"Release her!" I shouted.

In one fluid move, the beast dropped the mangled prey, pounced on massive paws, and landed directly in front of me. Meager distance stood between us, but terror filled the empty space between.

As though mocking me, the beast dipped its large head and touched its snout to the dulled tip of my drawn arrow.

Images of my youth flashed behind my eyes, flickering like shooting stars in the heavens; fleeting mental pictures of my old home and family, of Ersule, of our life together. The visions passed so swiftly, I slammed my eyes shut to keep them from fading.

Ersule. A rush of heat swept through my limbs. I opened my eyes.

The creature crouched low, narrowing eyes boring into mine like molten iron burning snow. Drenched fangs dripped fresh blood upon the ground, and the vile, dizzying stench of animal breath and gore wafted up my nostrils. My fingers twitched, and the creature growled and lunged forward.

A large paw slammed into my chest, the massive blow sending me crashing to the ground on my back. The creature rose over me, its hideous face in mine, feral loins poised to attack. I fought with balled fists, hitting hard and knocking the beast about its pointed ears and head. Fur coated my tongue, and the wild animal scent scorched my nostrils.

Then the monster bit into my neck.

Gray blasts of labored breath rose above me as I cried out in excruciating pain. It came down upon me again, sharp teeth piercing my shoulder. Within seconds, life drained from my limp body in a flood of moist warmth.

Scraping my fingers across the forest floor, I felt a lichen-covered branch amid damp ferns. With my vigor all but gone, I wrapped my hand around the wood and cried out with all I had left, "To the fires of hell *shall you go!*" and hit the beast as hard as I could with one solid blow to its massive skull.

A harrowing yelp pierced the night. Birds fluttered from treetops, shrieking wildly as they fled. The creature pulled away and stared down at my body as I struggled for breath.

The image before me blurred. I blinked once, twice, unsure of what I was witnessing. Lying on the ground with my body and soul resigned and given up to God, I whispered a prayer and watched as the beast's thick fur shortened until it completely disappeared beneath pale skin.

"Dear God … " I murmured, repeating the prayer.

The creature's male genitals came into view beneath the wavering moonlight defying the thick canopy of evergreens above. Pale hair emerged on his skull and grew long, covering his broad shoulders like a blanket of corn silk. His massive muscles smoothed to a soft, rippled sheen, and the fangs and ears receded as though they had never been there at all.

The man-beast placed his hands on his hips and slowly arched his back. He moaned as bones crackled and crunched as if snapping back into place. Craning his long neck, he thrust his shoulders back, and his lean, naked body suddenly stood straight as one of my arrows.

"Lord in heaven," I whispered.

He lifted his face to the gleaming light above, rubbing his head where I had struck him.

Transfixed, my jagged breathing slowed. By all appearances, what stood before me was a man no different a creature from myself.

I slowly rolled to my side, coughing up fur, and I heard him laugh quietly at my misery. Weak and bewildered, I whispered the only thought that came to mind. "How is it possible you are both man … and beast?"

The imposing man held his chin high as he slowly stepped forward. He cocked his head, assessing me as though I were a hog before slaughter.

"How is it you are not afraid of what you have seen?" he asked.

Dizziness seized me, and my stomach turned as if maggots roamed inside my gullet. "I am afraid." I gripped my belly and gradually sat up. "Whatever you are, go now and leave me in peace. I want no trouble." The taste of his feral fur sat wedged inside my throat like a loaf of stale bread. Again, I coughed and spat on the ground.

Undaunted by his nakedness, he sat on a fallen log spread wide across the forest floor and stared at me.

"You have no idea what you have awakened," he said. "What is your name? How old are you?"

I furrowed my brow at the absurdity of the questions under such circumstance. "I am eight and twenty years."

"And your name?"

"Rudliff." I sighed heavily. "I am Derek Ulrich Rudliff."

A slight smile tipped the corners of his thin lips. "That's quite the mouthful. Do you wish to know how old I am?"

"No," I managed to choke out. "Hell no." Gripping my churning belly, I narrowed my gaze and glared at the naked man-beast who had nearly killed me only minutes earlier.

Under the soft glow of moonlight, small shadowy lines etched his pale forehead. He cleared his throat and jutted his chin out. "How are your wounds?"

I felt for the open wounds on my neck and shoulder but found no evidence of my injuries, nor did I feel any sense of pain. I gasped. "How … how can this be? Who are you — *what are you?*"

"My name is Koenig," he said, "and I am over two thousand years of age."

"Two thousand?" I snorted and shook my head. "Absurd."

Pale eyebrows rose high. "More absurd than a man-beast?"

'Tis a valid point.

I slowly stood and brushed the wet leaves and dirt from my tattered trousers, stunned I no longer felt the effects of the brutal attack.

Koenig arched his neck, his nostrils flaring, expelling swirls of vapor into the cool air. "Upon you I detect the scent of a woman. The moon is still high, and I have yet to satisfy my hunger. Take me to her."

"Are you mad? I … I will *not*. I would rather die than take you to my wife!"

Koenig's expressive eyes softened, the furrow between his brows disappearing. He slowly shook his head. "What you do not understand, young Derek, is that by the full rise of the morrow's moon you will be mortal no longer, and your woman as you know her now will matter naught."

The muscles along my jawline throbbed. "It's you that does not understand. My wife is my essence. She is my *life*. I will never, *ever* —"

"Take me to her." Koenig stepped forward and glared at me. "I insist."

Icy fingers of panic crept along my spin. I lifted my chin. "Do with me what you will, but please, spare my wife."

"Is it a deal you ask of me — a bargain? Is that what I am

hearing?" He stroked his chin with long, nimble fingers and slowly paced around me.

Tears stung the back of my eye sockets. "Yes, a bargain. Take *me*. I will do whatever you ask as long as you do not touch her. What must I do to appease you?"

Koenig's tongue darted out, moistening his lips. " 'Tis ancient warrior blood I taste in your veins. For this, I must spare you, but your wife —"

"Do not spare me if you are to take the life of Ersule. Take me, but spare her." I moved in with balled fists. "I am prepared to fight for her!"

He looked at me as though I were no greater threat than a common fly and said, "I admire your courage, but … "

I frowned. "But *what?*"

He sniffed the air, his nose held high, facing in the direction of my home.

"But if I do not take her, then you must. And if you choose not to kill her, I promise, I shall slay her myself, but not before I ravish her first."

Eyeing him from head to toe, I snorted with disgust. "Why? Why would you do such a vile thing?"

"I do not expect you to understand. Not yet."

He was serious. Deadly serious. I lowered my hands to my sides, my shoulders curling. "I beg of you —"

"Do not beg!" he shouted. "It is beneath you. You are *Werewolf* now."

With those words, my heart sank like a rock in water.

He glanced at the gleaming moon before his penetrating gaze fixed upon mine once again.

"You have been bitten by a royal, bitten by a *Were* king, no less."

I lunged forward. "It's not possible!"

He caught my arms and held me tight. " 'Tis more than possible.

Have you forgotten what you have witnessed this night? There is no fighting this, young Derek!"

His terrifying words rebounded across thick trunks of trees, echoing in all directions, sending night creatures scurrying to safety amid low-lying brush.

I stood motionless, paralyzed with fear and dread, his lean arms enveloping me like a cold blanket.

"Listen to me," said he. "Had it not been for the blood running through your veins, I would have devoured you on the forest floor and taken your wife by now."

I raised my chin, my eyes glaring into his. Between gritted teeth I asked, "And what has stopped you?"

Koenig's expression softened under the subtle glow of moonlight. He sighed, unbound my arms, and stepped back.

"I have my reasons."

"My God, what reasons could you possibly have? Tell me."

Koenig inhaled loudly, deeply, and exhaled in slow, shallow breaths. "With the rise of the morrow's moon, your transformation will begin from man to the beast known as *Werewolf*—"

"No, no." I shook my head. "This cannot be true."

" 'Tis true, Derek," he said evenly. "You must wait for the transformation. Before the end of the morrow's moon, you must sink your teeth into the neck of your beloved. You must drain her until her veins run dry."

"I cannot. I will not." I covered my ears. "I will hear none of this!"

Koenig boxed my hands from my ears in a flash as though I were an insolent child. I froze, willing myself not to cower before him.

"I am offering you a choice. This is a great honor among our kind. You must do this if you wish to reunite with your wife again." He hemmed in closer. "Listen. You must drain her blood until you feel her veins run dry," he repeated. "It will be unbearably hard, for you will be tempted as an emerging *Were* to eat her flesh, to rip her to shreds and devour her whole, but you cannot. *You must not.* In return, you shall be rewarded."

I dropped my chin upon my chest, my shoulders wilting. Every part of my body told me the man-beast spoke the truth. Already, something inside me felt different, as though I were unwell with fever, but somehow stronger, more alive with the surge of warmth surging through my limbs.

He dipped his head and placed his hands upon my curled shoulders. I looked at him with eyes brimming with tears, needing his compassion, but I could not speak.

"Here me," he said in a voice barely above a whisper. "I know this is difficult, but in the end there *is* a great reward. Your wife shall return to this earth as a mortal in three hundred years, perhaps a few more, perhaps a few less —"

"Three hundred years!" I jerked from his grasp and spat at his feet. "I cannot do this. I will *not.*"

"I am offering you a choice. You may roam this world without your beloved mate, or you can do as I have told you and wait for her return." He shrugged. "The choice is yours."

"Certainly you do not expect me to understand."

He tilted his chin, examining me from head to shoe tip.

I thrust my chest forward. "Why do you look at me in such a manner?"

A lean finger wiped the last of my blood from his chin.

"I am amazed at my great fortune tonight."

"Great *fortune?*" I scoffed. How in God's heavenly name could he say such a thing? I fought back stinging tears, threatening to surface.

"You will understand, I promise. After you kill your wife, you will wait for her rebirth. You will know the instant she is reborn. From the moment she enters this world again as an infant, you will sense her whereabouts at all times. Her scent will cross great mountains, oceans, and continents. And while you may lie in wait to reclaim her, you may not do so until she has reached the age when you took her life."

My head pounded as though a mallet were striking my weary brain with each word he spoke. I swallowed hard, demanding the screams forming inside my throat cease.

He studied my face. "How old was your wife at her last birthday?"

My mind racing in every direction possible, I raked my hands forcefully through my hair. "It was only a week ago. She turned three and twenty."

"Any children?"

I sighed and lowered my head. "No."

"And so it shall be. You will wait until she has reached three and twenty, and then you must win her once again."

My sweet young wife, to die at such a young age and by the hand of her husband? *Such an unspeakable nightmare.*

"Look at me, Derek."

I forced myself to look into his eyes.

Koenig raised a slender finger. "When she returns to the human world again, she will have no memory of you. She will be drawn to you for reasons she does not understand, but you will have to fight for her and win her love once again."

I laughed hideously, in a tone I didn't recognize as my own. "Ah, but you are wrong. Ersule could never forget who I am, not in this life *or* the next."

Moisture formed in the corners of Koenig's eyes. "You will be up against many odds, Derek. This is a harsh world. Beware. You have heard of wolves among sheep. The opposite is true, as well. Watch for sheep among wolves, for they can be just as deadly." His gaze narrowed. "Above all else, you must never forget you are man and wolf. My royal line has merged with your warrior blood, and I have allowed you to live. From this day forward, you will be a noble among wolves."

Warm tears sliced my chilled cheeks. "I am *no* warrior." I bounded toward the comforts of home and yelled into the darkness, "It is not true — none of this is true!" But as my veins pulsed with the rhythm of an ancient tribal drum, I knew, deep within my soul, Koenig spoke the truth.

"There is no fighting this!" he called into the darkness.

I refused to turn around as I ran home, for I heard the terrifying sounds behind me of the man-beast transforming once again, howling like a great wolf in the shadowy forest.

I made a dash for the creek and washed the sticky blood from my face, neck and shoulders. When I reached home, I paused before opening the door. Crouched over, hands upon buckling knees, trying to catch my breath, I heard my hound growling behind the door, inside the house.

"What is it, *Hund?*" Ersule asked the hound. I rose up, stiffened my spine, and thrust open the door.

Ersule sat crouched by the fire stirring the cauldron and smiled. "Ah, you are later than I expected. I was afraid something might have befallen you." She smiled. "Sit. I have prepared a meal."

My wet tunic stuck to my skin and smelled of blood and creek water and God only knows what else. "One moment, my love," I said, walking swiftly to the bedside.

Hund followed me, sniffing at my heels, his ears flattened. I reached down to pat him. He yelped and his tail drooped, arcing between his trembling legs as he cowered like a newborn lamb to the floor. I frowned at his strange behavior and promptly changed into clean garments before my wife came to investigate.

Ersule rose from the fire and walked toward the hound and me. She placed her hands on her hips and stared down at the mangy beast.

"*Hund*, what troubles you?"

I swept my wife into my arms and hugged her close to my chest. I buried my nose against her head and breathed in the sweet scent of her freshly washed hair, hinting of rose water. I wanted to shout, to cry, to tell her of my plight, but words would not form.

"You smell of the damp woods tonight." She pulled away, holding my hands at arm's length. "Come sit. I have cooked us a delicious rabbit."

Ersule led me by the hand to my chair at the small table and served me a plate of stewed rabbit and a tankard of ale. Numb, disoriented, lost within my own body, I grew instantly famished by the smell of freshly cooked meat wafting into my nostrils.

"You seem especially hungry tonight." She sauntered behind me and wrapped her arms around my shoulders. Nuzzling the nape of my neck, she asked in the spiciest of tones, "Perhaps it's not only food you desire?"

I stuffed a wedge of warm bread in my mouth to silence the scream forming inside my throat. I patted her arm, avoiding her gaze, and guzzled two warm tankards of ale while she left to freshen herself.

My heart burned with sorrow. If the man-beast spoke the truth, by the end of tomorrow, my wife would be dead.

A sudden flush of fever surged through my limbs. I desired Ersule, craved her more than anything in the world. Her warmth. Her touch.

Her love.

She had lit a candle next to our bed and lay waiting under the quilts, gazing at me with eyes like smoldering emeralds.

"Is something troubling you tonight?" she asked.

I unclothed myself and slid into bed next to her. Unable to meet her inquisitive gaze, I pulled her head against my chest. "No trouble, my love."

Ersule flinched. "You're burning hot. Are you not well?"

Fever. But not from the horrendous, dreaded epidemic, I assured her. I lied and told her a simple ague had set upon me from my long day in the fields in the damp cold of outdoors.

She eyed me with suspicion, smiled impishly, then snuggled closer. "It must be fever. Your eyes are a deeper shade of blue tonight."

Ersule's cool body against mine sent warm blood hurling through my veins, forcing my heart into a frenzied dance inside my chest. Muscles tightened; my groin heated, and I instantly grew rock hard. I exhaled in jagged breaths as I slid my hand along the gentle curve of her waist, working my way up to her full breasts. Relishing the feel of her soft nipple pebbling against my palm, my breath hitched deep within my throat as I turned to face her.

She breathed against my throat. "I missed you today."

"I love you, Ersule. I will always love you."

"And I you, my love," she whispered.

I slid my hand down the small of her back, memorizing her soft skin against each callused fingertip. Trailing my fingers across her smooth buttocks, I found my way to the plush center between her warm thighs.

With a touch as light as a cloud, she brushed her fingers along my shaft, and I instantly quivered.

I gently slid a finger inside, readying her, and climbed above. I looked deeply into her arresting gaze, committing to memory the green eyes framed by lashes as fine as ebony lace, and thrust myself within her depths.

I gripped her bottom, plunging deeper, nuzzling her supple neck she so generously exposed for me. Tears welled in my eyes. "You are my life," I managed to whisper.

"And I'll love you for all eternity," she breathed against my throat.

For all eternity! My heart soared when I heard those words from her sweet lips. Surely, this was proof that Koenig was mistaken. My Ersule would always love me — *love me* — for all eternity, for she had said so herself.

Chapter Two

Erin pressed her back against the upholstered chair and laced her fingers across her lap. "Father, I'd like to speak to you about —"

The new employee poked his head inside the office door. "Excuse me, sir. Do you want me to go ahead and cover last night's shooting on Hewitt Avenue?"

Edward Richland frowned as he contemplated the question. "Yes. Yes, go ahead and cover that one, too, David."

"Right, sir. I'm on it."

Edward nudged his wire-rim glasses upward and busied himself at his desk with pen and paper, clearly ignoring his daughter's determined glare.

"Father?" Erin asked, tapping the toe of her shoe on the floor. Regardless of the excuse her father would undoubtedly furnish, she intended to plant herself in his office until her position was made clear.

"Mmm hmm."

"Father, I'm *talking* to you."

He peered over the edge of his glasses. "And what's with that tone?"

She heaved a sigh. "You know what I want. How many times must I ask?"

He removed his glasses, placed them on the desk in the designated spot, and rubbed his thick eyebrows. "Erin, we've been through this a dozen times."

A slice of autumn sunlight slanted through the window, illuminating the colorful braided rug near her feet. She rose from the chair and paced to the large window facing the snowcapped Olympic Mountains beyond the bay.

"I'm tired of these trivial pieces you've been sending my way." She pressed her forehead to the cool glass and sighed, fogging up the window. "A cow wandering into McGinty Hardware — please, that's *not* news."

Her father's usual pessimistic retort did not come as expected. The contemplative pause filled the small office.

She smiled and turned toward him. "I hear all the papers in the county have women on staff now. For heaven's sake, Father, Missouri Hanna herself started the *Edmonds Review* and look at her now with her *Votes for Women* magazine. Do you really want to be a man behind the times?"

He inched his chair away from the desk and stood next to her. "Seems these women's suffrage rallies have put a lot in your head."

Erin smoothed an errant ebony tendril back into place and glared into her father's eyes. "Nothing's been 'put in my head.' I attend the meetings and rallies, yes, but that's because I choose to do so. I'm for the women's vote because it's right and just. Our voices need to be heard, just as much as a man's does."

He rolled his eyes heavenward. "My daughter, the suffragist. What next?"

She closed her eyes and rubbed her throbbing temples. "Why must we constantly go back and forth about this?"

"Is this what you want? *A career?* Does it mean that much to you?"

She opened her eyes and studied the deep lines traversing his forehead. Clearly, he had her best interests at heart, but his outdated misgivings about a woman's place in a man's world irritated her.

"It does mean that much to me. You *know* it does. Why did you send me to the university if you had no desire to see me succeed? You know I can work as hard as your male employees and do just as good, if not better, work." She resisted the urge to jerk away when he placed his hands upon her shoulders.

"You know why I sent you back to New York. Getting you out of Everett was the best thing I could do for you at the time, considering —"

"I know. You're right about that." She slipped away and gazed out at the foam-covered waves greeting the rocky shore below. "I'm not disagreeing. Leaving here was for the best. But I'm back now, and I wish to work. But not if it means you'll only send me on simpleminded pieces. At least rotate me in with the men on important news."

Her father opened his mouth to speak, paused, then said, "Are you sure you don't want to find a successful husband, settle down, and have children? Most women your age are content with such a life."

"Father, do stop. Haven't you realized I'm not like most women?"

He gazed out the window. "Of course I've noticed. You've been blessed with your mother's beauty and an air of sophistication beyond your years." He shook his head and sighed. "But you have a restless temperament."

A restless temperament.

Erin struggled to keep from blurting the words forming in her throat. If yearning for more than the usual trappings of marriage that befell most females her age was considered restless, then yes, he was right. Women like her, desiring a career and to make it in the world on their own rather than disappear into domestic oblivion, were often frowned upon, considered impudent and selfish by much of polite society. It was a constant uphill battle with conventional men, and even some women, for that matter, but it was a fight she was determined to win.

"Well, you're very old-fashioned, Father. Just because you married Mother when she was eighteen doesn't mean I'm a spinster at the ripe old age of twenty-three."

She didn't wish to rock the boat with him, but standing her ground on this matter was important. She had already offended him the week before after refusing his offer to throw a grand party for her birthday, where he had planned to invite the "finest eligible bachelors" Everett had to offer. Wanting no part in his last-ditch attempt to marry her off, she refused with a resounding "absolutely not," causing a heated grimace in reply, but it was he who was behind the times, not she.

"Sometimes I'm at a loss for words with you." He sank in his chair, placed his glasses back on his thick nose with a flick of his finger, and thumbed through a stack of papers on the desk. Exhaling heavily, he said, "All right. Have a seat."

"Seriously?" She dropped in the chair in front of him and leaned forward. "What do you have for me?"

"David's already on top of the shooting." He examined a piece of paper then extended it across the desk. "Here are the possibilities for today. Take your pick."

"Take … *my pick?*"

"That's what I said. Take your pick." A single bushy eyebrow rose above the wire rims. "But I'm agreeing to this on a temporary basis, and we'll see how you do."

Before he had time to change his mind, Erin snatched the papers he extended and examined them. *Let's see:* Fire at Kennedy residence on Hoyt. *That's sad.* Loose pigs from Baylor farm seen swimming in the slough. *So what?* Everett Elks hold fundraiser. *More of the same.* Wolf prints spotted at Evergreen Cemetery, graves disturbed. Vandals paint bridge. *Wait. What was that? Go back.*

Wolf prints spotted at Evergreen Cemetery, graves disturbed.

She pointed at the paper. "I'll take this one."

He leaned across the desk and examined her choice, his brows knitting together. "Are you sure? It's cold around there — lots of walking, not to mention possible wolves."

"I'll be fine! I —"

"All right." He raised his hands and smiled. "No need to bite my head off."

She folded the notes, stuffed them into her leather satchel, and kissed his ruddy cheek. "I'm on it. You won't regret this."

A gentle mist fell from the steel-gray sky. Erin was glad she had chosen to wear her leather boots to the cemetery as she sidestepped the copious puddles. While gloomy weather often kept citizens indoors cozied up by a warm fire, she tended to be just the opposite.

Arriving in the bustling mill town when her father founded the local newspaper, *The Everett Messenger,* the new surroundings had taken some getting used to. Accustomed to the vibrant metropolis of New York, the budding young city of Everett, Washington, with its fertile farmlands, abundant timber, and constant clamor of buzzing sawmills, felt as far from civilized society as one could get. She hadn't realized just how much she enjoyed the cool, marine weather of Washington until she had gone back to New York for her studies.

The East, with its sweltering summers and freezing snow had grown tiresome and predictable. And as each college term blended into the next, she had longed for the biting winds sweeping across Port Gardner Bay, chilling her face; missed the scents of lush green ferns growing in damp earth below overgrown fir and cedar trees humming an ancient tune as she walked below. Yes, the Pacific Northwest had grown on her.

As she approached her mother's graveside, she noticed the small granite tombstone had acquired a hefty dose of moss within the engraved rock since her last visit. She bent low, holding the flowers she had purchased earlier, and laid the fragrant bundle at the foot of the headstone.

Ella Mae Richland. Loving wife and mother.

She traced the etchings with her gloved fingertip, scooping out the green lace clinging to the carved stone. Glancing around the grounds, she noted the cemetery appeared nearly deserted. At the entrance, an elderly couple exited the grounds. In the distance, a figure stood near the large pyramid-shaped Rucker Tomb on the hill above.

She examined her notes. *Now where are the wolf prints?*

She followed the directions, leading her to a section of freshly-dug, unmarked graves piled high with loose brown dirt.

"It's a dang soggy mess today, ain't it?"

Erin spun around and came face-to-face with the disheveled cemetery caretaker. "Oh, you surprised me. Thank you for meeting me, Mr. Avery." She pulled a notepad and pen from her satchel. "What can you tell me?"

He scrunched his nose and scuffed his boot in the moist dirt. "Well, this ain't the only time I've found wolf tracks, mind you, but it's the first time they got into graves."

"Coyotes, bobcat, it could be anything besides wolves, don't you think?"

He snorted. "Oh, no, Miss. It's wolves all right. Come take a gander at this."

She followed as he walked over a section of inlaid headstones several yards away from the path.

He stopped, crouched low, and pointed. "See, they start here. These ain't no coyote or bobcat — these here are wolf prints, and big ones at that."

Erin hiked up her skirt a few inches and bent down. She inserted her entire hand within the paw print and still had room to spare. "My goodness."

He cocked his head south. "I think they come in through them thick woods."

She turned, surveying the well-kept grounds. "And the disturbed graves are where?"

"Back on over here. Now, watch the mud, Miss."

She followed behind him.

He called over his shoulder, "When I came out this morning and saw the tracks, I followed them. Took me here."

He stopped abruptly and Erin nearly bumped into his back. "Inside this grave's a young woman. Died just a few days ago — buried yesterday." He jutted his whiskered chin forward. "I found what was left of her under that maple over yonder."

"What was *left?*" Erin suddenly felt parched as her gaze followed in the direction of his bony finger.

"Yep. She'd been chewed up to pieces. I tossed my breakfast putting her back in the grave and filling the dirt back in." He grimaced and quietly said, "Sorry about the gruesome details."

The contents of her stomach curdled. "So, what you're telling me is that the wolf, or *wolves,* dug her body out of the ground and … ate her?"

"That's exactly what I'm saying. Only it wasn't just her — there are two more. All buried within the last three days."

She noticed three large mounds piled high with fresh, brown dirt. "What about the caskets? How could they get through those?"

"Metal caskets seem to be safe. Looks like it's the plain wood ones they can sniff out and claw and chew their way through. All of them dug up corpses were six feet under in simple pine boxes."

"Wouldn't that be hard for a single wolf to do? Have you seen more than one? A pack, perhaps?"

Mr. Avery's thin lips twisted with contemplation. "I can't rightly say for sure. I know I've seen one wolf, a big one, and I think it's the same one each time." He rubbed his nose and coughed. "But there've been a night or two when I had a little too much fun down at the saloon. I thought I saw more than one on them nights. Was the beer, I told myself, but now I wonder. Still, this is the first time around here wild animals have taken to diggin' up and eating the dead."

Dizzying nausea threatened. Erin drew a cotton handkerchief from her pocket and held it to her nose. "Thank you for your time, Mr. Avery. If you don't mind, I'd … I'd like to walk around the grounds and take notes for the newspaper."

The darkly clad figure she had spotted earlier came into view near the Rucker Tomb. It appeared to be a man, a tall man, in a heavy coat or cloak. "By the way, who is that man over there?"

The caretaker spun around. "Huh? What man is that?"

"The man over there by the pyramid." She looked again, but the man was gone.

"Sorry, Miss. Best I can tell, nobody's here right now but us."

Erin glanced again. Sure enough, no one was there. She cleared her throat and forced a smile. "Good grief. I suppose these long days of work must have me seeing things."

A crooked grin spread between the caretaker's lips. He removed his cap and scratched the top of his balding skull with long, yellow fingernails. "I best get on back to work. You take your time and get all you need."

"Thank you kindly for your time, Mr. Avery."

Erin walked the path, looking for missed clues, thinking about the familiar people buried here. William Mescher. He'd requested that his body be entombed in his couch after his death. Her father had sent a clipping of the article to her in New York. Then there was poor Margaret Quinn, shot in the street by her drunken husband.

Her murder had caused quite the scandal as women rallied in support of dry laws, followed by the bungled execution of her husband. There were graves of people she remembered reading about just this past March. The Wellington Avalanche victims. Ninety-six killed. A real tragedy. Worst avalanche in United States history. During a fierce snowstorm, while passengers slept in the rail cars at the depot waiting to get through on the track, the huge avalanche struck without warning.

"A magnificent tomb, don't you agree?"

Erin gasped and spun toward the deep voice.

The tall man wearing a dark coat took unhurried steps toward her. "I'm sorry if I startled you."

Her heart thumped like a drum against her chest. "Sir, I … I didn't know you were there."

"Again, I apologize if I frightened you." He angled his chin toward the tomb, his gaze fixed upon hers. "I've been admiring this granite tomb. It's unique."

"Yes, yes it's quite impressive," she said, finding it hard to regain her composure after such a start.

"I don't believe I've had the pleasure." He held out his hand.

Struck by the intensity of the sapphire blue eyes gazing into hers, she instantly felt off balance as she inched her feet forward and offered her hand. "Erin Richland. I'm … .I'm with the *Everett Messenger.*"

He clasped her hand longer than she deemed appropriate, and she heard the breath hitch within his throat.

"Derek Rudliff. I'm delighted to make your acquaintance."

Where had she heard that name before? "Wait. Rudliff as in *Rudliff Land and Timber?*"

He smiled and released her hand. "Guilty as charged."

"It's a pleasure meeting you, Mr. Rudliff." She surveyed the handsome stranger from head to toe, her gaze pausing at the brilliant smile below a smooth, neatly-trimmed mustache.

My, my. Derek Rudliff. Up until now she had thought the owner of the giant company was nothing more than a phantom, just another investor or corporation from outside Washington State. While she had never laid eyes upon the attractive Mr. Rudliff before today, the name was certainly a familiar one within the city. Names like Hill, Weyerhaeuser, and Rudliff — these were the Northwest's great timber barons, and with their vast land holdings and bustling sawmills along the waters came immense wealth and prestige.

He cocked his head. "And what brings you to a cemetery on such a cool, drizzly day, if I may be so bold to inquire?"

"Oh, yes." She paused, still captivated by the unique shade of his eyes. "I'm working on an article for the newspaper, but I could ask you the same thing."

He smiled and arched an eyebrow. "I must confess, I enjoy cemeteries, day or night."

She frowned. "That's rather macabre, wouldn't you agree?"

"Perhaps."

His eyes narrowed to indigo slits, and her breath instantly caught deep inside her chest. He watched her as though studying every inch of her face, every pore upon her skin, even her every breath. His gaze moved leisurely to her mouth, her throat, settling upon her covered breasts.

He cleared his throat, and his gaze snapped toward the tomb. "You must admit there is beauty in such a piece."

She silently cursed her burning cheeks. "Um, yes. It is beautiful." She joined him at the wall of the thirty-foot tomb and placed her hand upon the cold granite. "This is the Rucker Tomb. Two local men had it built to honor their mother."

He turned to face her, his vibrant gaze holding her in place against the wall like an invisible embrace. Unblinking, she watched as his tongue leisurely moistened his full lips, how the hint of evening stubble accentuated his masculine chiseled facial structure, how —

"And what story would lead you to this cemetery on such a day?"

His question breaking the spell, she blinked and said, "Oh, yes. I'm hunting wolves."

He coughed and fingered his coat collar. "Excuse me? Hunting … *wolves*?"

She smiled. "Well, not actually *hunting* wolves. It's an article — for the newspaper."

A dazzling white smile brightened his face. He dipped his head and leaned toward her, his gaze narrowing. "I'm relieved, Miss Richland. For a moment there I thought I might have to flee for my life."

Erin laughed louder than she had intended, but the man had a way about him that made her deliciously giddy and nervous all at the same time. As was her nature in conditions that felt out of her control, she rambled, saying, "Oh, yes, I can imagine a man of *your* stature must occasionally need to play the part of a wolf. Or, so, I would imagine … in your business dealings, that is."

His eyebrows jumped. "This is true, more than you know."

Her lashes fluttered uncontrollably, and she cast her gaze downward. "And how long do you plan to stay in Everett, Mr. Rudliff?"

A long pause filled the near silence, causing her heart to stop dead in her chest. She peered up, meeting his soulful eyes.

"I hope to stay a good while. You see, the construction on my home here was recently completed."

"Is that so?" She cleared her throat. "I don't believe I've seen you around town, Mr. Rudliff."

The edge of his mustache curled upward, and he took a step forward. "Please, Miss Richland, call me Derek."

A surge of heat rushed across her neck and cheeks. "Ah, yes. And where in Everett do you plan to reside … Derek?"

"My home is on Grand Avenue. I've just recently moved in."

She recalled seeing a lovely home on Grand under construction during the course of the last year. "Is it the new one — the one practically hanging over the cliff overlooking the bay — *that* house?"

He placed a hand in his trouser pocket and cocked his head. "It is. You know of it?"

"Why, who around here doesn't? The house is absolutely beautiful. I'd heard an investor owned it, but I —"

"Then you must come see it, Miss Richland," he interjected, his eyes deepening in color.

He brushed an errant strand of hair from his forehead, and Erin spotted the thick silver ring on his finger.

"In fact, I'm having a party week after next to christen the new place, so to speak. Mostly close friends and associates of mine. Please, say you'll come."

Erin wondered what Frederick would say about the invitation. With her father's incessant prompting, she'd felt obligated to see Frederick on more occasions that she liked since her return to Everett. Frederick Dimsdale tended to be more overprotective than jealous when it came to other men, but something told her that he would be more than envious once he laid eyes upon Derek Rudliff.

"I'll try to be there." Her gaze snapped to the ring again. "Will your wife be there, as well?"

His eyes shifted to the ground, and his broad shoulders curved forward. "My wife … she —"

Erin took a step forward. "Oh, I'm so sorry. I … I didn't mean to pry."

He lifted his chin and met her gaze. "It's all right, Miss Richland." His brow furrowed into a deep ridge. "My wife passed away, but it was long ago."

"I'm sorry for your loss," she said, though her voice barely rose above a whisper.

He studied her in the most unusual manner, as though waiting for her to articulate further. Above them, a black raven perched on a high branch of a cedar tree squawked wildly, magnifying the awkward silence swelling between them.

Derek cleared his throat and checked his pocket watch. "As much as I'd like to stay and talk, I really must be going." He returned the timepiece and stared directly into her eyes. He raised a single eyebrow and smiled. "I'm not a man who compromises the reputation of a lady. I'll send you a formal invitation and escort you to the party myself."

She squared her shoulders and lifted her chin. "I'm a modern woman, Mr. Rudliff. I assure you I go where and when I please. An escort won't be necessary. I'll be there. You can count on it."

"Then I'll send you the details this week." He smiled and bowed in an exaggerated sweeping gesture. "Until we meet again."

"Indeed," she said formally, smiling in return.

He turned to walk away, and a brilliant idea flashed through her mind. "Oh, wait, Mr. Rudliff … I mean, *Derek*. I almost forgot —"

He turned. "Yes?"

"Would it be possible if I arranged for a photograph of you — for the newspaper. I imagine many citizens would be —"

"No. It's not possible." The deep ridge between his brows smoothed. "What I mean is, I prefer no pictures of myself. Privacy is important to me."

Erin blushed and waved her hand. "Yes. Yes, of course. You're right."

The large raven on the branch above screeched and took flight in a sudden blast of glossy, black feathers.

"I'm sorry, but I really must be going, Miss Richland." He nodded formally. "Good day."

THE autumn moon towered high in the sky, and a lace coverlet of fog spread across the water below. From the parlor widow, Erin peered out at the tall ships, schooners, and fishing boats, their lights flickering like tiny floating candles woven into the gray mist.

"Almost time for dinner," Maggie called from the back kitchen.

Erin noticed the dining room had been set for three. "Will someone be joining us this evening?"

Maggie entered the room and placed a crystal wine decanter in the middle of the long walnut table. "Your father's invited Mr. Dimsdale to dine with both of you tonight."

As if on cue, a swift knock rattled the front door. Erin went to answer it, calling over her shoulder to the servant, "I'll get it, Maggie."

She looked out the peephole. Frederick stood on the porch, top hat in one hand and an oversized umbrella in the other. She sighed and opened the door.

"Good evening, Erin. It was kind of you to invite me to dinner tonight."

She cleared her throat and managed a suitable smile. "Come in. Let me take your coat and hat."

Frederick entered and perched his drenched umbrella against the plaster wall in the hallway. He reached into his vest pocket and pulled out an envelope. "I have something here. I wanted you to be the first to see it."

She opened the envelope and pulled out a folded piece of paper. "What's this?"

Frederick's brown eyes gleamed, and his thin lips disappeared as though controlling a wily grin. "You'll see."

She unfolded the paper. It was a signed business agreement showing Mr. Frederick Dimsdale as the new owner of a company.

Frederick twisted the ends of his bristly mustache to waxy points. "You're looking at the new owner of the Northwest Tugboat Company. I have plans to make it the largest fleet in all the Northwest."

Erin patted his arm and hung his coat and hat. "How lovely for you, Frederick. You must be very proud." She gestured for him to have a seat on the parlor sofa.

He stood in place, his brow deeply ridged. "But, I thought you would be —"

"Ah, Frederick, so glad you could make it, my boy," Edward said, descending the staircase from the second floor.

Frederick hastened past her. "Hello, sir." The two men shook hands. "I wouldn't miss an evening with such charming company."

Erin felt Frederick's narrow, predatory eyes seeking hers. She cleared her throat and turned on her toes toward the dinner table. "Shall we, gentleman?"

Maggie lumbered through the swinging door and served bowls of clam chowder and a basket of fresh baked bread. She poured white wine into the crystal glasses before heading back to the kitchen.

Frederick sat and clutched the lapels of his jacket. He thrust his chest forward. "Sir, I was telling Erin that the sale is finally complete. I'm officially the new owner of Northwest Tugboat Company."

"That's delightful, Frederick." Edward eyed his daughter. "Did you hear that, Erin? A proprietor of his own company — and a large one at that. Let's have a toast, shall we?"

They clinked wine glasses, and Edward said, "To Frederick, may your new business venture be prosperous and your life full and rich."

Frederick held his glass up and eyed Erin over the rim. "Hear, hear."

Judging by the lump in her throat, Erin wondered if she were swallowing the entire loaf of bread whole. She sat silent, fidgeting with her cloth napkin under the table while the two men talked at length.

After what felt like an eternity, Maggie removed the soup bowls and returned with plates of stuffed, roasted chicken and vegetables.

"Did you have a chance to tell Frederick the story you're working on for the paper?" asked her father.

"No, no, I haven't." She took an extra-long sip of wine and turned to Frederick. "You see, Father has graciously allowed me additional work at the paper."

"That's lovely. What sort of work?"

"Well." She looked at both men who sat hanging on her every word. "I went to Evergreen Cemetery today working on —"

"That dismal place — what on earth for?" Frederick interrupted, before shoveling a fork-full of chicken in his mouth.

Edward waved his hand dismissively, "Oh, I told her it would be dreary there today with all the mud and rain and Lord knows what else, but you know her, Frederick."

"Both of you, I'm not a child," she said. "There's a story there, a mystery, really, and I find it terribly exciting."

Frederick grunted. "A cemetery? Exciting? Well, I certainly find *that* hard to believe." His thin lips twisted in a smug smirk.

Erin hemmed in closer to the table. "You can poke fun all you want. Apparently, there's a bloodthirsty wolf in the city — perhaps even a pack — and it's not the first time the footprints have been spotted in the cemetery."

"All wolves are bloodthirsty, my dear," Frederick declared.

Erin willed herself not to laugh at his asinine statement. "That's true, I suppose. But it's the first time corpses of the recently buried have been dug up."

Frederick gasped, and his eyes bulged wide. "Dug up?"

Erin's gaze narrowed, and she summoned up her most dramatic persona. "Yes, dug up, ripped to shreds, and then *devoured.*"

Frederick dropped his fork on his plate. The sound echoed across the wood beams of the tall ceiling. He turned to her father. "Pardon me, sir, but you've allowed Erin to romp recklessly through a cemetery with wolves on the loose?"

Edward Richland raised his hands. "This is her choice. I'm tired of fighting with her."

Frederick's gaze snapped to hers. "Erin, this isn't safe. Tell me you're done with the story and moving on to something more —"

She sucked in her cheeks and took a deep breath. "More what, Frederick? More ladylike? More *what* exactly?"

Edward cleared his throat and cocked his head toward the back of the house. Craning his thick neck he called, "Maggie, we need more wine in here!"

Frederick's brows knitted together, and he leaned toward her, whispering, "Perhaps we can discuss this later."

Erin glared back. "Yes, perhaps we should."

"Oh, Erin, I almost forgot," her father said. "David tells me you ran into the elusive Mr. Derek Rudliff. Is this true? I have always wanted —"

Frederick slammed his fist on the table, and his face glowed crimson, quickly turning to purple.

"Oh, my Lord, I think he's choking!" Erin shouted.

Edward shot up and came behind the younger man. With a balled fist, he hit Frederick between the shoulder blades repeatedly, but nothing seemed to be working.

Erin stared into Frederick's face, turning a deeper shade of violet. "Father, he's still choking! Do something!"

Edward growled and hammered harder against the younger man's back. Suddenly, Frederick's entire body stiffened like an iron rod, and he fell backwards in the chair to the hardwood floor. A loud grunt followed, echoing across the room, just as a wedge of potato soared from Frederick's mouth, landing on the center of the dining table with a lifeless thud.

Frederick lay coughing and gasping for air at Erin's feet. She stood over him, hands on her hips. "My heavens, are you all right?"

Frederick growled and looked away. "Yes, I'm fine."

Edward thrust his hands in his thick gray hair and darted for the back of the house calling out, "Perhaps you should lie on the sofa a moment or two, Frederick. I'll get you a fresh glass of water."

Erin helped Frederick up and led him toward the sofa.

He jerked away and smoothed his vest. "I said I'm *fine*."

"My heavens," she murmured under her breath, irritated at his abrupt manner. She tilted her chin high, fanned out her skirt, and sat on the sofa. "Well, it's just that you gave me a fright."

He exhaled in shallow breaths and sat next to her. "I just swallowed wrong, that's all. I'm fine now." A wry smile slowly spread below his shiny mustache. "I must say, it was worth the discomfort to see you fret over me."

He took hold of her hand, his clammy grasp moistening her palm like a tepid wet rag. She shook her head. "Don't be silly. I wasn't fretting. I merely —"

He squeezed her hand and leaned closer. "Now tell me more about this chance meeting. Who did you say it was, a Mr. Rudliff, was it?"

Erin frowned, caught off guard by his interruption and sudden change in demeanor. "Well, all right. Where was I?"

"You said you saw Mr. Rudliff. Derek Rudliff, is that correct?"

"Oh, yes. Yes, Mr. Derek Rudliff. That's him. I wanted to arrange a photograph of him for the paper. Perhaps write a story on the man and his business, but he wasn't the least bit interested."

Frederick's eyes narrowed, and the muscle along his jawline pulsed. "I see. And what did you think of him?"

Careful not to stir up his protective nature, she frowned and waved her hand. "Oh, he was pleasant enough but a *dreadful* bore. Not at all my sort."

Frederick's grip loosened. She seized the opportunity, snatching her hand back in a flash.

The lines on his forehead smoothed to a polished sheen resembling damp clay. He leaned closer, smiled, and whispered, "I can't tell you how happy I am to hear that, my dear."

Chapter Three

Bedburg, 1589

I awoke at the break of dawn praying that what happened in the forest the night before had been nothing more than a horrifying nightmare.

My senses told me otherwise.

As I surveyed the room, my surroundings appeared more vibrant and detailed. I could hear the soft rustle of nature stirring in the forest in the distance; feel the warmth of the rising golden sun upon my body, though no rays of sunlight entered the small room. Somehow, I felt more *alive.*

I looked at Ersule sleeping beside me, and my stomach twisted into a knot so taut I thought I would retch. I gazed at her peaceful slumbering form, amazed that such a beautiful, loving creature was mine — *all mine.* Thinking back to Koenig's words, I sighed heavily. Ersule was my world, and all I desired was to spend any remaining time I had left as a mortal man with the love of my life.

But Ersule had other plans.

"I'm going to the creek to wash clothes today," she said.

My fingers stiffened, and I dropped the spoon in my bowl of porridge. I seized Ersule's hand, keeping her from rising from the chair. I swallowed hard and said, "The early morning chores were particularly demanding today. Perhaps the wash can wait another day."

"Perhaps not," she said, smiling. "Have you seen your clothes of late? With the autumn rains and the grueling harvest there's much to wash —"

"Then I'll go with you," I offered far too quickly. I silently cursed my abruptness, hoping I didn't arouse her perceptive nature. I forced a smile. "We can take a long walk while our clothes dry. Perhaps pack some food and —"

"That's a lovely idea, but … " She rose from her chair, came behind me, and wrapped her lithe arms around my neck.

"But?" I urged, keeping my voice steady.

"*But* you promised me you would go into the village and bring back the flour from the mill."

I patted her hand. "Surely that, too, can wait."

She rested her chin upon my shoulder.

"I truly need it, Derek," she said in a teasing, pouty voice. "Not a bit remains after yesterday's loaves."

Ersule rose up and sauntered past me. My gaze followed the delicate sashay of her willowy hips defying the modest brown skirt and soiled apron.

She crouched by the fire and placed a log among the fading embers. Gazing over her shoulder, she said, "I'll do your wash, you get my flour, and then we'll have time together later. 'Tis a bargain?"

Gazing into her emerald eyes filled with tender love, I was her prisoner. My eyes shifted to the floor. I cleared my throat and whispered, " 'Tis a bargain."

I carried the basket of laundry upon my shoulder as we walked to the nearby creek past the rolling meadow. Ersule's widowed mother and several of the neighboring women had already arrived at the pebbled banks, scrubbing laundry and laying out the wet garments to dry on large rocks and stumps warmed by the sun. I smiled and nodded, joining in the feminine banter, but I remember not a single word I uttered, for the gentle sounds of the natural world had changed, grown louder, sharper, more succinct. I wanted to cover my ears, for the harsh, steady hum surrounding me hurt them.

Ersule busied herself beside her mother on the sun-filled bank with a brush and bar of lye and urged me on my way. "Go on now," she said with an impish glint in her eyes.

With a heart as heavy as the sack of crushed grain I was sent to retrieve, I left her side and hurried toward the village. The sooner I arrived, grabbed the flour and returned, the more time I would have with my wife.

As I neared the village square, I heard a commotion. Following the noise, I came upon a large crowd shouting curses.

I nudged Fritz, the village butcher, and asked, "What's happening?"

Frowning, he mouthed the long-stemmed wooden pipe dangling from his lips and fingered his long beard. "Haven't you heard? The wolves attacked again in the middle of the night. Just this morning, bloodied livestock and human body parts were found in the woods, in meadows, even in garden beds."

My throat went bone dry. "I see," I murmured. I hemmed in closer, my heart twitching like that of a wounded hare. I listened as frightened citizens talked of hunters running into the forest with crossbows and flintlocks, shouting in fury with their bloodhounds on the trail of the ferocious wolves.

Fritz plucked the pipe from his mouth and leaned in. "This is bad. Very bad, indeed."

I forced a nod, excused myself, and headed for the mill. Just as I retrieved the flour and thrust the heavy sack over my shoulder, the miller's elderly wife poked her head inside the door.

She fingered her tattered woolen scarf. "He's coming back!"

The old miller's cloudy-gray eyes widened. "Ah, the boy's returned," said he, before hurrying toward the boisterous crowd with his wife on his heels.

Curious, I followed and made it just in time to see a lad of no more than three and ten emerge from the woods.

Tired and winded, the slender boy brought word that the bloodhounds had finally cornered their prey. He told how the hunters and barking hounds had given chase and come upon a solitary large wolf. As the breathless huntsmen stood with hoisted bows and flintlocks aimed squarely at the creature, the wolf suddenly stood on two legs and removed a belt of thick fur from around its waist. Then, before the huntsmen's eyes, the wolf miraculously transformed into a mortal man.

Demanding answers and reckoning, the panicked crowd erupted into roars and shouts.

While trying to absorb the boy's incredible revelation, I curled my shoulder forward and lowered the sack to the ground. I thrust my hand through my hair, waiting for the hunters to emerge from the forest.

Could this man-wolf the hunters cornered be Koenig?

The time waiting passed swiftly, for my mind raced in a flurry of frightening thoughts and horrid images. Finally, the hunters emerged from the forest. To the crowds' astonishment, as well as my own, the hunters brought forth a neighboring farmer, and a story of unimaginable evil began to unfold.

Peter Strubbe, a man of about forty years and average in every possible way, told of a fondness for blood and black magic from the time he was twelve years of age. He had sold himself to the devil, body, mind, and soul, and the wicked devil made him a promise in return: to bestow upon Peter whatever his twisted heart desired. He declared his wish had been to become a creature capable of satisfying his bloodthirsty desires.

Horrified, I stood in place and listened as he told of dozens of rapes of women and young children, even murders, including his own son, which he committed in the guise of a mighty wolf.

A rush of heated blood pounded in my veins. His words stung

my ears until they burned like fire, and I shook in my shoes with such fear and dread.

Dear God in heaven. What will become of me?

Unable to face Ersule, lest she perceive the consuming terror in my eyes, I placed the flour in the root cellar, made my way to the fields, and busied myself with the hoe and spade. Soon thereafter, a neighbor approached me in the backfield.

"Can you believe it, Derek?" asked he.

I assured him that I had not heard the latest news.

"Ah, the magistrate ordered Peter be bound and laid out on a large wheel. With burning pincers, his flesh is to be *ripped* from his bones. His arms and legs are to be crushed with the blunt end of an axe, and his head chopped off and placed upon the town pole. And, to ensure every speck of evil is eliminated, his carcass will be charred to black ashes."

Bile rose in my throat, and the darkening clouds above seemed to close over my head. If Koenig had spoken the truth, I would undoubtedly face the same fate if caught.

I bid my neighbor farewell and set out on heavy feet to bathe in the lake and gather my wits before returning to Ersule.

Sitting upon a boulder at the water's edge, I watched the ginger glow of the setting sun as it dipped below the horizon. My heart sank as I envisioned my precious wife, gone from my life for three hundred years.

Three. Hundred. Years.

I needed to see Ersule. I needed to touch her, feel her. I needed to know she was *mine*.

With weighted arms, I shook out my garments, dressed, and walked home. Soon I would know if what Koenig spoke was truth or lies.

Ersule greeted me at the door with her customary smile, but her expression instantly turned into a puzzled frown. "Where is the flour?"

The flour! I waved my hand. "Oh, yes, I … I left it in the cellar. I'll get it in the morning."

The hound looked into my eyes, yelped, and darted out the door.

"Come back inside!" I shouted.

Ersule pressed her hand to my arm. "Let him go. He's acted in a disturbed manner most of the day."

She crouched near the fire and placed a skewered chicken above the flames. "Ale?"

Dancing firelight lit the room, sending finger-like shadows clawing at the stone walls. With my head held low, I nodded and removed my shoes.

Ersule whisked them away and laid the shoes by the glowing hearth to dry. "Tonight I would like wine," she said merrily as she proceeded to pour a tankard of ale for me and wine for herself.

I gazed out the small window at the rising silver moon. Instantly, my stomach twisted as I turned toward the other window and watched as the last trace of the glowing sun set below the horizon.

Then I heard the wolves.

"Do … do you hear that?" I asked.

She arched a raven brow. "Hear what, my love?"

"Do you hear the wolves in the forest?"

She tilted her head, listening. "I hear no wolves. Drink your ale. You must be tired."

I was never surer of anything in my life. It was a pack of wolves and they were calling *me.*

With each somber howl from the group, I felt the marrow quiver deep within my bones. I ate heartily, but the more I ate, the hungrier I became; the more I drank, the thirstier. I was thankful Ersule sat enjoying her wine, humming a cheerful ditty, filling her tankard twice more.

She rose from her chair and took my hand in hers. "It's time for you to join me," she said with a playful lilt in her tone.

I gulped the last of my food and washed it down with the remaining ale. I cleaned my face and scrubbed my hands in the bucket.

She dried my hands with the linen cloth, blotted my face, and led me by the hand to our bed. "Come," she whispered.

Guided by the sultry cadence of her words, I found comfort in the familiar play of seduction we had shared since our wedding night. I lay upon our bed, folded my arms behind my head, and watched as she unclothed herself down to her sheer nightdress.

With delicate, unhurried fingers, she pulled the pins from her long hair and sat next to me on the bed. With a smile upon her full lips — the same smile that had melted my wary heart so long ago — she gently removed my socks, then my trousers, undressing me as though I were a helpless child. The deep glow of rising passion grew within her gaze as she ran her hands inside my tunic, fingering the hair on my chest.

I lifted my neck from the pillow as she guided the tunic over my head. "You're a vixen tonight," I said.

"Your vixen," she whispered in a tenor as sweet and spicy as honeyed mead.

She slipped into bed next to me. My hot skin against hers felt like flames scorching satin, causing me to instantly stiffen. The moment she whimpered with yearning, blood charged through my veins, rippling through muscles, surging like errant sparks of fire into my limbs. The chicken carcass, the stale ale, the wine, my sense of smell and hearing, all seemed to grow tenfold. The taste upon my tongue and the slow increase of saliva suddenly intensified.

I flinched and pressed my back into the bedding. The fragrant scent of her hair, the sight of her dusky nipples beneath sheer fabric, the subtle curves of her body, all called to me. And the moment she pressed her lips to mine, I trembled.

The transformation Koenig had spoken of was happening. I could feel it, altering me from the inside out. I slammed my eyes shut and summoned strength to fight the crushing physical urges threatening to overwhelm me.

But the growing wolf clawed inside my belly, begging to emerge.

She guided her hand between my legs. With every ounce of my body and soul, I tried to silence the rising beast, but the creature within took hold in a sudden, violent jolt.

I grabbed a thick strand of Ersule's hair, wrapped it around my hand, and pulled her head back, exposing her bare neck. She moaned, aroused by the intensity of my desire.

In a flash, my hunger for her grew fierce. I stared at my trembling hands and watched in horror as my fingernails grew thick, long, and brown. Spiked hairs thrust forth from my knuckles like blades of dark golden grass.

Ersule shut her eyes as her body gave way to rising passion. With her neck laid bare and only a whisper away from my quivering lips, I salivated, drooling like a mad hound as I stared at the thick cord of blood pulsating inside her neck, *beckoning me.*

"Derek," she murmured. "Such an animal you are tonight."

Such irony!

"Do you love me, Ersule? Tell me you love me and only me." I swallowed hard. My voice had grown deeper with the visceral changes threatening to consume me.

She moistened her full lips. " 'Tis only you I love," she whispered against my neck in a voice as passive as that of a mourning dove.

My thirst for the taste of her flesh was rivaled only by my instinctual desire to take her — to claim her — to keep her mine for all eternity.

I spun her around face down on the bed, and spread her arms wide across the quilt. She yelped playfully, and I was thankful beyond words that she had drunk liberally of the wine.

I cried out as my body tightened and teeth grew within the bone of my clenched jaw. She flinched at the sounds above her and tried to turn, but I pushed my morphing hand down, keeping her head pressed firmly against the bedding.

"Derek!" she whimpered, her voice muffled against the bedding.

"Ahhhh!" I groaned as my limbs swelled into mounds of smooth muscle beneath growing trusses of fur. My hands changed before my eyes into the mighty paws of a wolf.

Ersule's nightdress slid up, exposing her smooth buttocks.

It was more than I could bear.

In one swift move, I grabbed her by the waist and forced her toward me on all fours. She cried out my name, but as the mighty beast within me burst forth, her distressed voice was drowned out by my deep growls of pleasure as I slid inside her. I plunged her sweet depths, repeatedly, sparing my innocent wife no mercy as I continued my fierce ravishing.

But there was nothing, *nothing,* I could do to stop the wild beast raging inside.

After I had my depraved fill, she went limp and flopped face-first against the bedding.

God, help me.

Had I killed her?

She slowly rolled over to face me. I scurried to the side of the bed, growling in a low hum and baring my fanged teeth. Terror dwelled within the emerald gaze fixed upon me, but she didn't flinch or attempt to flee.

My mortal self, body and mind, was slipping away, evolving into a vicious, murderous wolf. I slammed my eyes closed, took deep breaths through flared nostrils, but try as I did with all I had left, I could not fight the emerging beast.

I forced my eyes open and stared at the luminous moonlight slicing through the window. With my world as I had known it all but gone, there was only one thing I knew with certainty: If I were to see my beloved wife ever again, the time had come to seize her life.

Like a young doe before slaughter, she lay quivering, tears welling in her eyes. Her lips trembled as she tried to speak. "It … it is you in there, Derek. I see you in those blue eyes, *your eyes*."

I hovered over her, my eyes fixed upon the artery pounding in a panicked frenzy within her neck, listening to her sweet vocal cords I knew I would crush within my powerful jaws.

With only a fragment of my mortal life left within me, I managed to speak in a voice I barely recognized as my own. "When the Angel of Death calls thy name, do not answer."

I held her down, my brown nails digging into her soft flesh, and sank my sharp teeth into the beautiful pulsing cord upon her neck.

Oh, dear God.

The feel of her warm blood surging into my mouth was surely like sweet nectar to a bee, succulent, luscious, *vital.* The rush of crimson liquid darted across my tongue, consuming me to the point I barely heard her final words.

"Come back to me. Come back to me, Derek."

I groaned like a whelping pup as her lifeblood pulsed against my thick devouring tongue. Small, errant drops dripped down her tender neck, falling like wet rubies upon my golden fur. Every part of my wolf body urged to bite harder, to rip and tear flesh from her bones as she lay dying. But deep in what was left of my mortal mind, I heard Koenig's words, "*You cannot … you must not.*"

I trembled, whimpering and growling all at once as my teeth nipped and grazed her neck. I willed myself to keep from slashing her to pieces and devouring her whole.

As I drew the last of her blood, I cocked my ears back and listened to the outside chorus.

"Prince Derek Rudliff. Join us," called my howling pack.

I looked one last time into the faded, lifeless eyes of what had once been my beloved bride. I licked the last of her succulent blood from my paws, then turned and leapt from the bed. With the vision of the brilliant moon shining through the window, I thrust my mighty head high, howled in reply to my awaiting family, and crashed through the heavy wooden door to join in the hunt.

AFTER feeding late into the night, I fled toward the forest to rest, where I happened upon Koenig curled on the ground. At the sight of his sleeping *Were* form, I felt a fierce bond of loyalty seize me unlike anything I had ever known in my mortal life. I needed to be near him, protect him, and keep him from harm.

I lowered my haunches, curled next to him, and nuzzled his cold nose. He nudged his eyes open a sliver, but even such a small effort appeared to exhaust him further. I sensed something was wrong, but as a newly emerged *Were* with much to learn, I thought my questions could wait until morning.

But I was wrong.

What Koenig had failed to mention earlier became painfully clear by first light.

I awoke in my human form, lying naked as a newborn baby, icy fingers of rain raking my skin. Koenig was on the ground, weak, fragile, having only partially transformed back to his human form. His pale, handsome head appeared that of a man, as was his torso, but his legs and arms were *Werewolf*.

I bolted up to sitting. "My king, what has happened?"

He heaved a heavy sigh and winced. "There is much to learn … so little time."

"But, what has happened? Tell me."

A slight smile tipped the corner of his thin lips. "I wish I could say my motives had been noble. They were not."

I moved in closer and smoothed his golden hair from his damp forehead. "Tell me. What ails you?"

His eyes paled. "I'm dying."

My heart cleaved into a million pieces! "But ... but you're a *Were* king. You're — *you're immortal,* yes?"

"There is a flaw in us all. What is important now is that I chose you. You are the one."

"But." I frowned. "I do not understand."

"You are my successor."

"Successor?" I scrambled to my feet. "*Me?* You jest. You're a king."

"I speak truth, Derek. 'Twas the warrior blood in you."

I paced the ground, scuffing up wet dirt with each forceful step. "I am neither royal nor worthy, and I am *certainly* not a warrior. How can this be?" I stopped in my tracks and stared down at his frail figure, awaiting his reply.

Koenig moistened his parched lips and closed his eyes. "The answer is not simple. You are royal now. That is what matters. My chosen successor must be worthy. He could only hail from the same royal court from long ago, or from the blood of the mightiest of all warriors who fought on her behalf." He coughed. "You, Prince Rudliff, descend from Hermann, also known as Arminius."

I'd heard of that name before, but where. From a dream, perhaps?

"He saved our people long ago from the Roman invaders. I fought with the mighty Chieftain. I tasted him the moment I sank my teeth into your neck. To be sure, I bit into your shoulder."

I scurried in and knelt beside him. "King, tell me more."

"What I did not tell you earlier, I must explain now. For you to rule I must die."

"*No!*" I shouted. "Tell me you speak lies."

" 'Tis truth I speak. There is only room for one king in our clan.

I have lived a long life. Too long. When I was bitten by King Ulnry all those years ago, I, too, was given a choice of taking the life of my wife so I might be with her once again. I chose unwisely and have regretted that decision for two thousand years."

"But … but why must you die? Could you not have chosen me to be a common *Were* and your life spared?"

"It is your bloodline that dictates what you will become in the *Were* world, just like anywhere else. I saw the love you have for your wife and was reminded of my immense loss." He sighed, expelling curled vapor in the chilled air. "I have missed her for so very long. This is my only chance to find her in another world."

I raked my hands through my hair. "Perhaps no other world exists."

"There are other worlds beyond what you see, young Derek. You will learn this."

Stinging tears filled my eyes to brimming. "Is there no other way?"

He sighed, expelling a swirl of mist into my face. "There is no other way."

I beat my fist against the brittle trunk of a dead hemlock.

"Listen to me." He coughed. "I'm weak. I haven't much time. There is more."

I stared into his eyes, salty tears burning my chilled cheeks. "Speak, my King."

"There are rules. A male *Were* may have any female he chooses to satisfy his needs, but you must commit to only one queen. You have chosen wisely. Your Ersule can be yours again. It will be up to you to make her your *Were* queen and part of our clan. Before you bite her again after the age of three and twenty —"

"What? I … I cannot! I cannot savagely bite her, not *ever* again."

"You *must*." Koenig's feeble voice trembled with resolve. He winced as chunks of fur fell from his legs, leaving behind open sores.

"This is very important. She must declare her love for you. It *must* come from her heart."

It must come from the heart. Those words echoed in my mind.

"There are more like us … different clans. They will try to work magic — try to strengthen their bloodlines with our stronger, ancient blood. Beware." He closed his eyes.

"Don't leave me, Koenig. I know not what to do. I'm just an ordinary man!"

A single eyelid opened a crack, and a small spark glinted within his pale blue eye. "You were always far from ordinary, Derek. You will know what to do. 'Tis in your blood. From now on, you will rule our ancient *Weres*. We are small, but we are strong."

Koneig's eyes shut again. I cradled his head in my arms and wept. A few moments later he spoke his final words.

"Let me go in peace. Do not mourn, for it is you who has set my dark soul free. Go now and rule, King Derek Ulrich Rudliff."

How long I sat embracing his handsome head, I do not know, for I was gripped with searing pain tearing straight through my heart.

Naked and my chest sore from choking sobs, I lumbered through the woods toward home. The door stood open wide, and my hound was nowhere to be seen. In our bed lay Ersule, still, lifeless, bloodied, and pale — just as I had left her.

Kneeling by her side, I cried like an infant as I gently washed the caked blood in her hair, her neck, her shoulders, and dressed her in her favorite lavender frock. After dressing myself, I buried her in the sunny meadow where the wildflowers grew in abundance each spring, turning the ground into a lush rainbow of vibrant colors.

Shrieks and shouts rang out, coming from the village square. I sighed and set out toward the commotion.

The wolves had attacked, and more mangled body parts had been found at daybreak. I knew the news to be true, for it had been I, along with my pack, who had hunted, killed, and devoured throughout the dark night until we were full and satisfied.

But we were no ordinary wolves.

Yet, it was the pathetic Paul Stubbe who would be racked, bludgeoned, decapitated, and burned on this day for the crimes against humans that my pack performed regularly.

With no explanation for my wife's disappearance, and my old life nothing more than a memory, it was time to go, time to leave my home of Bedburg, the only home I had ever known.

I would wait with the patience of a saint for the rebirth of Ersule. Just as Koenig had said, I would make her mine — claim her as my queen — no matter what happened in the next three hundred years.

Chapter Four

Everett, Washington

"Oh, there you are. I'm heading out." David dropped an envelope on Erin's desk. "While you were gone, this arrived. I'll see you tomorrow."

"Yes, all right. See you tomorrow," Erin murmured absently, staring at the return address on the envelope.

Rudliff, Grand Avenue.

The envelope had been sealed with an ornate burgundy wax stamp. Inside was an engraved invitation on thick parchment.

"A costume ball on Halloween," she whispered.

Lord. She had been unable to stop thinking about Derek ever since they had met at the cemetery. With the way his arresting blue eyes assessed her body, he was not an easy man to forget. More importantly, no one had written a story about him in the local newspapers. With a little luck, perhaps she would be the first. After all, an exclusive interview with Mr. Derek Rudliff could launch her career.

She rose from the chair and gazed out the tall window overlooking the bay. Derek was hosting a costume ball, likely a grand event. She would need to give some thought to her costume. She sighed and rubbed her chin. Perhaps something wicked and fun would be in order.

"Hello, dear, you busy?"

Erin turned toward Frederick's voice at the door.

"Your father said I could see my way to your office."

I'm sure he did. She summoned up a warm smile. "What brings you here today?"

He entered the office and stood in front of her desk. "I was down at the dock finishing up on business dealings and realized I was simply famished. May I take you to lunch?"

"I'm sorry, I've already had lunch. Perhaps another day."

His brows knitted together, as his gaze fixed upon the invitation sitting on her desk. "What's this?"

"Oh, that." She rose from the chair and waved her hand. "It's nothing important."

"The return address says Rudliff on Grand. Tell me you've had no further involvement with that man. He has a scandalous reputation. I know. I've checked."

She folded her arms across her chest and heaved a sigh. "You've *checked?* Good heavens, Frederick, are you now my father? I said it's nothing. It's just a note — a thank you note."

"I'm sorry, Erin. I simply want what's best for you. I'm just trying to warn you. From what I've heard, the farther away a woman is from Rudliff, the better."

She rolled her eyes. "And just what have you heard? Enlighten me."

Frederick's eyes bulged wide. "Well, I cannot give details because I'm a gentleman. But allow me to say he has a rather unsavory reputation, having been spotted in sordid establishments and gambling halls near Chestnut."

The muscles along her jawline pulsed. "That's it? He's *'been spotted'*. Many of the men you employ go down there on a regular basis. In fact, if memory serves me, didn't you once need help getting home from that area after a 'gentleman's party'?"

His cheeks flushed crimson. "That was different. My cousin was to be married the next day —"

She took a step forward and poked a firm finger in his chest. "And God forbid a woman walk near that area, right? What would you and your scamps think of that? Would you prefer she were hanged? Or would a scarlet letter sewn upon her bosom be enough?"

His mouth flopped open. "Sometimes your words astonish me, Erin." He paced to the window and gazed toward the distance. "I didn't want to tell you this, but your father has been most concerned about your independent nature. He told me you've recently taken to going out in the buggy at night and on long walks unchaparoned."

Erin held up her hands and shook her head. "Excuse me? Have we suddenly gone back to the Dark Ages? What is it with you two?" She dropped her arms to her sides. It was no use. Nothing she could say or do that reeked of feminine independence would ever please him.

She softened her stance, taking pity on the poor narrow-minded lout. He and her father were exactly alike — both schooled in old traditions, both from families whose women sat idle, watching as the world passed by, too busy mending their husbands' socks to fulfill their own dreams before passing away.

He took her hands in his. "Forgive me. Your father and I just want what's best for you. While I won't forbid you to associate with Rudliff, I will —"

"Forbid me!" She snatched her hands back in a flash. "I can't talk to you about this anymore. I have work to do. Can you find the door yourself, or do I have to show you out?"

"Erin, I —"

"Just *go*." Tears stung the back of her eyes. "Go now before I say something I may regret."

Frederick pursed his lips into a tight seam and nodded. "Very well." Starting for the door, he paused and turned around with a menacing glare. "But this matter is far from over."

WITH her long dark hair and green eyes, attending the costume party dressed as a black cat seemed the perfect idea. Wiltse's Mercantile carried a wonderful assortment of costumes this time of year, and finding the perfect fuzzy, feline ears had been easy. The slinky black dress and feather boa she had worn to the hospital charity ball months earlier were still hanging in her armoire. Tucked away in her cedar chest were black satin slippers that would complete the ensemble.

Erin glanced at the pink roses from Derek, perched in the crystal vase on her bureau. The fragrant bouquet, delivered to her at the newspaper, had come as a complete surprise. Somehow, she had known exactly whom they were from before reading the small-attached card, thanking her for making him feel welcome in Everett.

The very next day, Derek had sent a telegram, insisting she allow him to send his carriage for her the night of the party. Given it would be an evening event, and on Halloween, no less, she sent word back accepting his gracious offer.

The knock on the door filled her tidy bedroom.

"Do you wish to wear the emerald combs, Miss?"

The combs. "Yes, Maggie, come in. I almost forgot."

The servant entered with a worn, black velvet box and opened the top. "These belonged to my grandmother, God rest her soul. She received them as a gift from an old beau in London many years ago. Apparently, they're quite old. I thought they would be perfect."

Erin rescued the lovely heirlooms from their box and brought them to her vanity mirror. "Oh, you're right — these combs are perfect." She stuffed them in her hair. Frowning in the mirror, she turned her head from side-to-side.

Maggie laughed. "Hand them over, and let me do it for you. Honest to Pete, you're all thumbs, just like your father."

Erin scowled and plopped down on the vanity bench. "I suppose you're right. Honestly, Maggie, I don't know how I ever managed without you while I was away at college."

"Oh, you did just fine, girl."

Erin watched in the mirror as Maggie brushed her hair to a sheen and removed a few wispy strands to hang from her temples, while the remainder hung down her back. The servant placed a dragonfly comb on each side so the emeralds sparkled luminously when the light hit them just the right way, accentuating the color of her eyes all the more.

"Just look at you now. I must say, you're one sultry kitty-cat."

Erin scrunched her nose and purred, and they both laughed.

The sound of iron hooves marching up the street sent Erin scrambling up to look out the window. "I think the driver is here. Can you get my coat?"

Erin slipped into her mother's calf-length mink. To keep the new style in place, she gently covered her hair with a silk scarf.

What arrived was much more than a simple carriage. Two tall, pitch-black horses, their manes braided into thick twisted ropes of horsehair, pulled a dark maroon brougham. Clearly, they were well-tended animals, for their coats had been brushed to a slick luster resembling black satin under the glowing street lamps.

The driver arrived at the door and tipped his hat. "Good evening, Miss Richland. Allow me."

He escorted her into the handsome, velvet-lined carriage. She ran her fingers along the plush seat, savoring the smooth texture against her skin.

Derek's house was a mile away, at most. To the west, menacing dark clouds loomed over nearby Whidbey Island. A threatening breeze blew across Port Gardner Bay, carrying the salty scent of the cobalt sea.

As they neared the final block, the wind kicked up with the approaching storm. Fallen autumn leaves and twisted, broken branches rustled in the streets.

The carriage turned on to Grand Avenue. Just up ahead, the massive cedar-shingled house with a second story turret stood before her. Perched high above the perilous cliffs, the mansion faced the islands in Puget Sound and the incredible fuchsia sunsets often greeting the western skies.

The driver reined in the horses. He promptly climbed down, tethered the horses, and opened the carriage door. With a leather-gloved hand, he escorted her along a cobbled pathway framed with boxwood hedges. Sheltered, fiery torches with bending yellow flames defied the gusting wind, illuminating the narrow path leading to the covered front porch.

Erin undraped the scarf from her hair and slid a loose curl back into place. "This place is truly amazing."

The driver's breath caught, his steel-gray eyes narrowing. Her chest slowly tightened as his intense gaze lingered on her face and hair for far too long. She reached up to secure any wayward tendrils, but each and every hair felt in place. Uncomfortable, she cleared her throat.

His gaze snapped away. "Yes, this place is remarkable, Miss Richland."

The coachman thumped the brass knocker on the massive double-doored entrance. An older woman with hair as white as fresh snow opened the door. Wearing a long black dress enveloped by a contrasting white apron, the slender woman wore a prickly scowl that would scare even the most persistent door-to-door solicitor.

She guided Erin's coat off and hung it in the entry armoire. "Come, Miss Richland. Master Rudliff has been expecting you."

Master Rudliff. Well, well. Erin stood in the enormous entry, craning her neck for a better view. The sprawling wood floors, clearly made from the finest Douglas fir trees, were so brightly polished she could see her reflection. Painted a rich color of deep taupe, the plaster walls exuded warmth below the imposing ornate crown molding and high-beamed ceilings.

Centered in the foyer was a round walnut table topped with a stylish vase filled with evergreen sprigs, twisted branches, pinecones, and winterberries. The fragrant arrangement smelled as if she had just stepped into a damp northwestern forest.

A tuxedoed butler wearing what appeared to be a mask similar to the one described in the new French novel *Le Fantôme de l'Opéra* arrived with a sterling tray of crystal glasses filled with sparkling liquid. "Champagne, Miss Richland?"

"Yes, please." She took a glass from the tray he extended.

"Allow me to escort you upstairs. Master Rudliff is expecting you."

Erin followed along the shadowy hallway that appeared to go on forever, leading toward the rear of the house. Trailing the servant up a wide staircase, medieval-style, candlelit sconces hung high upon the dark, paneled stairway, lit their way. Music filled her ears. She looked up and saw Derek standing at the top of the steps, dressed as what appeared to be a gothic count.

"Good evening, Miss Richland. I'm delighted you accepted my invitation."

Reminding her of a handsome effigy, his body towered over hers as she ascended the last step. She gazed into his eyes, as he reached for her hand and whispered a kiss upon her knuckle.

He tilted his chin. "I must say, you make a particularly lovely feline. Your eyes are especially green tonight, like the exquisite emeralds adorning your hair." His gaze narrowed. "The dragonfly combs are unusual. Wherever did you find them?"

A warm flush rushed to her cheeks. She fingered the combs in her hair. "Oh, I just borrowed them for tonight. Apparently, they're quite old and from London."

A single eyebrow rose. "From London, you don't say. Most interesting," he said, leaning forward, surveying the combs more closely.

She smoothed her hair. "I … I believe they're one of a kind."

"Yes, I think perhaps they are." He flashed her a dazzling smile.

Derek made a handsome nobleman. His slicked back hair looked longer and darker than she remembered, giving him a sharp, almost sinister, appearance. He wore black trousers and a crisp white shirt framed by a blood-red vest. A long black cape with red velvet lining completed his costume.

Gesturing with a forward sweep of his arm, he asked, "Shall we?"

She nodded. He touched the small of her back, sending a jolt of warmth clear up to the nape of her neck as he guided her into a large room.

"Oh, my," she said, entering the dimly lit area. Far larger and more open than she would have expected, the room felt massive with the enormous windows that reached from floor to ceiling, overlooking the bay. Band members, dressed in white tuxedoes, congregated in the corner with instruments. Their hands and faces were painted bright white with thin, black etchings around their eyes and mouths, making them resemble human skeletons.

An oversized, linen-covered table stood in front of the tall windows. A selection of wines, appetizers, and desserts sat off to one side. On the opposite end, a huge roast beast of some sort rotated slowly on a fiery spit. Next to the meat, an assortment of freshly-baked breads lay in wooden baskets lined with black linen cloth. She cast her attention to the magnificent ice sculpture in the shape of a large, predatory wolf, dead-center. Icy, crimson punch flowed between bared, pointed fangs before dribbling into an oversized sterling punch bowl.

All around the room people mingled in extravagant costumes: Marie Antoinette and King Louis the XVI, Caesar, Cleopatra, Napoleon, wicked pirates, and a creepy assortment of witches, goblins, vampires, wolves, and medieval warriors. In every direction, the fantastic costumes worn by the guests made her feel as though she had gone back in time.

"I have some friends I'd like you to meet." Derek led her across the room toward the couple dressed as Marie Antoinette and King Louis the XVI. The king, seated on a damask divan, rose when he saw them approach.

"Derek. A splendid party, my friend." The middle-aged man with a stocky build dipped his head and smiled. "And who might this splendid creature be?"

Derek draped his arm over the man's shoulders. "Edgar and Charlotte Eberhart, I'd like you to meet Miss Erin Richland."

Charlotte angled her chin and nodded gracefully under her immense white wig. Erin noticed a thin, white scar traversing the woman's right cheek and another across her slender neck.

"Enchanted," Edgar said, bowing formally. "I was hoping it was you, Miss Richland. Derek has had fine things to say on your behalf. Do I understand that you work at the *Everett Messenger?*"

Erin nodded and smiled. "I'm delighted to meet you both, Mr. and Mrs. Eber —"

The queen gasped. "Dear girl, please, we're simply Edgar and Charlotte. We so despise being addressed formally." She crinkled her nose. "It makes us feel more ancient than we already are."

"Let her speak, dear." Edgar leaned forward. "As you were saying, Miss Richland?"

Erin cleared her throat. "Oh, yes. You see, my father owns the newspaper, and I've recently bullied him into giving me more responsibility. So, the short answer is, yes. I work at the *Messenger.*"

"That's splendid, my dear," Charlotte said, snapping her fan open with a flick of her pale wrist.

"And have you found the mischievous wolves at the cemetery you seek?" Edgar asked. "I do hope it's not a breach of conduct that Derek told us about the wretched animals wreaking such chaos."

Erin looked at Derek for a moment before turning toward Edgar again. "No. No, of course not. The authorities have already been notified, and the caretaker will be on the watch for any more suspicious activity."

"Excuse me, sir," the white-haired servant interjected. "I must speak with you a moment."

Derek's gaze shifted from Erin to Charlotte and finally back to her. "Excuse me a moment." He turned to his servant. "Yes. Yes, of course, Mrs. Schauss."

Erin watched as the two walked toward an unoccupied corner, talking in hushed tones. She smiled and turned toward Charlotte. "Mrs. Schauss appears rather serious."

Charlotte snorted and lowered her fan. "You could say that." She tilted her chin. "Edgar, perhaps Miss Richland would like some of the divine party punch. Something tells me it would be to her liking."

Edgar's eyes narrowed to slits. "Perhaps not, Charlotte. It's possible our gracious host would like to offer her a glass himself."

Charlotte sighed, raised her chin, and snapped her fan open.

"It does look refreshing," Erin said, attempting to lighten the moment. "I'll just help myself."

Edgar leaned forward. "Oh, but the champagne is delightful, my dear. Perhaps you would like more —"

"Let her drink what she chooses, Edgar." Charlotte lowered the fan and smiled. "Women these days know exactly what they want and what's best for them. They certainly don't need a man making decisions on their behalf. Isn't that right, Miss Richland?"

Erin smiled, delighted to have found a woman in the room with similar insight about the modern world. "Indeed, and well said. Excuse me a moment."

As she strolled toward the table, she saw Derek and Mrs. Schauss still conversing in the corner. The servant gestured dramatically with her hands while Derek stood tall and rigid, his lips pursed tightly together, shaking his head.

"Hmm. I wonder what that's about." She reached for a chilled silver goblet, held it under the fountain, and watched as the fluid dribbled like liquid garnets into the metal cup.

Suddenly, Derek was by her side.

"Is the champagne not to your liking?"

She flinched and placed a splayed hand across her chest. "You startled me."

"I'm sorry. I … I didn't mean to frighten you." He gestured toward her goblet. "Perhaps a different champagne — or wine — would be more to your liking?"

She glanced around the room, taking notice that everyone appeared to be drinking from the chilled goblets. "That's not necessary."

A band member in full tuxedo fanned out his tails and took a seat behind an organ. Without pause, the band began playing a haunting gothic piece. The butler turned the lights off so only the candelabras and faces of the skeleton band glowed, giving the eeriest feel to the darkened room.

Ignoring the chill creeping up her spine from the evocative music, Erin smiled. "You've outdone yourself, Mr. Rudliff. This is impressive. I'm almost frightened."

"I enjoy hosting a good party now and then." He took a step forward and placed a hand in his trouser pocket. "But please remember, Miss Richland, my name is Derek to my close friends."

The nervous flutter of her eyelashes tickled the top of her cheeks. She lifted her gaze to his. "Is that what we are? Close friends?"

The color of Derek's eyes deepened. "I'd certainly like to think so."

His eyes followed her every move as she took a healthy sip from the goblet. His tongue darted out and moistened his full bottom lip.

Instantly, the tiny hairs at the nape of her neck twitched.

"You'll have to tell me how you like the punch. It's an old family recipe."

Erin tilted her chin and licked her lips. "It's very good. Different. Earthy." She drank more, allowing the liquid to linger against her tongue, trying to determine the unique flavors before swallowing. A solitary drop dripped from her lip, landing on her chin. "Oh, I'm so clumsy —"

"Allow me." Derek pulled a silk handkerchief from his vest pocket and blotted her chin, his dark pupils narrowing in on her lips.

"Good thing I didn't come as an angel dressed in white."

He gazed into her eyes. "Do you like it?"

"The punch? Oh, yes, very much." She drank from the goblet again.

Derek reached toward her chalice. "Ah, ah, now, not too much. It's rather potent for those unaccustomed to its unique —"

"Nonsense," she said playfully, furrowing her brow. "Everyone's drinking the punch. It's delicious."

His eyes widened as she downed the rest and set the empty goblet on the table. "Erin, you must —"

"Derek. Another grand party."

Derek turned. "Ah. There you are." He patted the younger man on the back. "I'd like you to meet someone special. Gregore, meet Miss Erin Richland."

Dressed as a Franciscan friar, Gregore smiled and bowed. "Delighted to meet you, Miss Richland."

She dipped her head. "The pleasure is mine, sir."

"There you are, Gregore. Come dance with me," called an approaching costumed woman.

Gregore's face brightened. He leaned in toward Erin, his eyebrows waggling, and whispered, "I love to dance."

And just like that, the playful friar was gone in a flash, whisked away by a chatty pirate wench.

Derek looked into Erin's eyes, his piercing gaze so intense the back of her eyes stung. He offered his arm. "Shall we dance, my dear?"

My dear. The sultry cadence of his words slid from his lips straight to a secluded place deep within her pelvis. "Yes, that would be lovely," she said automatically, still captivated by the intensity of the eyes staring back at her.

Leading her toward the center of the room, Derek slid his hand along the silken fabric of her dress at the small of her back. Within seconds, they were moving across the dance floor. Costumed guests, sitting off to the side, whispered with one another. Soon, couples joined in on the dance floor.

Erin gazed up into Derek's eyes. "I suspect you've done this often?"

"Done what often?"

"Danced like this. Like an expert."

His fingertips dug into the sleek fabric as he swept her across the room in a waltz, his cape wavering behind him as if flying on its own.

"I'm not an expert, but I have done this several times over the years."

The thought of him dancing with other women needled her. She quickly brushed the ridiculous reaction aside. Derek was devilishly handsome and terribly wealthy. Surely, he'd had many opportunities to dance with women. Still, she couldn't help but wonder if he looked at the other women with the same soulful gaze when they danced, the kind of contemplative stare that made a woman feel as though they were the only people in a room.

Had the house grown warmer? A sudden flush of heat spread like tiny sparks of fire seeping into her skin.

Derek guided her, but her feet felt as though they had gone

numb, moving on their own, while the penetrating warmth probed every inch of her skin.

The steady drizzle of rain outside intensified, as though suddenly closing in around the house, surrounding them, the showers pounding the roof like a blaze of gunfire. The wind wailed, howling like a mournful dog across the eves. The pace of the music increased, grew louder, the beat deeper, more powerful, echoing across the wooden floors as Derek glided her around the floor, over and over, keeping with the rhythm.

Beads of moisture formed across her neck as costumed guests hemmed in closer, dancing with curious smiles, then quickly retreating. Bodies moved in, then out: Marie and Louis, Napoleon, Abe Lincoln, a vampire dancing with a ghost. As the music intensified and the drums beat with the rhythm of her racing heart, guests glided by, smiling and nodding, but others stared as if grimacing before darting away. An angel and a wolf danced nearby, moving within inches of them. The wolf lurched toward Erin, bared his teeth and snarled, then whizzed away.

She gasped and gripped Derek's broad shoulder. "Is … is it hot in here?"

His eyes narrowed. "Not particularly. Are you feeling all right?"

Warmth slithered like a serpent through her veins. She fanned her face. "I think so, but would it be all right if we got a bit of fresh air?"

Derek stopped in mid-step and looked out the set of large windows. Her gaze followed his. In the distance, dimly-lit ships bobbed like tiny, floating candles in the rough sea below.

"The storm is fierce outside," he said with a frown. "But I know where we can go."

He took her hand and led her through a back door to a covered porch overlooking the bay. Immediately, the wind seized their clothes, and his cape swirled like a winged bat taking flight. She reached up, holding her fuzzy ears in place as the gusts whipped wildly about.

"Over here." He escorted her under cover.

She pressed her back against the cold cedar wall, relishing the cool sensation against her heated skin beneath the dress. Spreading his cape, he moved in and towered over her for extra protection.

Beneath the soft glow of the porch light, her head felt as though it were bobbing like the boats in the distance. The punch, the storm, his masculine presence looming over her, all of it made her suddenly breathless.

He stood in front of her, their bodies inches apart. Through his clothes, heat radiated from his skin, sparing her from the biting wind. Towering treetops of massive evergreens bent and bowed; twigs snapped like brittle bones, and large branches crashed to the ground nearby, echoing across the tall bluff.

Derek's eyes remained fixed upon hers, glowing like an azure sea in a tempest. His nostrils flared as though catching an invigorating scent within the swirling current of air.

She closed her eyes and inhaled his unique virile scent of bayberry cologne and the rich, earthy aroma of the northwestern forest. God, how she wanted to wrap her arms around his broad back, breathe in that wonderful scent that was all Derek, and pull him into a deep, passionate kiss.

As if he had read her mind, she felt the scratch of his mustache on her upper lip as his mouth came down upon hers. He kissed her gently at first, his lips closed, but when she responded with a soft moan, he softly coaxed the seam of her lips open with his tongue. The kiss intensified, growing passionate, heated, seductive, as he wrapped his arms around her in an embrace, pulling her hard against his broad chest.

Erin gave into the intimate embrace while the storm swirled like a beast breathing cold air down the back of her neck. She wrapped her arms around his neck, the tips of her toes barely touching the ground, as her tongue joined his, dancing with the frantic beat of her heart.

A violent rush of icy wind ripped across the bay, slapping her hard across the cheek.

Oh God.

She withdrew from the kiss and pressed her cheek to his. "Derek, this … this isn't like me," she whispered. "I don't know what's come over me."

He slowly pulled back, his heated gaze fixed upon hers, deep blue eyes boring into hers as though speaking on some unearthly level.

The soothing tempo of stringed instruments from inside the house suddenly changed to a feverish pace, the drumbeat matching the thumping beat of her racing pulse.

She closed her eyes as Derek slowly leaned in and kissed her again. Urgent hands slid around her back, his fingertips digging into her skin, sending fevered heat down the length of her spine as his tongue explored her mouth. His taste, her pounding heart, the warm serpentine dance slithering up her backbone, all called to her on some primal level. The next thing she knew, her body fell limp in his arms.

"Come now," she heard him whisper as he lifted her in his arms and carried her through the back door.

The fevered music, his strong arms carrying her, the heat penetrating her skin — she felt as though she were spiraling, her mind and body detaching from one another, every part of her existence seeking solace from the storm.

The anxious look in Derek's eyes made her heart pound so hard she could hear the harsh whirl of blood beating inside her ears.

"Derek, I feel so … strange."

"It's all right. Everything will be fine," he whispered against her cheek.

Her vision blurred, the surroundings growing hazy, the walls slowly moving in and out. Set against the primal music playing at an excited pace, sounds of muffled laughter echoed across the tall ceilings and polished floors.

She clung to his neck as he deftly carried her through a long, darkened hallway. They passed candlelit rooms, doors ajar, each one with what appeared to be blurry scenes of fur and half-naked women sprawled out on red satin sheets.

He came to the end of the hall and kicked the door open wide. She gasped at the sound of the heavy wooden door slamming against the wall. Lying within his arms, another rush of heat swept through her entire body. Was this all her wild imagination? The punch?

Oh, God. Perhaps I've gone mad.

Through hooded lids, she surveyed the candlelit room as he placed her down upon the large bed. Her body went limp as a rag doll as she melded into the thick mattress. His gaze narrowed as he hovered over her, his outstretched arms perched at each side of her shoulders. "Erin."

Had he just called her name? She tried to focus on his deep voice and the candlelight flickering in his black pupils as he gazed deeply into her eyes. "Derek, I … I feel so hot, so … "

His lean body perched above her, his sensual scent, the seductively lit bedroom — all merged with the heated, sexual sounds coming from other rooms.

Desire rushed through her veins, warming her face, her neck, her breasts. Her hunger for his touch grew so fierce she could barely breathe beneath the pinching corset. "Kiss me. Kiss me, Derek," she whispered.

A seductive smile spread beneath his mustache. He rose up, removed his cape, and tossed it on the leather bedside chair.

His gaze wandered the length of her body. "Now, where were we?"

He slowly slid above her, gentle hands brushing away the wispy tendrils of her hair that had fallen against her cheeks.

Lifting her neck from the pillow, she whispered, "Kiss me."

He stared into her eyes, his gaze so penetrating her heart skipped a beat, then two.

"My pleasure." In a flash, he slipped a hand beneath her neck, and pulled her into a deep, passionate kiss.

Every inch of her skin grew sensitive, ignited with longing so intense she felt as though she were burning from the inside out. She pulled from his lips, breathless with desire, and kissed his neck. "This is madness," she whispered.

"My God, woman," he breathed against her ear. "You have no idea how much I want you."

Inhaling his scent, her heart bounded to life. She raked her hands through his thick hair, down his back, across his broad shoulders.

Derek moaned a low, throaty growl as his large hands slid across the curve of her waist, her hips, her thighs. He moved his pelvis, rubbing slowly, rhythmically against her.

Was it her imagination, or did her heart match the tempo of the pounding drums?

"I want you," he breathed against her earlobe.

She moaned in reply and moved her hips, joining his seductive pace.

His hand glided down the length of her silky dress, inching the fabric higher. She gasped when he reached her sensitive naked thigh.

Urgent fingers slipped beneath her garter, heated fingertips digging into her inner thigh as though branding her with his touch. Her entire body trembled, breath catching deep within her chest, as she groped for the top of the bed.

"Erin, my sweet."

His husky voice seemed to call to her from every direction as his fingers inched inward. She closed her eyes and moaned when a solitary finger penetrated her depths. Arching up, she pressed her palms against the thick mahogany headboard.

His moustache scratched her bare neck, and a gritty moan hummed against her throat. He paused for a moment. Did she hear a hushed groan?

Like a quill to an inkwell, his finger penetrated her again. And again. She bit down on her bottom lip, stifling the escaping moan, as he slowly withdrew. His hand slid up the thin fabric of her dress, reaching her covered breast.

The animated sounds of heated pleasure and whimpering moans in the nearby bedrooms added to the intensity of the pounding music and her growing desire, threatening to consume her entire body. He trapped a taut nipple between two fingers, and she cried out.

In a flurry of fabric, they discarded their clothing, tossing the garments to the floor with hasty abandon.

She lay on the satin sheets in only her silk garters and black stockings. He stood above her, stark naked, his hair tousled, and as powerfully virile as anything she could have imagined.

His jet-black pupils narrowed as he scanned the length of her near-naked body. His nostrils flared. His shaft stiffened, and her breath caught so deep within her throat she thought she would faint.

He sank in the bed next to her and gently pulled the emerald dragonfly combs from her hair, fingering the heavy ebony mass spilling across the satin pillows.

He reached for a thick strand and rubbed it between his fingers. "You're so lovely." He positioned himself above her, slowly inching down until his full body lay on top of her. "So *very* beautiful."

The matt of curled hair on his chest tickled her breasts. Heated breath scorched her neck as his hard shaft pressed against her belly, making the yearning for him almost unbearable.

Derek kissed her hard, demanding, his strong hands roaming along her hips, her torso. He cupped a breast, kneading the sensitive skin and circling her pebbled, erect nipple.

He pulled from the seductive deep kiss and trailed his tongue down the slender column of her throat. Kissing her neck, his lips lingered at her racing pulse point before blazing a path to her breast. His tongue darted out, dancing like the devil around fire as he licked and sucked the sensitive skin and trapped a peak between his teeth.

A jolt of electricity seized her body, narrowing in on her moist, heated core. "Oh, Derek," she moaned.

He slowly maneuvered his hand down her torso, stopping between the apex of her legs. Firm fingertips dug like claws into the flesh of her inner thighs, and just as she cried out, he slid a finger inside, silencing her.

"You're so wet," he whispered against her throat, "so very ready."

His voice. His touch. It all felt familiar, yet so far away, like an old dream she couldn't remember the longer time passed. The music rose to a fevered pitch; squeaky violins shrieked, and fingertips pounded on the organ, echoing across the tall ceilings. She closed her eyes as sounds of nearby laughter, panting, and growling reverberated inside her head.

"Make love to me, Derek," she said, the words floating from her mouth as if someone else had spoken them.

He inhaled jagged breaths against her throat. Slowly, he positioned himself so that the tip of his shaft sat at her moist entrance.

"Are you sure? There's no turning back after this," he whispered.

She answered with a nod and squirm of her bottom, wetting the smooth tip of his manhood.

In one single plunge, he went deep, so deep she gripped the

post of the bed and cried out, her sounds of pleasure instantly extinguished by the frantic music growing increasingly louder. Pouring rain pelted the closed window, and pounding fists hammered from somewhere outside the bedroom walls, merging with eerie echoes of hissing and laughter.

He slid within her depths, riding with her, against her. She cast her gaze toward the firelight scratching the dark walls and ceiling like twisted, deformed fingers.

He plunged deeper, his hips moving with precision, faster, harder, the pounding on the walls echoing inside her head.

"Derek." She moaned, breathless with yearning, drawing closer to the edge of sweet release.

"Erin. My sweet, sweet angel," he whispered against her ear.

He wrapped his hands in her hair and swept her into a deep kiss. His limbs tightened, and the last thing Erin saw was a blast of blinding white light as they climaxed together, their sounds of passion drowned out by the storm and the frenzied echoes coming from all directions within the large house.

The music stopped dead; the sounds from the nearby rooms instantly silenced.

They lay wrapped in each other's arms, legs tangled in a puzzle so familiar it frightened her. She tugged the coverlet to her chest and looked in his eyes. "God help me, Derek. I hardly know you."

Darkness crept into the bottomless depths of his eyes. He sighed and pulled her against his chest, gentle fingers slowly combing her tangled hair.

Drifting to sleep, enveloped in Derek's strong arms, she gazed through half-closed lids at the emerald dragonfly combs perched on the night table, winking like mischievous dancing fireflies.

Chapter Five

France

"*Derrrrreck . . .*"

The brilliant light ahead beckoned, but I was being led back, gently pulled into a swirl of somber gray mist, obscure images, low humming voices, and throbbing pain.

"*Derek*, come back. Come back to *me*."

I tried to focus on the familiar whisper. "Ersule."

" 'Tis I. Breathe, my love. *Breathe*."

Fighting the pain seizing my chest and the overwhelming need to gag, I suddenly gasped and drew air deep within my constricted lungs.

"Yes, my love. That's it. *Breathe*."

An apparition shrouded in a graceful glow came into focus. She was standing over me in a white dress, smiling, her green eyes glistening like moist emeralds.

"Ersule, my angel," I whispered through parched lips. I tried to reach up, to touch her lovely pale face gleaming down at me, but my arms would not move.

The aroma of rose-scented hair, dried in the summer sunshine, lingered in my nostrils as she slowly drifted away, floating like a delicate feather in a gentle wind, her image fading into the harsh backdrop of unforgiving stone walls.

"You must live, my love. You must stay strong, for us," her dreamy voice called.

You must stay strong for us. I watched as her waning image slowly disappeared with a gentle gust of summer air wafting through the open window.

"Ersule. Ersule, do not leave me."

Something icy cold was placed over my forehead and eyes.

"Hold on. Hold on, King," whispered a familiar voice.

I squinted my covered eyes, but even such a small task was more than I could physically bear. A long sigh above me filled my icy blackness.

"The purple is fading, and the fever has broken. You are going to live, King," said the gentle, reassuring voice of Gregore.

I inhaled deeply. Then again, forcing vital air into my weakened lungs, just as Ersule had asked.

"Ersule."

Gregore whispered against my ear, "What is that you say?"

"She … she was here."

"Rest, you must rest, my King."

A steady hum of low chatter filled my ears before I fell into the empty darkness of overwhelming exhaustion.

Contrary to folklore, we *Weres* were vulnerable creatures. While immortality was possible, in a harsh, unpredictable, world, there were no guarantees. As fate would have it, another wave of the Black Death, the vile illness that had scoured the continent many years before, resurfaced. I was the first to fall prey inside the secluded stone house in the wooded Vosges Mountains. One by one, the disease ravaged our human bodies. For those of us who survived the horrific ordeal, our inner beasts only grew stronger and more erratic.

Vividly green and rich with fir, pine, and spruce, the rounded summits of the Vosges held abundant prey. When our appetites called for more than the usual deer, wild boar, and fox, additional game was readily accessible in the lower landscape dotted with pastoral animals and unwary farmers.

One evening while drinking from a cool stream, I inhaled a scent that instantly made the fur along my back bristle. I ordered the pack upstream near the waterfalls, but they were quick in detecting the heavenly aroma. I yipped again, but the males bounded forth ahead of me, the seductive scent of females drawing their urgent attention. Before I knew it, I, too, was instantly spellbound and followed on their heels.

Edgar howled at the *She* wolves grouped before us in a circle of thick red fur, reeking with desire. Panting and weaving in a frenzied dance, his nails clicked against the crisp fallen leaves on the forest floor. His nostrils flared, his tail whipping about in a seductive dance worthy of tempting even the chilliest female Lycan.

Despite the excitement, the chill to my marrow warned me these were no ordinary wolves. For years I had heard stories about the *Loup Garou*, a near-extinct, ancient clan of French *Weres*. By all accounts, this band of *Weres* had been a formidable force of nature before the slaughter of their king, the mighty Beast of Gevaudan, who had terrorized South-Central France. The lucky members from the *Loup Garou* would have fled into the night, away from the royal huntsmen, nobles, and French army that sought to hunt them down. Like us, for survival, the remaining pack members would have quickly moved on.

A red-furred *She* wolf pranced haughtily before me with her tail held high. She wandered around me on hefty paws, assessing me, nostrils flaring, her suggestive brown eyes glowing deep amber. She lifted her snout and scratched the dirt in front of my paws.

Fear and desire flooded my wolf veins, making every movement feel as though my limbs were filled with sand. Within moments, instinct swelled within my loin, a detail not lost on the eager *She* posturing before me.

The *She* leaned forward and nuzzled my neck, affirming herself as the leader of her pack and that it was me she desired.

I turned toward Edgar. He mistook my questioning gaze as a sign of affirmation, suddenly yowling and mounting an agreeable *She*.

My gaze darted side to side, my nostrils flaring, searching for the competing scent that might free me from this powerful *She* threatening to unravel my lucid sensibilities. I lowered my snout, finding it most curious there were no rival males within our vicinity.

As though the *She* sensed my hesitation, she hunkered down, then pounced and bit into my neck, drawing blood. She bit down again, hard, snarling, making it clear that she was the *Alpha* of her pack and had laid claim.

There was no ignoring the *Alpha*, nor did the base, impious part of me want to. But something told me this particular *She*, who set her sights upon me right from the start, was not to be taken lightly.

I bared my teeth and bit into her hindquarter. She let out a mighty yowl. Her predatory eyes narrowed, boring into mine.

As soon as the *Alpha* presented herself to me once more, I mounted her. Holding her in place with my strong paws, I bit into her neck with razor-sharp teeth. She moaned and yapped with excited passion. With sounds I recognized as both man and beast, I slid inside her heated depths and stared at the towering moon slanting through the treetops as I poured my seed inside her.

A month later, while sealing the outside gaps between the rocks of our stone house, I heard something approaching from behind. Wiping my muddied hands upon my trousers, I turned.

"I must speak with you," said Edgar, a solemn expression drawn upon his face.

I frowned and asked, "Is something wrong?"

After a long pause he said, "My future mate calls."

I exhaled louder than expected, thankful it was nothing serious. Containing a smile, I explained to the romantic *Were* that a male need not commit to a mate unless *he* has chosen *her*. To my surprise, Edgar informed me that this particular *Were*, the *She* he had mounted in the woods a month earlier, was indeed the mate of his choosing.

"Her name is Charlotte," he said.

"Edgar, dear Edgar. But you are not of the same clan."

He sighed heavily and lowered his head.

I placed my hands on his wilted shoulders. "I know there are few to choose from these days, but is there not a female within our own pack to your liking?"

Edgar's jawline pulsed. He turned to walk away. "I knew I should not have come."

"Wait," I said. "Don't leave heartbroken."

He lifted his expressive blue eyes to mine.

"Is it Charlotte who would join us, or the other way around? I will not part with you, Edgar, and not for one moment do I believe the *Alpha* would agree to Charlotte taking leave."

His eyes paled as he turned and walked away.

My heart shattered into pieces, for he was like a brother to me.

Gregore emerged from the dense woods in full sprint. Carrying my Jaeger rifle, he headed straight for me.

"There's a pale, red-headed woman in our territory — walking down by the lake."

I did not need my powerful senses to know to whom the red hair belonged. I grabbed my rifle from Gregore. "Stay back with the pack," I said, before heading to find the trespassing *She* on my own.

I reached the wooded bank of the lake and spotted the *Alpha* sitting on a fallen log in her human form. Her hair hung in a blanket of red waves cascading down her back, and she was dressed in a flowing gown of jade green.

Rising slowly, she stared me squarely in the eyes. "I must speak with you," she said, her brown eyes soft and poignant.

She was more beautiful than I would have expected. "You have crossed into my territory." I stiffened my spine. "I must ask you to leave."

She sighed as she approached, a demure smile spread across her generous lips. "Surely, you cannot turn away your mate."

I snorted. "I am not your mate, woman."

Her ginger eyebrows curved high. "After I allowed you to take me as you did a month ago, and so vigorously I might add, you most certainly chose me as your mate."

My muscles tensed. "I did no such thing. I am a *Were* king and may choose whomever I wish, whenever I wish for my own needs. You met my physical needs — nothing more."

She rushed forward and slapped me hard across the face. "Do you know who I am?" Her sharp voice carried across the lake. "I am not to be trifled with!"

I gripped the rifle so hard my knuckles turned white. "Pray tell, woman, who might you be?"

She placed a single finger upon my shoulder and walked leisurely around me. "I knew *you* were royal the moment I inhaled your scent, King." She stood before me and leaned forward. "Do you not know royalty when you see it? When you *smell* it?"

I took a step back. "It's no concern of mine whether you are royal or not."

" 'Tis the line of Koenig that runs through your veins, is it not?"

My heart stopped dead in my chest, resuming seconds later. "It's not your concern," I replied coolly, though my voice barely rose about a harsh whisper.

"Ah, but you are wrong." She inched closer, her eyes narrowing, boring into mine. "You see, it matters a great deal."

My blood chilled.

A small smile rested upon her lips as she closed her eyes and turned her face heavenward. "You are so very naïve, young King. I am older … wiser. 'Twas Koenig I approached years ago with an offer to blend royal bloodlines. But as you are well aware, he has since passed to the other side after he chose his successor — *you.*"

"Blending royal lines? You speak nonsense, woman. Be gone with you before the setting of the sun." I turned to walk away.

"I am Queen Regine Delacour of the Court of Count Fredelon de Toulouse, and I have claimed you as my mate, King."

The pulsing muscles in my jaw pounded with pain. I spun around to face her. "I don't give a damn who you are. I grant you until the setting of the sun, Madame. If you are not gone from my territory, I will set my hunters upon you."

She seized my arm in a flash, digging her nails deep into my skin. "You cannot leave me. You cannot simply abandon me. I am a queen, and I'm older than you. I have claimed you, King. It is a great honor for him I choose, do you not understand? *I claim you.*"

I shook my head. "Unhand me now, woman. You mean nothing to me. Go before I kill you myself."

Her fingers dug deeper. "But —"

I eyed her firm grasp, my gaze slowing rising to meet hers. "I have claimed another. Be gone with you."

Her russet eyes narrowed to mere slits, her nostrils flaring. She removed her grip. "I do not detect the scent of a *She* other than myself upon you. You speak lies."

"As I have already informed you, Madame Delacour, I am taken."

"I am not *Madame* Delacour. I am *Queen* Regine Delacour — *your queen.* Do you hear me, King?"

I waved my hand above my head in a dismissive manner and turned to walk away.

"Listen to me," she called. "I am the only *She* capable of bearing offspring. Turn away if you wish, but I will find you again, for it is I who carry your *Were* child within my womb, and you shall *never* be allowed to walk away from that!"

My legs turned to weighted sand, nearly crumbling beneath me. I stiffened my knees, and tried not to fall as I turned to face her, shouting, "You lie. No female *Were* can conceive!"

"So young you are." She approached and ran her finger across my pulsing jawline. "Had you been older — wiser — you would have already learned that I am not your ordinary *She*. I have certain abilities the average *She* does not. I assure you, I am very capable of conceiving, and I have done just that."

"Therefore, because I am young you chose to trick me, fool me, *deceive me?*" I shouted. "Are you so vile that no king would have you before me?" I turned toward the lake, my hands balled into clenched fists.

She scurried in front of me, her expression a blend of determination and panic. "King — do not be foolish. We can rule all the clans — you and I. By mixing our stronger, ancient bloodlines we create a higher species. Don't you see? This is for our survival."

"I tell you, I will have none of it. I do *not* claim you. I belong to another."

"Then it is you who speaks nonsense." Small flashes of gold glinted like sparks of fire in her eyes. "It is I you belong to now," she said, jerking her chin haughtily. "I have chosen *you*."

"I will never be yours!" My roaring voice echoed across the water.

"We shall see about that." She turned to leave. "Ah, before I forget." She spun on her shoe tip to face me. "It seems my *She*, Charlotte, has fallen for one of your *Weres*. Unless you begin to see things my way by the time of the birth of our royal child, I will see her dead."

I moved in and gripped her arm. "Are you so cruel — so wicked?" I spat at the ground near her feet.

She jerked from my grip and sauntered away. I stood frozen. In the distance, I heard her shout, "It is I, Queen Regine Delacour, who has claimed you. Never forget that!"

The following month, while Gregore, his older brother Franz, Edgar, and myself were returning from the village with supplies, I heard desperate cries. Sounds of frantic footsteps rushing through the dense woods followed, slicing through the serene glow of the setting amber sun filtering through the treetops.

Edgar sniffed and sprinted toward the noises.

"What's happening, King? Shall we follow him?" asked Franz.

I, too, had picked up the scent. "No, 'tis a private matter, I believe."

We heard heavy feet tromping on the path behind us. A moment later, Edgar appeared carrying an unconscious, bleeding woman within his arms.

"Help me! It's Charlotte!" Edgar shouted. "Gregore, quickly, lay the blanket down. Franz, help me with her."

Both men scrambled into action. I crouched next to Charlotte, my blood instantly going cold.

Charlotte's neck had been slashed on the right side, and a deep gash carved into her cheek. These were not the injuries caused my jagged jaws or fierce claws, as I was accustomed to seeing, but clean and deep, made by a sharp tool.

I examined her injuries. "Charlotte, what has happened?"

Her soft brown eyes opened to narrow slits. Silvery trails of tears ran down her bloodstained cheeks. "I did nothing. She came at me."

Edgar growled and shot up. Raking a hand through his hair, he scuffed the dirt with his boot, sending a clod flying. "Who has done this to you?"

"My queen. Queen Delacour. She has gone mad, mad with revenge."

"Revenge?" asked a wide-eyed Edgar.

Charlotte's eyes rolled back in her head. Edgar knelt by her side and took her hand in his. "Stay with me, Charlotte."

"A royal *Were* shall be born on this night," she murmured. " 'Tis my fault she must bear this alone. She scrunched her eyes shut. "She ordered the pack to hold me down, and she cut my face. I screamed for her mercy, for I knew not of what she spoke. Just as she slashed my throat, I turned my head and fought her with all I had. I ran as fast as I could."

I felt the heat of Edgar's angry eyes boring into me. "Bring her quickly," I said, avoiding his penetrating gaze.

Once inside, Edgar pulled me aside.

"King, I do not wish to be disrespectful, but do you know of what Charlotte speaks? Is there a noble *Were* to be born? Did you know of this?"

'Twas then I told Edgar how I had been fooled by the Alpha *She*, how I was unaware of the queen's royal blood or the magic power she possessed to conceive. I explained of her trap and devious trickery, and how I thought the very idea so preposterous, surely she spoke only lies.

His eyes softened. "Oh, King."

"I never believed she would carry out her threat." I begged for his forgiveness for my ignorance on the matter. As a king, I knew it was beneath me to plead, but I did so anyway, for Edgar was not only my loyal subject, he was a true friend.

That night, in the distance, I heard the *She* clan's mighty howls of victory piercing the night sky as they welcomed a new *Were* — a prince, into their clan.

Under the bright glow of the moon above, I shrieked and bellowed as my body contorted, twisting from man to beast. I welcomed the flashing, searing pain, for surely there should be a price to pay for my ignorance. Every part of my distorted body crawled with warning, screaming for survival, the sensation so strong it seeped into the deep crevasses of my soul.

Just as I knew in my heart and soul that the sun would rise and fall each and every day, I also knew it was only a matter of time before Queen Delacour and the new prince, *my son,* would seek vengeance and power, and they would never rest until they saw me dead.

Chapter Six

Everett, Washington

Erin stepped on the stool and ran her fingers along the high shelf.

What did I come here for again?

A week had passed since the costume party. Seven days since she'd last seen Derek, and each and every day since then her mind had gone blank at the most inopportune times. She shook her head in an attempt to flush the steamy images from her mind, but all she could see were their tangled bodies consumed with passion.

A flush of heat burned her cheeks. Never, *never*, had she been so forward with a man, so *accommodating*. Yes, it had been years since she was a virgin, thanks to a certain English Literature professor at the university, but bedding someone purely for the sake of a frenzied roll in the hay was not in her usual repertoire.

She winced, wondering what had passed through Derek's mind when he learned she had left in a taxi carriage early the next morning before he awoke. And when she demanded the flowers he'd had delivered to her office the next day be sent back with the deliveryman.

To purge the relentless contemplations, she had yielded to Frederick's persistent requests for her company, just to keep her mind occupied with something else. She quickly realized that by allowing the prosperous Frederick Dimsdale to court her, more journalistic work managed to come her way. All week long, her father had given her the task of writing increasingly significant articles for the newspaper.

Frederick had taken her to fine restaurants, the theatre, walks in the parks, all while he talked incessantly about himself and his new burgeoning business. It was a bitter tonic to swallow with his constant chattering and coddling, but he did have a way of making her feel decent about herself again after her brazen romp with Derek.

"Ah, there you are."

She closed the door and stepped off the stool. "Hello, Father. I was just getting some supplies."

"Well, I'm glad I found you. I have two items for you to work on."

Her eyebrows rose. "Anything exciting?"

"I certainly think so. First, I heard from the sheriff. Seems Mr. Avery from the cemetery was found dead this morning."

Erin gasped. "Dead! How?"

"How dead? Very dead." He smiled.

Erin swatted his arm. "Father, that's terrible. You know what I mean. What happened to him?"

"Not exactly sure. The police suspect it was a wildlife attack." He winced. "It's pretty gruesome, and get this: More wolf prints turned up at the cemetery."

"So, they're back again." She frowned. "Any graves disturbed this time?"

"I don't have the details." He placed a hand on her shoulder and looked her squarely in the eyes. "I thought I'd leave that up to you."

She cleared her throat and tried not to smirk. Her father knew she had just scheduled a date later in the week to attend the theatre with Frederick. In his eyes, she had grown more responsible by allowing the eligible young businessman the pleasure of her company.

Erin slowly shook her head. "I can't believe this is happening in the city. Poor Mr. Avery. It must have been horrible."

"I know. My thoughts exactly. Perhaps the poor fellow went fast. That's all we can hope for now."

"I'll get right on that story after I finish the article on the Women's Suffrage Vote. I'm almost done, and then I'll stop at Delia's shop for some flowers for Mother's grave."

Her father's gaze softened. "You're very good about doing that."

"Well, I still miss her."

"I know you do, dear. So do I." He pulled her to his chest and rubbed her shoulder. "Now, chin up. I want you to interview the man who found Avery's body — see what you can come up with. His name and address are in my office."

"Is he an Everett man?"

"He's local and lives nearby. Never heard of him, though. I want you to go to the cemetery first." His bushy brows knitted together. "But I don't want you to go there alone this time. Take someone, perhaps Frederick, and see what you can come up with."

"All right." She turned to walk away then spun on her toes to face him. "Wait. You said there were two things."

"Oh, yes, how could I forget?" He clicked his tongue and rapped himself upside the head. "None other than Mr. Derek Rudliff has agreed to an article for the paper. You know how I've wanted to get an exclusive on him."

Her mouth flopped open, and she stared wide-eyed at her father.

His eyes brightened. "I know, my thoughts exactly. Isn't this fantastic? But, he's agreed with one caveat."

"And that is?" she managed to squeaked out.

"It must be you who conducts the interview. Apparently, you made quite the impression on him. Of course, I told him you'd be delighted to do the interview, and that you could meet him whenever his demanding schedule allows."

Her stomach twisted. "Um, yes, of course. I'm … delighted."

ERIN buttoned her coat and lifted her face to the warming sun. Daylight grew short and the nights were especially long and dark these days, so it was easy to discover the incredible beauty of the Pacific Northwest when the sun came out to play.

First stop, the florist. She greeted her friend at the counter. "Good afternoon, Delia."

"Erin. It's good to see you, honey. Are you here for some flowers for your mama again?" Delia flashed an impish grin and whispered, "Or are you coming here to reclaim those flowers you sent back from Mr. Rudliff?"

"What?" Erin held back a smile. "You're so bad for bringing that up."

Delia's perfectly tweezed blonde eyebrows arched high. "Well, what on earth were you thinking? Ever since that man moved into this city, he's been all the talk with the women. You have seen him, yes?"

Oh, I've seen him all right. "Yes, I've caught a glimpse of him here and there."

"Well, my dear, I think he's positively dreamy with those brilliant blue eyes and wild dark-blond hair. I could just sop that man up with a buttermilk biscuit. But *you.* You must have made quite the impression. He spent a fortune on that bouquet I put together. When I informed him that you sent them back well … well, he was stunned to say the least. Finally, he told me to take them home myself."

"And did you?" Erin asked far hastier than she had intended. Her stomach knotted with the thought of her flowers ending up with another woman who stood in front of her gushing about them.

"Well, of course I took them home, you silly girl. And they sat on the dining table the entire week. Since you apparently didn't want anything to do with him, I sent Mr. Rudliff a thank-you card in return. I was hoping I'd hear from him again, but no." She sighed extravagantly. "The story of my life."

Erin smiled. Delia never had any trouble mincing words. "I missed you at the Suffrage Club meeting the other day. Are you coming tonight?"

"Yes, I'll be there. But my poor father's not doing so well. Pneumonia. Course this damp November chill hasn't helped any. But I'll be there."

"Good. We need all the help we can get. Members of the Bible clubs have had daggers out for us lately. I just don't understand why these women can't get it through their thick heads we're doing this for them, too. For all women. Makes my blood boil sometimes."

Delia's gaze softened. "Yes, honey, but change often needs to come in small chunks for some people. My parents don't understand my passion in this matter, either. I suppose they're just old-timey."

The bells on the shop jingled. Erin turned.

"Ah, there you are, Erin. Your father said I would likely find you here," said a beaming Frederick.

Mumbling under her breath, Delia fled with an audible swoosh of her thick skirts through a curtain leading to the shop's storage room.

Erin stepped forward. "I was going to fetch you in a bit. Did Father tell you I was heading to the cemetery?"

"He did, and I'm here to give you a lift. You know how I feel about your traipsing around that dismal place, but as long as I'm with you, I promise not to complain." He twisted his waxy mustache and smiled. "Besides, I have a surprise for you. Close your eyes."

"Oh, you know how I hate surprises, Frederick." She sighed and covered her eyes. "But if I must."

He led her by the elbow to the large display window. "Open them."

Out front stood a brand new carriage parked at the edge of the street. "Oh, Frederick, it's truly a handsome carriage. Is that yours?"

"And now I have my own driver, as well. After you, my dear."

Delia emerged through the curtained doorway. "Are you two leaving?"

"Oh, wait." Erin patted Frederick's arm. "I almost forgot." She looked about the store. A copper bucket bursting with pink carnations sat at the edge of the wooden counter. She jutted her chin forward. "I'll take a dozen of those."

Delia wrapped and tied the vibrant bundle with a delicate yellow ribbon. "Y'all have fun now."

Frederick guided Erin by the small of her back and closed the shop door behind them.

Erin cast her attention to the brightly-polished carriage. A short, stocky man she had seen with Frederick down at the docks sat perched up high, holding leather reins in his gloved hands. "When did you find the time to purchase this?"

Frederick opened the door and waggled his brows. "Oh, I've had it ordered for quite some time. I wanted to make sure my business dealing went through. I received it just today. Next time around I plan to order one of those horseless carriages everyone's raving about."

Erin entered the enclosed carriage and ran her hands over the rich leather seats. Frederick scooted in next to her. "It's truly lovely," she said.

They headed down Broadway with Frederick waving out the window at everyone he knew along the way. Erin laughed. "You're incorrigible, showing off in your fine new carriage."

Frederick Dimsdale grinned, his white teeth gleaming beneath the bristly mustache, clearly charmed by her spirited teasing.

By the time they neared the cemetery, Frederick had catalogued all of his recent business accomplishments, and Erin couldn't wait to get out of the carriage and stretch her legs.

"And I told that bad-tempered old man, 'you can't afford *not* to do business with me.' And he said —"

"Watch where you're going!" the coachman barked. He reined in, and the horses came to an abrupt stop, sending Erin lurching forward.

Frederick poked his head out the window and screeched at the offending coach driver, "Dammit! Watch where you're going, man! You nearly killed us!" He reached for Erin's arm and steadied her back on the seat. "Are you all right, my dear?"

Erin recognized the disheveled coachman passing hurriedly in front of them. It was none other than Derek's driver who had picked her up at home and driven her to the costume ball. She slumped in her seat and nudged the brim of her hat over her brows. "Yes, I'm fine."

"Some people," Frederick growled. He rapped on the ceiling, and his coachman urged the horses along.

Once they stopped, Erin retrieved her satchel from under the seat, and she and Frederick exited the carriage. "Here." She handed him the leather bag. "Mind this for me. I'll be right back. I want to put these flowers on my mother's grave first."

He took a step. "I'll go with you."

Erin thrust her hand out. "Thank you, but no. It's nothing personal, Frederick. I prefer to visit my mother alone."

He cleared his throat. "Oh, yes, of course, dear. I completely understand. I'll be here when you return."

"It's just over there." She pointed. "See the pyramid tomb? Near there."

A light breeze carrying the scent of the salty bay blew gently across Erin's face as she hiked up the hill toward her mother's gravesite. She sighed and laid the flower bouquet against the weathered granite headstone. Instantly, the vision of her mother appeared in her mind's eye. She could still see the serene, oval-shaped face framed by blonde hair that used to shine so brightly in the sunlight. In every image, her mother wore the same simple gingham dress covered with the usual beige apron tied around her slender waist. Fortunately, the memories of her mother had faded very little over the years.

"Sweet dreams, Mama." She kissed her finger and placed it on the cold headstone. As she stood, movement passed behind the large pyramid-shaped tomb up ahead. Curious, she held her breath and slowly put one foot in front of the other and headed toward the crypt.

He was standing with his back to her, but the dark-blond hair brushing against his frock collar and the unmistakable tall, lean build gave his identity away immediately.

Her breath caught deep within her chest, and a voice inside her head poked and prodded, begging her to turn and quickly walk away. But something deep inside urged her feet forward. She swallowed hard, recalling the intensity of Derek's sapphire eyes the night of the party, and how the very thought of looking into those blue depths again beckoned her headfirst toward the tomb where he stood. Each advancing step felt as though she were moving in slow motion through an evocative dream she could no longer recall.

She stopped in her tracks. *Oh, dear Lord, what am I doing?*

She slowly stepped backwards. One step … two steps … three. She spun around on her boot tips to flee undetected and stepped on a crisp, weathered pinecone. *Crunch!*

She froze.

Derek turned. "Oh, Miss Richland." He stepped aside, and a woman suddenly came into view. Apparently, she'd been there all along, her smaller body concealed by his larger frame.

Erin took a shaky step backwards and swallowed the lump in her throat. "Oh, I'm sorry. I … I didn't mean to intrude." A rush of heat burned her chilled cheeks.

Derek slowly approached and reached for her hand, his azure gaze locking upon hers. "Nonsense, Miss Richland. Your charming company is most refreshing."

She accepted Derek's hand, but her gaze snapped to the well-dressed female marching toward them. Clearly, the striking woman was new to the area. With her long, wavy red hair and unique brown eyes, Erin would have noticed her around town.

Erin squared her shoulders, released Derek's hand, and stepped toward the advancing woman. "I don't believe we've met."

"Miss Richland, I'd like to introduce you to an acquaintance of mine," said Derek. "An old friend … from France. Madame Regine Delacour, meet Miss Erin Richland."

"I am most pleased to make your acquaintance, Miss Richland," Regine said, her accented words rolling like silk from her tongue.

Derek cleared his throat. "And what brings you back to the cemetery, Miss Richland? Another story — for the newspaper?"

Erin wrenched her gaze from Regine's lovely face and turned toward Derek. "Um, yes. More trouble, I'm afraid." Behind her, she could hear Frederick grumbling unintelligibly as he watched her from the cemetery entrance below.

Derek lifted his chiseled chin and glanced over her head. A single eyebrow rose. "It appears someone is trying desperately to get your attention." His gaze lowered, his piercing eyes locked upon hers. "A beau, perhaps?"

Erin ripped her gaze from Derek's and peered over her shoulder. Frederick stood beside a man. She faced Derek, matching his sharp, insistent gaze. "Oh, him. He's just a good friend … like your Madame Delacour, here."

"*Touché*, my dear." Regine stepped forward, slipping between the two of them. She smiled and brushed a wayward auburn tendril behind her ear.

Frederick called out again.

Ignoring Regine's intrusion, Erin looked evenly into Derek's eyes. "I had best be on my way."

"So soon?" he asked, his brows furrowing. "But you've just arrived."

Regine looped her arm within Derek's, her radiant eyes glinting with smug amusement. Derek's stance instantly stiffened, and the muscle along his jawline pulsed.

Madame Delacour tilted her chin and glared at Erin. "Perhaps we'll have a chance to meet again, Miss Richland. Derek has agreed to show me around the area."

Erin's chest tightened. "Is that so?" She raised her chin high and avoided Derek's gaze. "Yes. Perhaps we shall meet again, Madame Delacour. I've heard Mr. Rudliff is very good at showing a woman a good time."

Regine lifted a gloved hand to her generous lips and laughed. "Oh, so *true*. You have heard correctly."

Erin cleared her throat, demanding the vile words coming to mind remained locked inside her head. She summoned a bright smile and said, "Good-bye, Madame Delacour." She nodded. "Mr. Rudliff." She turned on her heels and started toward an awaiting Frederick, her heart beating so hard she thought it would burst. "I'm so stupid," she quietly muttered, "*So. Very. Stupid!*"

Frederick shuffled forward with her satchel in hand. "I've been calling for you. I'm afraid the policeman here has some rather distressing news."

The chubby policeman standing next to Frederick nodded. "Hello, Miss Richland."

Erin retrieved a notebook from her satchel. "What can you tell me, Officer?"

"Well, as much as I hate to say it, we've definitely got a predatory wolf."

She pursed her lips and frowned. "And you're sure it's a wolf?"

"Absolutely. Look here." He showed her the paw prints leading south from the forest. "Appears to be a lone wolf — no other prints except these. No graves were disturbed, but the animal sure did a number on the caretaker."

Frederick chimed in. "Not that I wish to see it, but is Mr. Avery's body still here?"

"No. What was left of him was taken to the morgue, poor guy. His throat had been literally ripped out."

Erin winced. "That's horrible."

"Looked like he fought back hard, too. Lots of fur and skin were found under his broken fingernails. The coroner took everything to the laboratory for microscopic analysis. Should have confirmation of what we're dealing with when the results come back."

"Have you spoken with the man that who found Mr. Avery's body?" Erin asked. "Mr. Henkle, is it?"

The officer removed his hat and wiped his brow. "Yeah, I sure did. The old guy's a mess."

Erin gazed around the grounds. "I was planning to interview him after we're done here."

"Well, you might check down at Dinkbottom's Saloon. Poor man was shaking in his boots last I saw. Said he planned on tying a big one on down there."

Erin was having a hard time catching the policeman's every word. Up above, she could see Derek talking with Madame Delacour. Her slender arms flailed about dramatically, while he stood tall, rigid, his hands on his hips. Whatever the conversation was about, by all appearances, it appeared heated.

She faced the policeman. "Thank you for your time, Officer."

"Yes, indeed, Officer, thank you," Frederick said, shaking the man's hand.

Erin took notes while stealing unnoticed glances at Derek and the attractive red-head in the distance. She stuffed the notepad in her satchel. "Let's go, Frederick," she said, glancing at the two walking away together. "I'm tired of being here."

No one answered the door at the Henkle home, so she and Frederick headed to the saloon. Erin followed Frederick through the swinging wooden doors, and the place instantly went silent. She nudged her chin high, glaring at the men seated at the bar staring at her. Seconds later, the low voices of chattering men resumed.

"What was his name again?" asked Frederick.

"Henkle. Wiley Henkle."

Loggers, draymen, millworkers, farmers, you name it, all the men eyed her with suspicion, as she walked around in her tidy attire, searching for an unoccupied table.

"Stay close to me," Frederick said, guiding her by the elbow toward the bar. "I hate having you come in a place like this. But I know you won't rest until you get this interview out of the way."

Frederick approached the bartender. "Sir, could you tell me if a Mr. Wiley Henkle is in your establishment?"

"You wanna drink?" the bartender asked, gnawing on a wad of smelly tobacco.

Frederick clutched the lapel of his jacket. "Ah, no, um —"

"I'm Henkle, what can I do ya for?" an elderly fellow said, holding a beer in one hand and a glass in the other. Three empty shot glasses with flies buzzing around the rims sat on the bar in front of him.

"Ah, hello, my good man." Frederick looped Erin's arm through his. "This is Miss Richland with the *Everett Messenger*."

Erin rummaged through the satchel for her notepad. "Hello, sir. I only wish a moment of your time. I have some questions about what you found today at the cemetery."

The old man's eyes widened to bloodshot globes. "I don't wanna talk about it." He poured the remainder of the beer down his gullet. "I don't ever wanna talk about it, ya hear me?" He reached into his pocket and tossed a wad of bills on the bar.

Erin took a step toward him. "But —"

The older man teetered on the edge of his stool, his breath reeking of tobacco and booze.

"Listen up, Miss. What I saw when I found old man Avery will haunt me 'til my dying day. If I was you, I'd leave this alone. Nothing but evil did that." His voice trailed off. "Nothing but pure evil."

Mr. Henkle stood to leave. Frederick reached out to steady the drunken lout before he could fall in a heap of soiled coveralls to the sticky hardwood floor.

"I got it," said Henkle, swatting Frederick's hand away as he started for the door.

Erin's heart raced. All she could see was opportunity heading for the saloon exit. Louder than expected, she quickly piped up. "But there were paw prints. Wolf prints. Did you see a wolf, Mr. Henkle?"

Henkle's bleary eyes wobbled around in their sockets as he struggled to focus. "Naw, I didn't see no wolf, but what I *felt* was real. And it was evil — dark as the devil himself, I tell ya. Now I have to get home to my wife before she sends the sheriff out looking for me again, so if you'll both pardon —"

Erin pressed her hand to his arm. "Would you mind if I arranged for a picture —"

"Picture? Hell, no!"

The saloon went dead quiet, and all eyes focused on the trio.

Henkle swallowed hard and sighed. "No picture. Now, please, just leave me alone, Miss."

He took a wobbly step forward and inched his face so close to Erin's, she felt tipsy from the fumes on his breath.

He whispered, "Pure evil, I tell you. What I saw was pure evil."

She and Frederick watched in silence as he turned and staggered out the swinging doors. She rubbed her arms, trying to smooth the goose-bumps creeping along her flesh.

Frederick sighed heavily. "Well, my dear, there you have it. The man doesn't wish to talk about it. End of story." He held his arm out, gesturing toward to exit. "Shall we?"

Erin nodded compliantly, but her mind sprinted in all directions. One thing was certain. This story was far from over.

She sat in silence next to Frederick and gazed out the carriage window at the crimson sunset bleeding across the bay. In the distance, a blanket of fresh snow covered the ridged peaks of the Olympic Mountains, thrusting boldly into the heavens above.

Frederick cleared his throat. "I don't mean to pry into your personal affairs, but was that Rudliff — at the cemetery?"

"Yes," she replied said coolly. "What of it?"

"No matter, really." He smoothed his mustache, twisting the ends to a sharp point. "I just find it odd that both times you've run into the man it's been at the cemetery."

Erin sighed. "And each time, I was there on business matters. Perhaps Mr. Rudliff has business to attend to as well."

Frederick snorted. "Business? Who was the woman with him — with the magnificent red hair?"

Having no desire to conjure up the mental image of the earlier impromptu gathering with Derek and Madame Delacour, she waved her hand and hoped a casual tone in her answer would avoid further questioning. "Just an old acquaintance. I believe she's from France."

Frederick snickered. "Hmm. Well, from where I stood, they sure appeared to be much more than acquaintances, wouldn't you agree?"

His assertion simmered inside her head, reaching a boiling point within seconds. She whacked him on the head. "You men!"

"Huh? *What?*" He flinched and rubbed the spot where she had just smacked him, his brown eyes wide with astonishment. "What did I say?"

Chapter Seven

London

Enchanted by a young prostitute he had known for only a short time, Franz hired a London artisan to create a unique gift of sparkling combs for her hair. Approaching the woman's humble home with the gift in one hand and a jug of fine Madeira in the other, he heard peculiar noises coming from within the small flat.

"I was confused," said a weary Franz. "I should have left right then and there."

"And what happened?" I asked, though instinctively I felt it was something horrific.

Franz ran his hands through his thick hair and sank into the upholstered chair. "God help me."

I knelt by his side. "Look at me. I need to know."

He tilted his chin and stared me squarely in the eyes. "I couldn't help it. I had to look. I maneuvered my way around the rose garden leading to the window." He closed his eyes. "I don't wish to talk about it. Please don't force me. It happened just last night. It's too painful —"

"But you *must*," I said decisively. "I sense we could all be in danger here, Franz. Am I correct?"

As though suddenly pulled from a deep dream, his steel-gray eyes opened wide. "I gazed through the window. She was with another man. She was fucking *him*, not me."

"You expected this whore, for whom you've developed a fancy, to be faithful to you, Franz? Is that what this is all about?" I exhaled heavily, relieved that I was simply dealing with nothing more than wounded pride.

He grumbled, shot up from the chair, and paced the room. "No, no, it's not that. I didn't turn away. I *couldn't* turn away. I listened to her moans of pleasure, sounds she had made with me. I watched the strapping young man mount her repeatedly in every position imaginable. Witnessing such a thing would be bad enough for any reasonable man, don't you agree?"

Before I had time to answer, Franz stopped in mid-step and stared me dead-on. "But that was not the worst of it."

My heart stopped. I marched up and seized his shoulders. "What happened? Tell me now."

"Rage seized me, King. Before I was aware of what was happening, I shifted below her window among the sharp thorns." Franz closed his eyes and bit down on his bottom lip.

"What happened next?" I asked, my voice sounding like I had swallowed grit.

Franz gazed at me with moist eyes. "The lovely creature never knew it was me."

My arms fell limp to my sides. "Dear God, Franz. What in God's holy name did you do?"

His words came at me in a slow wave as he told me how he had lunged through the opened window and torn out the throat of the man heaving above her. Franz ravished the woman, and while she lay begging for mercy, he ripped her to shreds, tearing her limbs from her torso with fanged teeth, and then tossed the dead, mutilated bodies into the Thames.

I gnawed on my thumbnail, pacing the room, my mind racing in every direction imaginable.

He placed a hand on my shoulder. "He was a lout and she a whore, King. Perhaps their bodies won't be found, or nobody will notice they are missing —"

"Christ in heaven, Franz, *think*! They were mortals. Someone will miss them!"

His shoulders slumped. "She was a lovely girl — whore or not — I truly cared for her."

I sat in the chair and planted my face in my hands, trying to remain calm. Then a horrifying thought surfaced. My mouth went so dry I could barely form the first word. "Franz."

A moist, soulful gaze stared back at me. "Yes, my King."

"What happened to the gift — where is it now?"

Franz scrunched his eyes shut and sighed heavily.

"Oh, dear God," I mouthed. "You left it there?"

He nodded.

The news of the prostitute's grisly demise made headlines in the newspapers. Apparently, the woman had left behind an infant daughter and hailed from an affluent British family. A handsome reward was offered to anyone who could bring the evildoer to justice.

According to the papers, the brazen suspect had left a clue — a small velvet box with emerald combs inside in the shape of dragonflies. Tucked within the box lay a bloodied message that read, *"Life is the childhood of our immortality,"* signed simply with the letter "F."

Bobbies and detectives, as well as average men seeking the monetary compensation, scoured the city looking for the heinous person capable of such a vicious crime, all while trying to decipher the "hidden message."

Her death had not been premeditated, nor was there a hidden message. Franz had merely meant to give the young woman a thoughtful poem by one of Germany's most renowned poets, Johann Wolfgang Von Goethe, along with the gift. Nothing more.

Our volatile beasts lurked within our human forms night and

day, always on the hunt, forever ready to seize a moment of weakness. This was exactly what we feared most, an unbidden shift brought on by raw, palpable emotion, capable of unleashing our inner demon, with no regard for time, situation, or setting.

It was only a matter of time before the unique combs would be traced back to Franz. For the survival of the pack, I insisted we separate until I came up with a plan.

Franz headed to Belgium, Edgar and Charlotte for Paris. Others in the pack headed for the small villages to which they had been accustomed during their early mortal lives. Gregore and I remained in London.

Influenced by 17th-century French and Italian masters, Gregore became an accomplished artist in both oils and sculpture. His works were invited to the finest galleries in London. I apparently had skills of another kind — for business. After paying Gregore back his initial investment, it took me only twenty years to become wealthy.

I owned two theatres, several flats, and a large country home in Gloucester. Still, with my newfound wealth and an increasingly busy social life, my heart ached for Ersule.

So many years had passed, but I could still smell her freshly washed hair laced with the scent of sweet rose, still see the glowing sparks of dancing candlelight in her emerald eyes after we joined in tender, passionate lovemaking, still feel her delicate fingers upon my skin.

Above all else, I missed her unconditional love.

After centuries of gloomy existence, my life had grown comfortable while the clock ticked away, counting down to the rebirth of my precious wife. Now, every evening before the setting of the sun, I sipped exquisite brandy, smoked fine cigars, and remembered Koenig's words to me.

Three hundred years. Perhaps more. Perhaps less.

Two hundred and ninety-eight years had passed since I had taken her life, and as each day drew closer to three hundred, I prayed Koenig spoke the truth.

But a full three hundred years need not pass.

The miraculous day arrived in late October of 1887.

While I reclined in a chair with a sharp blade grazing my throat, held by my Parisian barber, a potent scent blasted into my nostrils.

My eyes flew open wide, my gaze darting around the small shop. When I realized Monsieur Beaudin had not spilled a bottle of heady cologne, I shot to my feet. "Oh, dear God!"

The barber seized his blade in a flash, but not before nicking my neck. "Monsieur Rudliff! *Je suis désolé ainsi!* I'm so sorry!"

I grabbed him by the shoulders and kissed his cheeks, smearing foamy blotches of shaving cream on his thin, wrinkled face. I ripped the towel from my neck, dropped coin upon the table, and fled as fast as I could down the outside stairs to my awaiting carriage.

"But Monsieur!" he called from the open window above.

I could barely hear his words, for I was consumed with the intoxicating scent — *Ersule's scent* — her same sweet fragrance of olden days, only more powerful, more seductive, unrelenting.

While my driver hastened home, I held my head out the carriage window, drawing in the familiar scent following me, calling me, beckoning me.

"Ersule," I whispered. "My precious Ersule."

The aroma shadowed me everywhere, every hour of every day. Within the month, I was able to narrow her tiny infant presence to somewhere in North America.

Still, my heart felt as heavy as the sack of flour I had retrieved from the mill all those many years ago in Bedburg. I would need to wait twenty-three years before I could claim my beloved wife and make her my queen.

Gregore and I had attended the opening of Buffalo Bill Cody's

Wild West at Earl's Court as part of the American Expedition for Queen Victoria's Golden Jubilee. Soon thereafter, he had suggested we visit America sometime soon. While I had entertained Gregore's idea, it was not until the rebirth of my beloved bride that I realized destiny had intervened.

But I feared leaving for America too soon, afraid if I caught sight of Ersule, even as a small child, I would not be able to resist the temptation of approaching her.

After much drink and deliberation, Gregore suggested we stay in London, accumulating our wealth for America a little longer while enjoying the social scene of England's most vibrant city.

I knew what Gregore suggested was logical and precisely what we must do. Simply put, with Ersule's unrelenting scent compromising my rational thinking, I could not be trusted.

But we should have left earlier than we did.

One night, I attended a lavish party. I spent much of the evening talking with a fellow German who had immigrated to America years earlier and was currently on holiday in London. The elder gentleman spoke excitedly about the prosperous brewing company he owned in the city of Baltimore, Maryland.

America. Again she beckons.

My mind bursting with the countless possibilities the elder man had mentioned in America, I retrieved my coat and hat from the attendant. Just as I was about to take my leave, the man approached and placed a hand on my shoulder.

"There's a woman in the library," he said. "The lovely creature says she wishes to speak to you directly."

Curious, I obliged, and he led me to the grand hallway and pointed me in the direction of the library.

"There you go, ol' boy." He patted me on the shoulder and winked.

I entered the candlelit room and upon seeing no one, I frowned and turned around to leave. I froze in place when I caught the familiar scent.

"Do you still not know royalty when in their presence?"

My heart stopped dead, resuming seconds later with a massive thud against my vest, nearly knocking the breath from my lungs. I closed my eyes and slowly turned.

Regine Delacour emerged from a darkened corner. Her long red hair was piled high on her head with ruby-jeweled combs woven throughout. Her perceptive brown eyes gazed at me with measured gentleness.

I closed the door and stiffened my spine. "My God, what are you doing here?"

"I could be asking you the very same thing."

I was at a loss for words as my gaze involuntarily wandered the length of her curvaceous body. She was lovelier than I remembered, and with the passing of time, my anger toward her had softened.

With the flick of her finger, she closed a book and placed it back in place on the library shelf. "Much time has passed, King, and our territories are no longer an issue."

She turned and stood before me in a red velvet dress, her breasts like two ripe melons spilling from the tight bodice. She took my hand in hers, and I instantly felt defenseless.

"It has been a long time, you and I," she whispered with a purr. "Come sit with me."

She led me by the hand to the divan. My pulse hammered like thunder against my throat. "Regine, I … I must go."

"You will *not* go." She gazed into my eyes. "You know I am a queen. You have no command over me without the full power of your pack to protect you."

"But —"

"Don't deny it, King. You need not try to convince me otherwise."

She was right. Without the full powers of my entire clan nearby, I was defenseless against an ancient Queen with the powerful influence of her female pack.

I took a deep breath and sat next to her on the divan.

She placed a hand on my knee. "You have not asked about your son."

"I have no son," I said, surprised my voice quivered.

Her ivory fingers slowly inched upward along the wool fabric of my trousers, toward my thigh.

"Ah, but you do have a son."

My shoulders slumped. I inhaled sharply and lifted my chin, trying my best to defy my overwhelming sense of defeat. "How can that be, Regine? A *Were* is the age they are turned *forever*. Is this son still a newborn infant? It's nonsense."

Her eyes softened with empathy at my apparent ignorance.

"Ah, I see. You do not know the details. I understand, King." She moistened her bottom lip with the tip of her tongue. "The *Were* child I carried within my womb would grow to be my age if female, and no more, and resemble me. If male, he would grow to his father's age, and no more, and resemble you."

Determined not to let her feel my growing arousal generated by her devilishly meandering fingers, I sighed heavily and inched away. "And you say you did indeed have this *Were* child?"

She drew closer, smiling, and leisurely adjusted my collar. "You know I did." She leaned in and whispered against my ear. "His name is Rudolpho. He is a noble wolf, King. Truth be told, he reminds me very much of you."

My hazy brain reeled with a muddled mixture of yearning, confusion, and dread. "Regine, I don't know what you want of me, but —"

"Ah." She placed a finger to my lips. "I have not come to fight with you — quite the contrary. I have come to make peace."

"Peace," I murmured, suddenly relieved.

She slid her fingers between my thighs. My limbs instantly tightened. She moved closer, her ample ivory breasts nearly spilling from her gown.

She angled her chin and quivered her ginger lashes seductively. "I want you to make love to me, Derek." Her fingers trailed within a breath of my hardening cock. "It's not so very hard for you, is it?"

Christ in Heaven.

The queen had overwhelming power over me, and she damn well knew it. I closed my eyes, but despite how hard I tried to push the thought of ravishing her like a wild dog from my mind, I grew so hard, I throbbed with pain.

"If you make love to me, I will never ask again," she whispered in my ear, her accented words caressing my earlobe like warm silk. She slid her palm over the obvious bulge in my trousers.

A husky, involuntary groan escaped my lips.

"More importantly, I won't divulge to the Royal Court you are the true father of Rudolpho. They believed me when I told them that he was sired by a mere commoner in Paris who ravished me after deceiving me into believing me he was a Celtic *Were* king."

"And the Court believed you?" My mouth hung wide open. God, how I feared the existence of the Royal Court, the shadowy faction of ancient *Weres* governing each and every *Were* clan on the European continent. From everything I had heard over the years, if they summoned a visit, chances were you would not survive to tell of it. Somehow, Regine had managed to survive. But knowing firsthand Regine's capabilities in her devious, insatiable quest for power and dominance, nothing about her surprised me anymore.

"Come now, King. 'Tis only you and me tonight. No one need know."

A warm hand cupped my shaft, straining against my trousers. She gently squeezed, and my breath hitched. "You … you will never ask this of me again, Regine? Never?"

"*Nevvver*," she whispered.

I trembled, breathless from her seductive touch. "You know I will always belong to another. *Always*."

Her eyes narrowed, golden sparks radiating from within the smoldering gaze. "I promise. I will never ask this of you again."

We left in my carriage. The entire ride home I gazed out the window, breathing in Ersule's scent, wishing it were she sitting beside me, dreaming it was her I would make love to rather than a woman I despised.

Arriving home, I immediately opened a bottle of wine. I needed the calming effect of alcohol on my rattled nerves. After pouring two glasses, Regine grabbed the remainder of the bottle and led me by the hand down the hallway in search of my bedroom.

She guided me upon my bed. I sat and drank liberally of the wine, watching as she slowly padded across the room, lighting candles, blowing each long match out seductively, while leisurely undressing herself down to sheer underclothes.

Hypnotized, I set my glass down and lay across the bed, my arm draped over my eyes. "My God, Regine. Do you not know the spell you have over a man? You could have any. Why must it be me?"

Warm hands slip up my legs to the buttons of my trousers. I removed my arm covering my eyes.

Regine was naked, long red hair spilling across her pale breasts capped with strawberry nipples. With a seductive smile no man on the planet could resist, she took my cock in her hand and gently stroked.

"I want you, King."

A hesitant groan caught deep within my throat.

"I have had no other since you," she whispered, her breath close to my shaft. "Do you know how hard that has been for a woman like me, my King?" She flicked her tongue out, moistening my tip.

I shuddered, the temptation almost too much to bear. "Regine, I —" She took me inside her mouth. "Oh, my *God*, Regine."

The woman was the devil, and I knew it, but I had no power to resist her. "Damn it to hell!" I swore under my breath, ripping at my clothes, my shirt buttons flying from the fabric, like spinning tops racing across the marbled floor.

With a smile as mysterious as that of Mona Lisa, Regine watched as I came unglued, flecks of gold flashing in her triumphant eyes.

I tossed my trousers across the room and grabbed her shoulders, hard, tossing her to the bed.

Lying naked on her back, she yelped playfully. "Tell me, King. Tell me this is a night I shall never forget." She arched her back and moistened her lips.

Every muscle in my body yearned for this *She* queen, but I would not — *could not* let her have such power over me. I would not allow her to rule me.

Not now. *Not ever.*

I forced a smile. "Oh, you most certainly will *not* forget this night, Regine. This I promise you."

In a flash, I flipped her onto her stomach. Her fiery hair hurled, settling like a red theatre curtain draping down her ivory back. With one hand, I pinned her wrists together and yanked her up by her waist to her knees at the end of the bed.

"Oh, my King!"

I planted my feet firmly in place at the edge of the bed. I spit on her arse, took aim, and dove deep inside her with a single hard plunge in a place she would never forget.

"Damn you!" Her head arched back, and she roared. "Damn you to hell, Derek!"

I leaned over and whispered in her ear. "You will get no seed of mine in your womb ever again, Madame Delacour, do you understand? Not now — not ever!" I grabbed her hair and jerked her head back. *"Do you understand?"* I hissed between clenched teeth.

The *She* vixen did not put up much of a fight for a woman who only moments earlier had been screaming for me to go to hell. In fact, she rode against me, laughing, mocking me. The damn feral bitch was fully enjoying herself.

"Go to hell, King," she laughed. "Go to hell!"

"You first!" I shouted, heated anger swelling inside me. I plunged deeper, harder, and I knew if I did not finish quickly, I would shift from blinding rage.

She cried out, her waves of passion gripping me like a throbbing vise. I yowled like a beast as I climaxed, and my knees all but buckled beneath me. After I had had my fill, I sat on the bed, shaking my head.

She lowered and rolled over to face me, her eyes moist. "No matter what you may think of me, I had no intention of forcing you to sire another royal *Were*."

I grunted. "I'm to trust you? It's because of you I already have an heir with a woman — no — a *She* I do not love." I slowly shook my head. "No, Regine. There will be no heir *and* a spare for you."

Her chin quivered. "Are you so hateful you do not wish to hear about your son?"

For some reason, her words cut me to the core. I sighed but gave no reply.

Desperation flooded her flushed face. She reached up and touched my hair. I slapped her hand away and glared into her eyes.

"He is, of course, your age now, and he looks like you, Derek. Rudolpho's hair is dark blond, like yours, but he has my eyes — brown and gold."

Hoping to wash away my vile sin, I rose and paced to the water closet.

"He is a fine prince," she called out. "A bit too independent for his own good, perhaps, but a fine *Were* noble, nonetheless. He knows his father is alive, but he does not know your name."

I ignored her.

"Are you listening to me, King? Rudolpho is anxious to rule one day. He will find you. You will meet your son someday, and you had better be prepared. Mark my words."

Mark my words. Her words reverberated inside my skull. I tossed the washcloth in the bowl and rested my head against the mirror in front of me. Queen Regine Delacour was ruthless. She could never be trusted, not ever. The farther away from her and Rudolpho I could get, the better.

I told Gregore of my misfortune with the *Were* queen. We both agreed it was best if we left for America right away.

He sold his paintings and sculptures, and I my theatres and real estate holdings. A week later, we boarded the steamer for America.

Chapter Eight

Everett, Washington

"Miss Erin!"

The urgent voice woke Erin from the puzzling dream. "Maggie?"

The servant opened the bedroom door and rushed in.

Erin slowly sat up in bed and rubbed her eyes. "What's the matter?"

"Your father's rushed off." Maggie yanked the bedroom curtains open. "It seems there's been a wolf attack."

"What — at the cemetery?"

"No, not this time. Over on Chestnut, and apparently the scene is horrific."

Erin scrunched her eyes shut and sighed, trying to rouse from her interrupted dream. "Are … are there any details?"

"I don't know anything more. You know your father. He rushed out the door. But judging from what I overheard, a woman was murdered."

Another murder. Erin scrambled from bed.

Maggie grabbed the chenille robe draped at the footboard and extended it.

"I'm going to need an extra-large cup of coffee to tackle this day, Maggie."

"Yes, Miss. Coming right up," the servant said as she swiftly exited the bedroom.

Erin slowly shook her head. *What the devil is going on around here? The graves disturbed in the dead of night at the cemetery. Mr. Avery shredded to pieces. Now this.*

After washing and dressing, she made her way downstairs to the dining room where Maggie had already set out a pot of coffee.

The servant entered with a plate of biscuits and gravy. "Thought you'd want breakfast before heading out."

Erin draped a linen napkin across her lap and watched as Maggie poured the steaming coffee into a cup.

The servant paused in mid-pour. "What do you suppose is happening around here?"

Erin gestured for Maggie to continue pouring. "I don't know. I really just don't know. Whatever it is, it's nothing this city has ever seen before." A cold shiver raced up her spine.

Maggie exhaled loudly. "And something tells me you plan to get to the bottom of this mystery, am I right?"

Erin forced a smile. "You know me far too well."

After breakfast Erin saddled her horse and headed for Chestnut Avenue. As much as she tried to focus on the task ahead, foggy images of her interrupted dream kept resurfacing. With each steady clomp of the horse's hooves, her heart kept beat as she recalled the faraway, dreamy vision.

Derek had been standing by her side near a sunny pebbled stream. Women in long woolen skirts sat crouched along the bank, smiling and talking to one another, while washing clothes in the flowing water. In the dream, Derek had looked the same, yet different. Dressed in modest, well-worn clothing and sporting a beard, his solemn face and poignant blue eyes had caught her by surprise.

But it was her own words in the dream that rang clear as a bell inside her mind now: "Go on," she had said to him in a chiding tone, waving him away with a dismissive swish of her hand. Yet as she watched Derek slowly turn and walk away, pebbly goose-bumps had raced across her skin, and the sudden feeling of dread made her wish she had told him … something.

Then Maggie's urgent knocks interrupted the dream.

"What was it I wanted to tell him?" she murmured, urging the horse to a slower clip as she approached.

Up ahead, policemen were shouting and waving their hands in a flurry, trying to keep the crowd of people away from the roped-off area.

She secured the reins to a weathered post and headed toward the swarm with her pen and notepad in hand. Just as she slipped underneath the rope, a policeman called out.

"Miss, get back behind the rope."

"I'm with the *Everett Messenger*," she said.

The young policeman grabbed her arm. "I don't care who you're with."

Erin glared at the firm hand gripping her arm. She lifted her gaze to his. "Unhand me, now. I'm a member of the press, and I have every right to be here."

Releasing his grip, his face flushed bright red.

She passed what appeared to be a body fully concealed with a wool blanket, lying at the bottom of the three-story brick building. Crimson stains seeped through the thick fabric. Her co- worker, David, was standing over the body, his arms crossed at his chest.

Erin approached him. "Looks like quite a story is brewing, don't you think?"

David appeared to struggle with wrenching his gaze from the covered body lying on the ground. "Erin." He frowned and shook his head. "Uh-oh. Wait a tick. What are you doing down here? Your father specifically told me he didn't want you on this story or anywhere near this part of town. There's talk about wolves."

Good Lord. It was too early in the morning for this nonsense.

She narrowed her gaze. "You men."

David's jaw flopped open, his arms falling limply to his sides. "What?"

She heaved a sigh and glared into his wide eyes. "You're new, David, so you don't know me very well. I understand you're just following my father's orders, and I appreciate that." She lifted a single eyebrow. "Now let me do my work. Where's my father?"

David's gaze darted from side to side. "Hmm. He was just here." He shrugged. "Heck, I don't know. He's around here somewhere. Do you want me to find him?"

She skimmed the faces of the panicked crowd. There was an important story waiting to be written. If she could get to the bottom of what had happened here before David did ... .

A slight woman leaning against the brick building captured Erin's attention. Tears sullied her pink cheeks, and her wilted shoulders heaved with quiet sobs.

"Erin? Do you want me to find him?" David repeated.

As Erin stared at the sad young woman up ahead, she felt as though she'd just entered a dark cave. Everything in her peripheral vision thinned to shadows except for the tearful waif-like creature standing alone, clutching a crocheted shawl draped across her shoulders.

"No," Erin muttered, stepping toward the young woman. "I'll find my father in just a bit." Erin ventured forward. "Miss?" She gazed into the despondent eyes staring back and realized the woman couldn't have been more than eighteen years of age.

With trembling fingers, the slender creature clutched her shawl shut and peered up with round eyes brimming with tears. "Yes, Ma'am?"

"Honey, are you all right?"

"No, no, no," she said, her soft voice trailing away with the cool breeze.

Erin jutted her chin toward the covered body lying on the ground. "Do you know what happened here?"

She sniffed. "It's Julie."

Erin stared at the blanket-covered corpse before turning her attention back to the distraught woman. "And you knew Julie?"

Sobs rocked the woman's upper body. "I did," she whimpered.

Erin rubbed the woman's shoulder, and her finger snagged in a hole of the threadbare shawl. "Do you wish to talk about it?"

The urchin lifted her moist gaze. "I … I don't know if I can."

Erin scanned the area, looking for a warm restaurant where they could talk. "Let me buy you some breakfast. I think —"

"No." The woman shook her head. "Please, I just need to go upstairs to my room."

Erin sensed the young woman knew what had happened. As much as she wanted valuable insight into this important news story shaking the city, she couldn't push the poor girl into talking with her, at least not yet. "I'll just leave you to your privacy, Miss. But if you ever need to talk —"

"You're welcome to join me upstairs." The waif cocked her head toward the brick building.

"Are you sure you want company right now?"

She pressed her hand to Erin's arm. "Please, come."

Erin followed quietly up the damp outside stairway leading to the third floor. Once inside, they walked a narrow hallway framed with peeling plaster from floor to ceiling. They stopped at a closed door. The girl reached up, retrieved a key from above the entry jamb, and opened the door.

Inside the small dwelling were two stools tucked under a drop-leaf table in the tiny kitchen with a hearth. Blankets hung on a tethered rope, separating the bed and small washbasin from the rest of the room.

"I know it ain't much. But I do have tea. Would you like some?"

Erin followed her into the kitchen. "Tea sounds lovely, but allow me to make it."

"No, no," she said with a firm shake of her head. "Sit." The girl knelt by the glowing embers of a dying fire, poured steaming water from a kettle into a bowl, and inserted the tea ball.

As the tea steeped, Erin sat on a stool, quietly observing the slight woman reaching into a copper bucket sitting by the hearth and placing a log on the waning fire. She said, "I just realized I don't even know your name. I'm Erin Richland."

Looking as though she had performed the same dull task hundreds of times before, the waif craned her willowy neck, leaned toward the embers, and blew gently until the log caught flame. "My name's Pearl." Without looking up she said, "And the body under the blanket outside? That's Julie. My older sister."

Her older sister.

Erin's heart sank to her toes. She rose from the stool and hastened toward the girl. "I'm terribly sorry for your loss, honey." She knelt beside her.

Pearl split the tea into two smaller cups and handed one to Erin before sitting on a stool at the table.

Erin took the seat opposite. "You know, Pearl is truly a lovely name."

Pearl snorted into her teacup. "It ain't my Christian name. Even Julie had her working name. She went by Lilly, you know, for the customers. Down 'round here, we're known as the White sisters: Lilly and Pearl White."

Erin's cheeks warmed. While she had suspected sweet little Pearl was likely a prostitute, she hadn't been sure until now.

Pearl sighed and lifted her gaze to Erin's. "You look like a fine woman, Miss Richland. What are you doin' talking to someone like me, anyhow?"

The question caught Erin off guard. "Well, I came here because

I heard something horrible had happened."

"But don't you know a lady's reputation gets tarnished to black ash if she's seen down these parts of town?"

Erin pursed her lips. "I don't care a whip about that. Truly, I don't. Besides, I work for the newspaper and —"

"The newspaper?" Pearl stood in a flash. "I … I don't want be in the newspaper. You hear me?" She paced the room, whimpering. Lifting her quivering chin she said, "I'm sorry, but I'm going to have to ask you to leave, Miss Richland."

Erin slowly rose from her seat. "I'm so sorry, Pearl. I didn't mean to upset you. I didn't come up here to —"

Pearl stopped in mid-step. "You didn't come up here to *what?*"

Guilt pierced Erin's belly. Indeed, she had thought about reporting Pearl's side of the story, but that idea had quickly faded once she realized the murder victim was Pearl's sister. "If you don't want your name in the newspaper, that's fine. Truly."

Pearl's eyebrows rose to pale arches. "You trying to tell me you didn't come up here to get a story?"

Erin couldn't lie to her. "Well, maybe, initially."

Pearl turned away with a sigh and gazed out the tall apartment window. "What happened last night. The sounds. I'll never get them out of my head. Never. The screams, the pleading." She covered her ears and flopped on the bed.

Erin rushed to Pearl's bedside, but appropriate words of comfort felt locked inside her throat.

"And then the sight of my poor sister lying on the ground and all that blood — *Oh, God.*" She lifted her head from the pillow, her gaze snapping to Erin's. "You're a proper woman, Miss Richland. Promise me you won't put me in the paper. *Promise,* or I won't say another word."

"Yes, yes, I promise, Pearl." Erin sat at the edge of the bed. "Truly, I won't."

Pearl rolled over and covered her eyes with the crook of her arm. "I'm all alone in the world now."

Outside, shouts from the lingering crowd demanding answers to the heinous murder rang out. Erin lifted her chin and gazed out the tall leaded glass window. Policeman shuffled the angry people away from the crime scene as an ambulance cart moved up the street, presumably with Julie inside.

Determined to get to the bottom of the murder of Pearl's sister, Erin asked, "What did you hear, Pearl? What *exactly* did you see?"

A large brown eye peeked out from below Pearl's draped arm. "Remember now, you promised you won't write anything about me."

"I remember."

Pearl's long drawn-out sigh filled the small apartment. "Last night, Julie and I were downstairs in the saloon. A man came in looking like a real fine gentleman, top hat, dressed in a suit that must have cost a fortune."

"Had you ever seen this man before?"

"No, but new clients had been coming in here ever since the building was bought by a new owner. Trust me, I surely would have noticed this man before. You probably know the rich-looking type, Miss Richland, but me and Julie, well, we have our regulars, and they don't look like him." She sighed and her arm dropped limply to her side. "The gentleman bought me and Julie drinks. 'Course he didn't know that our new boss just puts apple juice in our glasses. Hell, if we had liquor every time a man bought us drinks, well ... "

Erin nodded. "Go on."

"Anyway, after he bought us the drinks he said he wanted something special."

"Something special," Erin repeated.

Pearl blushed. "Well, he wanted both of us — me and Julie, together, for the night. We're sisters, so we ain't never, well, you know, not *together* — "

"Yes, yes. I understand," Erin said, hoping to move the story along quicker.

"Julie told him it would cost him big. There was something in the handsome man's eyes. Wild lookin' eyes, he had. I got real nervous. I wanted to pull her aside and talk to her a minute and tell her how uneasy I was feeling."

Erin cocked her head. "And did you?"

"Yeah." Pearl sniffed. "I got her alone, behind the bar, and told her I didn't trust the man. She laughed and told me not to worry. Said she'd take care of him herself. She liked the idea of being with a well-dressed gentleman with money. It was a pleasant change from all the loggers and mill workers, she said. I looked at him sitting at that table with an arrogant smile and those wild eyes of his. I begged her not to do it, but there was no arguing with Julie. She always did what she wanted, when she wanted, and that was the end of it. At first he put up a fight. Demanded the two of us. But after she whispered something in his ear, he smiled and nodded. After that, I called it a night and went upstairs to my room."

Erin frowned, trying to piece together all the information Pearl had just relayed while combining it with Maggie's announcement about a wolf.

Pearl sighed wearily, fresh tears moistening her eyes. "But that wasn't the end of it. Next thing I know, I'm being woken up in the dead of night. I hear Julie next door, and there's more pounding against the wall than usual, if you know what I mean."

Oh, Erin knew exactly what Pearl meant. The mental image of Derek's naked body hovering above her, his azure eyes seducing her, rendering her powerless, flashed through her mind. Instantly, a flush of heat raced across her neck and cheeks.

Pearl's eyes softened. "Oh, Miss Richland. You sure you want to hear this?"

"I do. I'm sorry, I'm just —"

"Only if you're sure. Fact is, I really don't have anyone to talk to anymore. I know we're strangers, but having you here helps."

Erin managed a smile. "I want to help. Go on."

Pearl closed her eyes. A single tear glided down the side of her face, disappearing on the dingy pillow beneath her head. "I was hearing noises against the wall. More grunting and groaning than usual. I didn't think too much about it at the time. Some men are, well, some men just have more vigor than others. But, then the sounds turned different, growling, heavy panting, muffled cries. I got real scared. I shot out of bed and quickly dressed." Pearl cleared her throat. "Then I heard cries. Sounded muffled, like he had Julie's mouth covered, then a loud growl followed. And it weren't like a growl from a man or a mangy ol' dog. It was like it was coming from … a beast."

"A *beast?*" The tiny hairs on the back of Erin's neck rose, and goose-bumps crawled across her flesh.

"I know. It sounds crazy, but I tell you, these sounds were *not* of this world. The pounding got louder, more violent. I ran out my room and knocked on her door. There was no answer, but I knew she was in there with him. I tried to open the door, but it was locked."

Pearl pressed the heels of her palms to her eyes. "Like always, her spare key was above the door jamb. Just as I placed it in the lock, I heard a howl —"

"A howl — you're sure?"

"Oh, I'm sure," Pearl said decisively. "Then the sound of breaking glass rang out, followed by a thud. I was so scared my hands shook as I opened the door. What I saw next … " Pearl's shoulders rocked as she wiped her moist, painted cheeks.

Erin pulled a handkerchief from her pocket. "Here, honey."

Pearl sniffed and blew her nose. "When I walked in the room, blood was everywhere. On the walls, the bed, even on the ceiling. I ran to the shattered window, and there, right on the ground below the street lamps was Julie, bloody, lifeless … dead."

Erin fought the urge to gag. "And where was the man?"

"I didn't see a man. I didn't see nothin' except a large wolf scampering away fast as the winter wind toward the river. Turns out, Julie'd been mauled — eaten alive — and the handsome man with the dark blond hair and piercing eyes was nowhere to be seen."

Darkling I listen; and, for many a time
I have been half in love with easeful Death,
Call'd him soft names in many a mused rhyme,
To take into the air my quiet breath;

— John Keats, "Ode to a Nightingale"

Part Two
The Guardian

CHAPTER NINE

America

I was in my *Were* form, panting wildly, rushing through a city park. Angry and famished, I pounced on the first unwary human I encountered, tearing unmercifully into my victim's slender throat. Gathering pools of dark blood surrounded me. Under the soft glow of a streetlamp, a shiny patent leather shoe dangled from my victim's small foot.

I dropped my prey and lunged backwards, recoiling like a snake. Shaking uncontrollably, I watched in horror as the little girl with coal-black hair stared back at me, her emerald green eyes fading with imminent death.

"Derek, if only you had waited," she whispered.

I woke in the steamer bunk with a start, drenched in sweat, frightened beyond measure. Trembling and weak, I gazed out the small window and watched the foamy Atlantic waves being ripped by the heavy wind carrying her scent straight to me. I reminded myself it had only been another nightmare. But something deep within my bones told me it was more than that. The disturbing dream was a reminder.

The animal inside me never sleeps.

I missed Ersule, missed her more than mortal life itself. Every day as her lovely scent wafted into my nostrils, I imagined what she looked like as a little girl. Did her ebony black hair frame eyes that sparkled like emerald jewels set before a fire? Was her ivory skin feather-soft to the touch, just as I remembered? While the sensation was unbearable at times, I stayed within the city of Baltimore, resisting all temptation to see her as a child residing in nearby New York. I dared not catch even a mere glimpse of her before she reached twenty-three, or I would be risking everything I'd waited centuries for.

Everything.

One evening at *The Horse You Came in On Saloon*, I met an elderly gentleman named Jeffrey Watt. We drank whiskey, smoked cigars, and played poker late into the night. With companies in Maine and Illinois, Watt spoke of his idea to expand his business in the West.

"The future is in the West, young man," he told me. "And I may have the perfect opportunity for such a man as yourself."

My mind wandered from the conversation back to the Wild Bill Cody Show Gregore and I had seen in London years ago. I had hung on Wild Bill's every mesmerizing word about the Great American West.

As Ersule matured, her scent ripened, and my temptation to see her swelled exponentially. She was now a girl of eleven, and she lived a mere two hundred miles away from me. After my brandy and cigar each evening, I would sit still and quiet, feeling the soft tick of her little heart deep within my chest, the beat mirroring my own.

So how could I move farther away from her now?

Sensing my hesitation, Watt explained, if I were interested, I need not move west just yet. Several years of acquiring more timberlands would be required before the logging could begin and the mills completed.

The idea appealed to me, more than I ever would have thought possible, and a delayed move out to the West certainly sweetened the offer.

Within a month, the necessary business papers had been drawn. All I had to do was travel to Maine, inspect my northeastern investments, and upon my approval and signature on the bottom line of the documents, I would become an equal partner in Watt & Rudliff Land and Timber Company.

Eager for excitement, Gregore insisted he travel with me, but with one special request. On the return trip, he wanted to stop at the museums in New York.

"Gregore, you're my dear friend, you know that, but I cannot possibly go there."

Pity dulled his brown eyes. "You have resisted for years, all while knowing she lived only two hundred miles away. New York is immense." He placed his hands on my shoulders. "I will keep you strong."

I slowly shook my head. "I don't know if I have the power to keep away. I struggle, Gregore. I fight each and every day."

But the more I hesitated, the more Gregore spoke excitedly of the museums and theatres, and when I saw the spark of life it brought to his eyes, I agreed with one caveat. We would stay in New York for two days and two nights only.

Our very existence within populated areas required a level of fluency. We had grown accustomed to our comfortable hunting grounds among the homeless wretches in the dark alleys of Baltimore, the pitiful vagrants no one ever gave the courtesy of a second glance. The full moon would occur by the third night, and we dare not temp fate by hunting in the unfamiliar alleys of New York.

In Maine we toured and inspected the mills, camps, and business ledgers. Upon the endorsement of my lawyer, I signed on the dotted line. I had officially become an American businessman and looked forward to celebrating with Gregore.

New York was unlike anywhere we had ever been. The large

city was similar to London, only more modern, more vibrant, with people out at all hours, day and night. Horse-drawn carriages filled the streets while people shopped, ate at the abundant restaurants, visited museums, or simply meandered through the large park.

The first afternoon we enjoyed a lavish lunch. Later, while admiring the collection at the Museum of Art, we stood in front of a marble sculpture designed by the artist Thomas Crawford, titled *Genius of Mirth*. I heard a guttural whimper from Gregore. He sighed, and I watched as a solitary tear dripped down his cheek.

"So beautiful. Look at the boy's young face," he whispered. "Not a care in the world." He turned and gazed into my eyes. "We were like that once. Do you remember being a child?"

I lowered my head. *Lord.* I hadn't thought about my childhood in so long, I wasn't sure it had ever truly existed.

I could feel Ersule's human presence nearby. The new sensation titillated me to the core. With her heavenly scent and close proximity teasing every inch of my physical being, I walked around the city feeling as though I were deliciously drunk. Following her aroma, I narrowed her residence to within a one-block radius. I knew she was close, a mere block away at most, and yet, I had a finer sense of control than I ever would have imagined.

New York was an eclectic city in every conceivable way. Humans of every shape, size, and ethnicity, were plentiful. Daily, people streamed into New York Harbor from all over the world to begin their lives anew. In this strange new city, perhaps we *could* blend.

The day we were to return on the train to Baltimore was the happiest day I'd had in more than three hundred years.

After breakfast I took a morning stroll through Central Park. I sat on a bench, gazing at the people going about their normal lives. Somehow, the scene made me feel mortal. I extinguished my cigar and broke off a piece of the biscuit I had placed in my coat pocket to feed the pigeons.

Instantly, my breath caught in my lungs, and my heart stopped dead. I raised my nose high in the air, sniffing at the familiar scent growing increasingly stronger. My heart suddenly rebounded with a massive thud against my starched shirt. I turned my head from side to side, my heightened sense of smell honing in on the delightful aroma. I narrowed my gaze.

There.

Oh, dear God.

It was she. A smaller version in a pretty pink dress, but it was definitely Ersule.

Raven ringlets of hair framed her ivory skin and sparking eyes. She appeared to be about eleven years old, fresh, innocent, on the cusp of womanhood, just as I would have expected.

Tears stung the back of my eyes, pooling in the corners, and I stifled the gasp threatening to escape my throat. I quickly slouched and tugged my hat over my brow.

"Mama?" Ersule called in the honeyed tone of a child's voice.

I peered from below the brim of my hat. Ersule stood staring at me, pointing.

Tightness seized my chest.

"That man is feeding the birds. Please, may I feed them, too?"

Her mother appeared delicate, reminding me of a gentle bird. Her chignon of fair hair peeked out from below a dark bonnet, and her physique was so slender she looked as though she could snap like a twig on an icy day. There was absolutely no resemblance whatsoever between the slight woman Ersule called "Mama" and the blossoming child.

"No, honey," said her mother. "I'm sorry, but I didn't bring anything to feed them today."

The little girl's ebony brows knitted together in a frown. "But I want to feed them, Mama." She crossed her arms over her chest and sighed heavily. I had to catch myself from chuckling aloud at her impish vitality.

"Erin, darling —"

Erin. Her name is Erin! I closed my eyes, and the tears I had tried to hold back dripped down my cheeks. I sniffed and swiftly brushed them away with the back of my hand.

Her mother bent low. "I've already told you, darling, I don't have anything. If you can't behave like a proper young lady, we'll have to leave." She took Erin's smaller hand, and they turned to leave.

My stomach twisted in a tight knot. Before I had time to contemplate, I called out, "Excuse me?"

The two spun around. The mother's face was poised with curiosity, but Erin wore a haughty smile upon her full lips, a smile so evocative it felt as though she had been wondering what had taken me so long. Her shrewd expression took me by surprise, and I instantly diverted my gaze.

"Yes?" The mother's pale eyes narrowed. "Have me met, sir?"

I stood, avoiding eye contact with the child. "No, Madame, I … "

"Yes?" she asked warily, clearly sensing my awkward hesitation.

Erin pulled her hand free from her mother's and took a step toward me. "The man is offering me some bread for the birds. Isn't that right, sir?"

Stunned by the child's boldness, I took a deep breath, trying to gather my wits. *What the hell was I doing?* I had no plan. More importantly, I had no escape.

I smiled and looked into her mother's eyes. "Yes, yes, that's exactly right. I have some extra biscuit here." I held out the crumbled biscuit, unaware I had been crushing it within my fist.

"That's kind of you to share." The mother turned to her daughter. "I think your offer would please my daughter very much, indeed." She nudged the child's arm. "Thank the kind gentleman, Erin." She looked into my eyes. "Your name, sir?"

"Oh, yes, my name. *Radcliff*." I coughed nervously, and my hands trembled as I divided the flimsy pieces of the biscuit.

"You must thank Mister Radcliff, dear."

Erin lifted her chin high and slowly approached me. With each step she took, I felt my chest squeeze like a tightening vise. She stopped directly in front of me and extended her small hand.

"Thank you, Mr. Radcliff. I'm Miss Erin Richland."

She shook my hand with a firmness I never would have expected from someone so small. I rubbed my thumb casually over the soft bend of her finger. Something invisible penetrated my skin with the subtlety of a bolt of lightning.

I flinched.

Erin looked directly in my eyes with startling intensity, holding my hand firmly and longer than I wanted.

She leaned forward and whispered, "Did you feel that, Mr. Radcliff?"

Dark clouds loomed over my head, and my vision dimmed to shadows. I ripped my hand free from hers, trying to keep my composure. Ignoring her question, I managed to choke out, "Open your hand, little one."

She presented her small hand, and I placed the largest piece of the biscuit in her palm.

Her eyes widened to dazzling emerald orbs. "Thank you!"

I watched as Erin skipped away, heading for a flock of cooing pigeons, leaving her mother and me alone in her joyful wake.

The sudden silence thickened the air. Dizzied, I gripped the armrest for support. "Your daughter is lovely, Mrs. Richland."

Her thin lips curved upward. "She's a delightful child — willful, but delightful."

I cast my gaze toward Erin, who giggled as she tossed pieces of biscuit into the flock of birds fanned out around her shoes.

Black patent leather shoes.

Dear God.

Beads of sweat formed across my neck and forehead.

"I'm sorry. I haven't introduced myself. "I'm Ella Mae Richland."

I wrenched my gaze from Erin and faced her mother. "Delighted to meet you, Madame Richland."

She gestured toward the bench. "Care to sit with me, Mr. Radcliff?"

I ripped my hand free from the armrest supporting me and sat. I blotted my damp forehead with my handkerchief. I needed to get out of there, but my numb feet would not move.

"And what do you do in New York, Mr. Radcliff?" Mrs. Richland asked.

I wedged the handkerchief back into my vest pocket "I'm … I'm visiting for a few days — business matters."

She sighed wearily. "You men and your business matters. My husband is a terribly busy man."

"Not too busy, I hope. Certainly he has time for two such charming females in his life."

She looked at me with a puzzled glare making me wonder if, perhaps, my comment appeared too lecherous coming from a stranger.

"He does the best he can," she murmured.

She suddenly coughed in a fit, and her eyes dulled to pale gray. "Oh my, I can't seem to shake this ague."

"Look at me, Mama!" Erin called, swinging her hands and chasing the birds. "Look at me, Mr. Radcliff!"

"You're precious, darling," her mother said.

I rummaged in my coat pocket and extended a clean handkerchief. She covered her mouth and another deep cough seized the woman's chest. I was about to speak up and inquire if she needed assistance, but she must have seen the question in my eyes, for she waved away my unspoken words.

"I'm fine now," she said.

I looked at the crumpled handkerchief clutched between her slender fingers. The crimson bloodstain contrasted fiercely with the white linen. My heart sank. Consumption, pneumonia, cancer? Whatever ailed her, I ached for the little girl who would undoubtedly lose her mother sooner rather than later in life.

"Ah, there you are," said a plump brunette darting straight for Erin. "And where might your mother be?"

"I'm right here, Maggie. It's all right."

The brunette's eyes narrowed as she approached us. "Ah, there you are, Ma'am."

"Maggie, this is Mr. Radcliff, a visitor to New York. He's enjoying our beautiful park."

Maggie cocked her head. "You don't say."

I felt the woman's concentrated appraisal of me from the tip of my head to the heels of my shoes. "Ah," I said, rising from my seat, offering it to the elder woman.

"Thank you, no. I'll stand," Maggie said. "What did you say your name is?"

Erin's mother shot Maggie a questioning glance.

I had no idea what irritated this woman. I clutched my lapels like a cock ruffling his feathers and said, "*Rad*-cliff."

She eyed me sharply and sighed. "Excuse me," she said, before heading back to Erin.

I sat back down and watched as the brunette vigorously brushed the dust from Erin's dress and shiny shoes.

Erin's mother leaned in. "Maggie's our servant. She can be abrupt at times."

A smile graced Madame Richland's lips, but something akin to sorrow seemed to radiate from her dull eyes.

I eyed the servant with the prickly disposition whispering something in Erin's ear. The child glanced at me before returning to feeding the birds.

A pit wedged within my belly. It was time to take my leave. Seeing as I was an unknown man among unchaperoned females in a city park, I had overstayed my welcome, anyway. "Well, I must be on my way, Madame Richland."

I had passed the test I had feared for centuries. I could be in the presence of reborn Ersule without compromising our future. As I turned to leave, the little girl saw me and tore away from the servant's grasp.

"Mr. Radcliff," Erin called.

She ran forward and hugged me around my waist. I froze in place, my heart racing like a wild winter wind. Could she feel it, too?

"Child! Behave yourself!" Maggie scolded.

I couldn't move.

Erin held tight and lifted her chin.

My breath caught in my throat at the sight of the arresting green eyes framed by ebony lashes gazing up at me. A clever smile arched her pink lips into a gentle curve.

"I've seen you in my dreams," she whispered.

And just like that, with the impetuousness of a child, she unwrapped her arms from my waist and ran back to the flock of hungry birds eagerly awaiting her return.

Chapter Ten

Everett, Washington

The question weighed on Erin's mind. Would Washington be the first state in the twentieth century to enact women's suffrage? Already, Wyoming, Utah, Idaho, and Colorado had seen fit for women to vote. With hard work and a measure of good luck, perhaps she would soon join the ranks of those allowed at the polls.

The Women's Suffrage Club had worked tirelessly getting the word out and their voices heard during the campaign. She attended public rallies and paid visits to granges, labor unions, and the Farmers Union. The most important work came from the door-to-door visits she made to mothers, grandmothers, wives, daughters, and sisters. It would come down to their influence on the men in their lives as they headed to the polls to vote.

Today was their last chance to make a difference. All morning and afternoon, she and Delia handed out flyers, knocked on doors, and talked to people on the streets. They had just left a front porch when a deep voice called out.

"Miss Richland."

Erin turned to see a coachman tugging the reins, pulling the horses to the side of the street. Derek sat in the back of the carriage.

"Oh, my God *almighty*," Delia whispered. "Would you look who's here?" She smoothed her skirts and puckered her lips.

Erin turned away on her heels and whispered, "Oh, my heavens, I don't want to see him."

Delia's lips formed a generous pout. "My stars. Why not? Have you seen what that man looks like?"

Erin turned up her nose and headed for the house next door. "Well, if you like him so much, you go talk to him."

"Oh, no, you don't." Delia grabbed Erin's arm and pointed. "Just look at him sitting all alone in the back of that fine carriage."

"But I don't —"

Delia spun her around by the shoulders, aiming her toward the carriage. Erin's gaze instantly locked with Derek's.

"Lucky girl." Delia poked the small of her back, urging Erin forward. "Well, go on — *get.*"

Erin stepped toward the carriage, one numb foot in front of the other, until she reached the coach door. "Good afternoon, Mr. Rudliff."

A dazzling smile spread beneath his mustache. "Good afternoon to you, as well, Miss Richland. Say, I was heading home and spotted you. Would like to join me for supper?"

She thumbed the last few flyers in her hand. "Oh, no, I can't possibly. I still have to hand these out."

He glanced at the scant amount of paper left in her hand. "That shouldn't take long. Perhaps you can hand those out later. I thought we could start the interview for the paper." Dark eyebrows arched high. "You *are* interested in a story, correct?"

She looked back at Delia, whose eyebrows waggled up and down. She turned to Derek. "I —"

He winked. "I promise I'll escort you home myself later."

Erin sucked in her cheeks, contemplating the situation. He looked devilishly handsome in his dark waistcoat and top hat, and saying no to those incredible blue eyes somehow felt *wrong*. On second thought, she did need to get that article for the newspaper.

"Sounds lovely. Yes, I'll join you."

He stepped out of the carriage and opened the door, towering over her by at least a foot.

"Splendid." He guided her by the arm into the polished brougham.

"Oh, wait." She stuck her head out the open door. "Delia, are you comfortable walking back?" She turned to Derek. "Perhaps this isn't a good idea. I really should —"

"Miss Delia?" Derek called. "May I give you a ride home?"

Delia meandered toward the carriage, her ample hips swaying in an exaggerated sashay. "Why, Mr. Rudliff, how very thoughtful of you," she said. "I need to check on my elderly widowed aunt two doors that-a-way." She pointed. "Perhaps another —"

"Ah, very well, then," Derek replied. "Good day."

He scooted in beside Erin and tapped the ceiling. Instantly, the driver snapped the buggy whip and urged the horses to a trot.

With every clomping hoof, Erin's heart thumped in reply. Moisture dotted her face and neck. *Oh, Lord, what am I doing here?* "Excuse me, Mr. Rudliff. I … I have to go. I forgot —"

A warm hand slid over hers, expressive eyes meeting hers. "Miss Richland." He paused. "*Erin*, calm yourself. It's going to be all right."

Something in his eyes reminded her of a faraway dream. She wrenched her gaze from his and snatched her hand back. "You don't understand."

"What don't I understand? That what we both feel at this moment is uncomfortable? I assure you, Erin, I understand more than you know."

The soothing tone of his voice calmed her. Just as her heartbeat slowed, a troubling thought intruded. What if the attractive red-head was there? "Um, will it just be the two of us for supper?"

"No."

Her stomach leaped into her throat. "Oh, I see. You know, I just remembered something. On second thought, perhaps —"

"My cook will be there as well as the butler. Is that a problem?"

"Oh!" she said, louder than expected. "No, no, of course not."

The horses trotted down the quiet street, pulling up to the large house sitting high above the bluff. Derek stepped out and escorted her along the path to the front door.

"Will that be all for now, sir?" his driver called.

"For now, Franz. I'll be calling upon you later when we take Miss Richland home."

"Yes, sir." He nodded and tipped his hat before descending the carriage to tend to the horses.

She scrunched up her nose and whispered, "Is it me, or is he rather sinister?"

Derek laughed so hard she thought the neighbors would hear. "Who, Franz? He is unusual, but I wouldn't say he's 'sinister,' per se. He's a good man, I assure you, but I suppose with that scowl he wears night and day he might appear that way to others."

Upon entering the grand foyer, the butler took her coat and hung it in the scrolled armoire. A sprightly, plump woman entered the room. "Ah, Master Rudliff, will there be two for supper?" she asked, wiping a wet paring knife on her crisp white apron.

"Yes, Hannah. Make that two for supper."

An old-world air of sophistication permeated the walls and tall ceiling of the massive home. Having been there during the costume party with the mass of costumed people and dim lighting, she had not been able to fully appreciate the unique setting until now.

"Oh, my," she muttered, walking down the hall and seeing the large windows facing the back. "I forgot what an extraordinary view you have."

Numerous sailing ships and small boats dotted the deep blue waters below. Centered in one of the large windows, the sun slipped low, spreading like a shimmering fan across the horizon, softening everything in its amber glow. To the left, majestic snow-topped mountains poked heavenward. And to the north lay the vast evergreen-laden island of Whidbey.

"So pretty," she called, turning and bumping hard into Derek's chest. She stepped back. "I'm sorry. I thought you were —" Secure hands caught her shoulders, settling her back in place.

Derek smiled. "No, it's all right. My fault. I was looking at the same view over your shoulder."

She cleared her throat. "What I was saying is, you have a truly lovely view."

He tilted his chin and gazed out the window. "It's beginning to feel more and more like a home every day."

They stood inches apart, yet a charged energy moved within the small space between them. Standing next to him, his tall, lean body next to hers somehow made everything around her feel brighter, more alive, different, and yet, so very familiar. She closed her eyes, welcoming the tingling sensation sweeping across her skin.

"Dinner is served," Hannah said, breaking the spell.

"Ah, thank you, Hannah." Derek turned to Erin. "Shall we, my dear?"

The long dining table had been set for two. Elegant china, silverware, linen napkins, and silver goblets tastefully adorned the crisp tablecloth. Hannah emerged with a sterling tray topped with grilled salmon surrounded by roasted potatoes, carrots, and turnips. The aroma was nothing less than intoxicating. The servant scurried through the swinging door and returned moments later, filling their chilled goblets with chardonnay.

"To you," Derek said, extending his goblet.

She smiled. "And to you."

Several minutes passed in silence. Finally, Erin said, "What do you think of the women's suffrage vote?"

His brow wrinkled into a deep seam, and his gaze shifted from hers. "I don't know if this is what you wish to hear, but I'm … I'm rather old-fashioned."

"Oh, I see." She sighed heavily. "So you're against it."

He eyed her over the rim of his goblet, his gaze so penetrating she wondered if he were reading her thoughts.

"Please don't misunderstand me." He set the glass down. "I'm not saying a woman's voice is less important than a man's. Quite the contrary." He took a hefty bite of his salmon followed by another drink of wine. "For example, if a woman wants to return flowers a man with only the best of intentions had sent her, she has every right to do so without so much as word, don't you agree?"

Oh, Lord. Did he really just ask that? She stared at him with her mouth agape.

He laughed. "What? The flowers I sent to you were returned *by you*. What can I say? I took it to heart."

Resisting a smile, she frowned and waved a finger at him. "Oh, I think you'll live."

"Back to the women's vote." He waved his hand dismissively. "So many men feel threatened by women. I can tell you from years of firsthand experiences, women are not only nurturers, they are also very deep thinkers."

Erin's stomach flip-flopped. Was he referring to his dead wife, mother, sisters, recent conquests? Perhaps the lovely red-head? She realized she really knew very little about Derek Rudliff, but the more time she spent with him the more she enjoyed his company.

She raised her chin. "Some men think if a woman votes she'll stop sewing their socks, minding the children, or discontinue preparing the meals. It's absurd, really."

He looked her squarely in the eyes. "Yes, but is it such a vile thought to know a man might prefer his woman above all else in the world?"

The soulful, penetrating stare caught her off guard. "But Derek. That is not what's at stake here. A woman can love and be loved, and still have a voice on issues that matter to everyone."

His eyes paled to a lighter shade of blue. "It's not that." He cast his attention to his dinner plate and poked a turnip with a fork. "I agree with you, but perhaps we should talk about something else."

Had she said something wrong? For a moment he had looked miserable, *heartbroken*. Had he been thinking about his deceased wife? After all, he still wore his wedding ring.

Wrapped in two thick blankets and sitting side-by-side on a lounger on the back porch, they drank brandy and watched the last of the setting amber sun. A majestic bald eagle flew overhead with a salmon clutched in its talons. Smaller birds flew in its wake, swooping wildly and pecking at the large creature, urging it to move on.

Erin set her brandy glass down. "So, you've decided to grant the newspaper an interview."

Derek set his glass down next to hers. "Ah, business talk now. I assume you heard my conditions?"

"You will only grant an interview if I do it, yes?"

"Yes." He leaned in. "But I must confess, Miss Richland. I know I said otherwise, but when I invited you here for dinner this evening, it wasn't just business I had on my mind." His eyes locked with hers.

She stared into the bottomless depths, his gaze so piercing she couldn't blink. "But … but you insisted that I conduct the interview and nobody else, correct?"

"I did, indeed."

I did indeed. Those three words had rolled off his tongue, smooth as polished silk, and just as potent as his masculine scent wafting into her nose. Those eyes, dear God, she could get lost inside their azure depths if she dared allow herself.

She ripped her gaze from his. "Why must it only be me?"

"It's simple, really. I trust you."

Derek was a man she barely knew, but his words of trust comforted her. "Why do I get the feeling you would prefer I conduct the interview on another day?"

He stretched and casually draped an arm across her shoulders. "You get that feeling because you're correct. Truth be told, another time and place would be much better. I'm enjoying this moment with you, Erin."

Feeling the heat of his arm across her shoulders, hearing him call her by her given game, everything felt so *perfect*.

Derek's eyes brightened. "I have an idea. Suppose with this exclusive interview I take you to my logging camps. Show you the ins and outs of the business — then to the mills. Give you an authentic firsthand experience."

Erin stared past him, imagining her byline in the paper, "*Erin Richland Granted Exclusive Interview with Timber Baron Rudliff— The Man, The Business."* Her father would undoubtedly allow her any story after that.

She smiled. "Well, going there would take care of the business side of Derek Rudliff, I suppose," she said. "But I'd also like to report about you — the man — what makes you tick. Who you are. Who you *really* are — make sense? If you would grant me the personal side of you as well, you would be doing me an enormous favor. Many citizens would like to know more about *you*."

"I hope that includes you," he said, fingering a thread of her hair that had come loose from her chignon. "I adore your hair worn down, like the night of the party. It's beautiful."

She gazed at the last spark of the setting sun glowing like a dying ember in Derek's eyes. God knows, she had been attracted to him from the very first moment she first gazed into the sapphire depths of his eyes.

She reached up and slowly pulled the pins from her hair and

shook it into a loose spill. The long ebony mass cascaded across his arm draped over her shoulders. "Better?"

"Much better," he whispered, taking a strand and rubbing it between his fingers. "So soft. So beautiful."

He spoke in a tenor as smooth as watered silk. For a split second, she felt as though she could see into the deep depths of his eyes, clear through to his soul. She craved his touch, and, by God, there was certainly no reason why she shouldn't kiss him. Yes, perhaps too much wine had been poured, but that was no excuse. She wanted him, simple as that.

She leaned in, and their faces poised mere inches apart. The invisible energy she had felt earlier floated between them again, swirling and stinging like the soft prick of tiny pins against her skin.

She closed her eyes.

Tender, gentle lips covered hers. He wrapped her hair around his hand, pulling her against his chest, kissing her harder, his tongue devouring the delicate depths of her mouth.

With a soft moan, she wrapped her arms around his neck and ran her fingers along the collar at his nape. She explored his mouth as their tongues joined in a sultry dance of seduction.

She inched away and whispered in his ear, "What *is* it about you?"

He moved her long mane aside and kissed the back of her neck. "How do you mean?" he whispered.

"I don't know how to explain it. You're so familiar and yet … you're not."

The darkness of night crouched around them, and the sounds of barking sea lions echoed across the water. Sharp squawks of fleeing gulls pierced the sky above, while the glowing ships bobbed gently in the current below.

"Not everything can be easily explained," he breathed against her neck.

He kissed her again, deeply, and she instantly melded into his embrace.

"Lord, woman." He pressed his lips against her cheek. "I so desire you." His hands slid across the small of her back, his fingertips digging in. "Tell me you want this as much as I do. Tell me you've thought of our previous night together just as I have."

His hands, his touch — her body responded, growing warm, flushing in all the right places. She slid her hands up his chest, gently fingering between the small buttonholes, touching the curls on his broad chest. She gazed into his eyes. "I do, and I have. I tried not to think of you. I was dreadfully embarrassed, but being with you here … now."

That was the truth, so help her God.

The entire week she could not focus, whether during a business meeting, personal time, or out with Frederick. More times than not, she would catch herself reliving their sensual journey the night of the party when they made love amid the strange surroundings in the house. The eerie costumes, the warming punch, the sultry sounds and hazy glimpses of pleasure in the other rooms — it was all so surreal, so primal, and not easy to push from her mind.

A lone great blue heron silently glided by, looking like a prehistoric pterodactyl, its massive wings and long, spindly legs weaving mightily through a rising patch of autumn fog.

Derek's hand brushed the side of her breast, and his mouth sought hers once again. He kissed her deeply, passionately, and a gravelly moan escaped his throat.

A dizzying wave of desire flooded her veins, flushing her chest and breasts. Sliding her hands up the firm length of his back, she returned the heated kiss, relishing the feel of his warm tongue dancing seductively with hers.

He scooped her up, blanket and all, and headed inside.

Erin gave no resistance — she had none — for she craved

making love as much as he did.

"Say the words, and we can stop now," he whispered, his eyes glowing in the soft candlelight of his bedroom.

She looked into his eyes and kissed his cheek in reply.

With a swift kick of his boot, Derek shut the bedroom door and gently laid her down on the silky bedding.

He lay next to her and stared into her eyes, his smoldering gaze holding her in place.

He dipped his head and gently kissed her forehead, the tip of her nose, her earlobe. "You're beautiful," he said, his breath searing hot upon her ear.

The touch of his hands, his mouth upon hers, his words, the uncomplicated moment, it was as though she was floating in a lovely dream.

His hand traced the small of her back, slowly curving across her waist, a solitary finger trailing up the side of her breast.

The liquor left her relaxed, her limbs languid, but her rising pulse hammered like a drum inside her chest. "Oh, I do want you, Derek."

With a smile no sane woman could possibly resist, Derek slowly rose and moved to the foot of the bed.

Frowning, she lay on her back and folded her arms behind her head. "Where are you going?"

"Just lie back," he said from the foot of the bed.

Unhurried fingers unlaced her boot, removed it, and massaged her ankle, slowly working his way down to her stockinged foot. She moaned.

He took his time and did the same for her other foot. While the massage felt divine, all she could think about was slipping into a hot bathtub to scrub away the grimy dust from walking outdoors all day.

She lifted her neck from the pillow. "This feels so wonderful, but I've been outdoors all day. I'm thinking —"

Derek looked up and met her gaze. "You're thinking you would love a nice hot bath."

That was *exactly* what she had been thinking. "If it's not too much trouble," she said, her body melting under the intensity of his heated stare.

He moved to her side, lowered down, and kissed her so deeply, passionately, she couldn't breathe, much less think clearly. "Derek," she whispered, sliding her lips from his.

"No trouble, my dear," he said. "When you're with me, you may have whatever your heart desires."

Candles had been lit, and a glass of brandy sat waiting for her on a small table next to the bathtub. The room had all the latest plumbing fixtures. A toilet, a sink, and the largest enameled cast-iron bathtub she had ever seen. No wonder it had taken so long to fill.

Derek handed her a fluffy chenille robe and excused himself, leaving her at her leisure.

On a tray at the head of the tub were body sponges and various shampoos and therapeutic body scrubs. She sipped the brandy and sank into the bath, allowing only her head to poke out of the water.

Who would have guessed? When she awoke this morning, she had no idea, never an inkling, the day would lead to another intimate night with Derek.

The last time she had been in his house, she had slipped out after they had made love, leaving him alone without so much as a goodbye. But unlike that night, her father would be home tonight and waiting for her arrival. With luck, Frederick would not come calling.

Erin frowned. *But then there would be Maggie to deal with.* The servant's bedroom faced the rear of the house, but the woman could hear anything and everything. Maggie had never asked her why she had returned home so late the night of the costume party, and Erin hoped it would stay that way.

She lifted her foot from the steamy bathwater, rotating her ankle, watching the water bead off her pale skin. She dipped the sponge in the water, soaking it, and squished it against her chest and neck. She sat up and inhaled the varied selection of soaps and shampoos, but the European rose-scented soap Derek had suggested tempted her the most.

The knock at the door startled her. She dropped the sponge in the water and folded her arms across her chest. "Yes?" she asked in a tiny voice.

"Is there anything else I can get you?" Derek asked.

What was it about Derek? Sure, he was devilishly handsome and incredibly wealthy, but there was something extra, something she couldn't put her finger on, something that pulled her in deeper whenever he gazed into her eyes or spoke with that voice laced with warmed honey, making her feel as though she were the only woman in the world that existed.

Dare I?

She cleared her throat. "I would love it if you would … wash my hair." The moment she uttered those words, she recoiled with embarrassment.

She stared at the brass doorknob. *Oh God. Oh God.*

Derek entered wearing a silken robe with a gaze so sinful it gave her warm skin goose- bumps.

"Well, *hello*," he said, accentuating the word "hello" so that it sounded terribly, terribly naughty. A smoldering cigarette hung lazily between two fingers.

Erin managed a smile and swished under the water, leaving only her head and neck exposed. Small waves sloshed over the sides of the tub.

He slid a chair across the floor and sat at the head of the tub, behind her. He extinguished the cigarette in an ashtray. "So, what will it be?"

"Excuse me?"

"Your shampoo of choice?"

Cursing the flush rising to her cheeks, she said, "Oh, yes, of course." She fingered through the tray in search of the one she had chosen. "This one. Rose, the one you suggested. It's wonderful." She reached behind with the bar and frowned. "I'm not exactly sure, but I think the scent reminds me of my childhood."

Silence filled the steamy bathroom. "Rose it is," he whispered in a throaty voice. He held his hand past her shoulder, and she handed him the bar.

Emboldened by the sultry tone of his voice, she dipped under the water, wetting her hair, and sat up. He gently gathered her ebony rope of wet hair, formed it into a ball behind her head, and rubbed the bar into the thick mass. Firm fingertips massaged her scalp while his thumbs kneaded the nape of her neck. She rose up a smidge, letting her arms dangle over the sides of the tall tub, and she caught sight of him twisting to peek at her breasts just below the waterline.

His hands moved slowly across the rounded pile of soap bubbles on top of her head, down her nape, his thumbs rubbing out the tight knots along her neck. He gathered suds and massaged her shoulders; his hands trailing down the front of her chest, gently brushing each pert nipple.

He stopped, and she heard the scraping of the chair legs across the floor.

He returned with a ceramic pitcher, dipped it into the water near her waist, and sat back in the chair. "You tell me if this doesn't feel wonderful."

Slowly, he poured the heated water through her hair, combing out tangles with his fingers. More water, more combing, more warm water running over her shoulders, her arms. Had she died and gone to heaven?

He stood and untied his robe, letting it drop in a sleek pile on the floor. Her heart stopped dead in her chest, and she had to keep from gasping out loud. Before her, Derek stood in all his handsome, naked glory and then some.

"Oh, um, do you want to come in?" She sloshed the water over the rim as she quickly moved to a higher sitting position.

A single eyebrow rose. "There *is* room for two. Do you mind?"

"I … " Of course she didn't mind, but he didn't bother to wait for her answer. He stepped into the tub, his long legs slipping alongside hers, occupying the opposite end.

He sank low, slipping under the water to wet his hair. She watched as he rose out of the water like the mighty Greek god Poseidon, raking his hands through the wet mass of dark blond hair. She couldn't help but stare at the beads of bath oil slicking his lean, muscled torso and the mass of damp curls on his chest.

His gaze narrowed to indigo slits, and he beckoned her with a single finger. "Come here."

She turned, looking over her shoulders behind her as if he were calling someone else. She turned back, and smiled, and whispered, "Who *me?*"

"Most definitely you. Come here." He reached under her arms and swirled her around so that her back pressed against his broad chest and her bottom sat between his sprawled legs.

Derek's unique masculine blend of bayberry and earth mingled with the rose-scented water, stimulating her senses. She glanced down, captivated by the way her long hair twirled like wet ribbons around his firm manhood, seducing him with the promise of more.

A lone finger traced the line of her jaw, trailing down, stopping at the warm, beating pulse point on her neck. His breath hitched deep within in his throat, and a soft moan escaped his lips. He pulled her hair to one side and kissed the back of her neck, her earlobe, trailing his lips across her neck.

Her heated pulse pounded so fiercely she was sure she'd

combust. Closing her eyes, she resisted the desperate urge to shudder as his teeth grazed her neck.

Her heart raced, beating wildly inside her chest, leaving her breathless, as hazy images flashed like shooting stars darting behind her eyelids. *I'm happy, deliciously happy. A warm room, stone walls, a hearth with a bright fire, blue eyes gazing into mine, large, fanged teeth!*

Gasping, she opened her eyes wide and shoved Derek's head away from her neck.

He groaned. "What —"

"I have to go. I must leave, *now.*"

He grabbed her arm, an expression of concern etched on his face. "You what? What's wrong?"

Despite the hot bathwater, icy panic raced through her body. "Derek. I'm sorry, but I … " She rubbed her temples and took a deep breath. "I just have to go. That's all."

She pulled from his grasp, stepped out of the tub, and snatched a towel. Her heart hammered against her chest, her mind racing with fleeting, disturbing images as she fled from the bathroom.

Derek marched into the bedroom with a towel wrapped around his waist. "Erin, what the hell is going on?"

"Nothing," she lied, her voice quivering. "I … I just have to go."

"You didn't have to go ten minutes ago." He reached out to her. "Come on, let's —"

"No!" She jerked away from his grasp. "I can't think clearly around you, Derek. I don't know what's happening, and I don't know what I'm doing here *with you.*"

In a flash, he was standing directly in front of her gripping her shoulders, hard, his eyes boring into hers. "Oh, but indeed you do know, Erin, you just need —"

"Don't touch me!" she yelled, twisting from his embrace, "I don't know anything anymore. Don't you understand?"

Judging by the injured look in Derek's eyes, clearly he did not understand. And why should he? Even she couldn't comprehend what was going on. Every inch of her body craved Derek, wanted him, *needed him*, and yet, pinpricks of warning now crawled across her skin.

She rushed toward the bedroom armoire for her clothes. Suddenly, her wet feet slid out from underneath her, sending her crashing to the hard floor.

The last thing she remembered before everything went dark was Derek lurching for her, shouting, *"Ersule!"*

Chapter Eleven

New York

"She was beautiful, Gregore. Positively beautiful," I said, trying to keep still in my seat on the train back to Baltimore.

"I believe you," he returned, though not as enthusiastically as I had hoped.

Poor Gregore. He tolerated my nonstop chatter, listening with the patience of a saint, but I suspected he had mixed feelings about my ordeal. And why shouldn't he?

By coming into contact with Ersule as the reborn child Erin, I had wandered into a hornet's nest of mixed emotions, coloring my rational thoughts. But I was sure he could be persuaded to relocate to New York after our short conversation earlier.

The night before, Gregore had wandered the quiet back streets of New York. Strolling past an alleyway, he heard music, lyrical melodies, reminiscent of our old days in Germany and France. Curious, he walked down the shadowy passageway, noting the music was coming from the basement of a large brick building. Dim light from a single small window illuminated the cobbled alley. Bending low to peer inside, he had felt a tap on his shoulder.

Turning toward Gregore I said, "We didn't have time earlier. Tell me more about last night. I want to hear about this man Dominic you mentioned."

Gregore's gaze snapped to mine, his face brightening. "Dominic." He tucked the magazine into the seat pocket, his gaze darting about, examining the seating arrangements of our fellow passengers.

He leaned in and whispered, "When I felt a firm tap on my shoulder, I was startled and spun around. Standing before me was a man." A smile spread across Gregore's face. "And not just an ordinary man, mind you."

I smiled. Gregore had an animated quality about him, gesturing with his hands, his expressive brown eyes gleaming.

"The handsome man had brilliant white teeth that glowed in the night and skin as pale as the dead." Gregore's gaze narrowed. "He said that a private party was going on inside the building, and I could attend as his escort."

"And did you?" I asked, though I had already heard this part of the story earlier.

"Well, of *course* I did. And Derek, you wouldn't believe how many of our kind are in New York. The *Others*, as they're called there, well, they've evolved — for the better — and they're unlike the vicious groups in the old days when we had to defend our territory."

I was intrigued. While I knew our kind resided in the United States, I dared not cross paths with them for fear of drawing attention.

"Do go on," I said.

"There were dozens upon dozens of patrons in the cool basement establishment. Every variety you can imagine — they're there. A bar, music, dancing, but most of all, the *Others* talked openly. I don't know how Dominic knew I was a *Were*, but he did. He told me his kind had been there for centuries and had evolved within the confines of the city. He said we, too, could sharpen the same 'skills'. They've developed protections we could only have imagined in our wildest dreams."

"And did you believe him? Did you sense any danger with this *Other*?"

The idea of living among progressive *"Others,"* all while I was close to Ersule, made my heart soar with possibility.

Gregore pondered the question. "I believed him. Think back. Remember how we used to speak, how our language has changed, evolved, with the passage of time? How we've learned to blend within society to the best of our abilities? But we are far from perfect. Surely, it must be possible to learn how to adapt further — for our protection."

"And you sense no concealed motives from this *Other* you speak of? *Dominic*, is it?"

"Yes, his name is Dominic. I sensed nothing like that with him."

I had to agree with the philosophy. In our mortal body we were vulnerable and always at the mercy of our unpredictable inner beasts. Perhaps in New York, with the help of the *Others* and their protections, we, too, could find the safety and security we desperately craved.

"I truly believe New York has more to offer us than Baltimore," said Gregore, "but … "

"But?" I asked.

"But are you strong enough to make the move to New York with Ersule so close?"

I was so excited I could barely breathe. Having been in New York and seen for myself what the glorious city had to offer, the idea of moving there actually made sense. Gregore had his love of the arts; our kind could live there among mortals, and I had my own obvious reasons. I inhaled deeply and exhaled in jagged breaths. "I've never been surer of anything in my life."

And that was the truth.

Later that night, I dreamed I was young lad of thirteen again, returning home with my younger brother, Hamlin, from a long day of hunting. The two of us were laughing as we ran toward home, our bags brimming with rabbit and pheasant. Having the spritely build of a ten-year old, Hamlin bounded forth ahead of me, eager to be the first to inform Mother of our successful hunt.

When I entered the door, Hamlin stood shaking uncontrollably in his boots, tears streaming down his face, and he had urinated in his trousers. Turning past his distressed gaze, I saw Mother lying on the dirt floor, her body covered in crimson from the waist down. Lying beside her and her blood soaked frock was her lifeless newborn baby boy, having arrived far too early.

Despite my anguish, I tried to sooth Hamlin, but nothing I said brought the boy comfort. Father had died in battle only two months earlier, sending my brother into hysterics for well over a month, and now Mother.

I swore at the screams forming deep within my throat, threatening to rip my heart to pieces. For Hamlin's sake, I squelched my pain and despair, and covered the lifeless corpses with quilts.

After quieting my brother with a warm drink and tucking him into bed, I set out to dig a grave in the meadow to bury Mother and our dead baby brother. When I returned for the bodies, Hamlin was nowhere to be found.

I had searched for hours, and just as I was about to hunt for him at an abandoned farm, I spotted something floating in the lake. My heart stopped quiet in my chest with dread. I ran as fast as my feet would carry me, but I already knew what floated in the murky water ahead.

Hamlin lay face down. I rolled him over and hugged his motionless body with everything I had, my body shaking uncontrollably. As the amber sun began to set over the water and the threat of darkness crept into my veins, I howled like a beast. My anguish and terror intensified with the lengthening shadows, and my wild screams and mournful cries echoed across the still water.

How long I held him, I do not know, but it was under a full moon that I buried him next to Mother and the dead infant.

After the burial, I drank ale. I downed the warm drink until my belly was so full I nearly retched. But no matter how much I drank, the numbness I longed for eluded me. I shed mournful tears, sobbing so hard each heave burned my chest.

I fled the house and ran into the night, caring not where my leather shoes would take me. I sprinted through forests, up hills, across farms and meadows. I ran until I could go no further and dropped to the ground like a heavy sack of yams.

When I opened my eyes, light surrounded me. I rubbed my eyes, trying to focus on the hazy image above me: A girl with shiny hair, black as a raven's wing, stood above me, smiling, in a field of grain under the scorching midday sun.

ONCE we arrived in New York, Gregore was eager to show me the alley establishment known as "The Blue Moon Lounge." Ever since he had told me of the place, I couldn't wait to see it for myself.

He gestured toward a dark alley. "It's down here."

The soft resonance of a mournful violin filled the damp, desolate passageway, beckoning me.

"This is where I met Dominic," Gregore said. "Right here."

A door opened, followed by footsteps heading up the darkened stairwell. Two women dressed in black passed us, laughing.

"Excuse me," Gregore said. "Is Dominic inside?"

I sank into the shadows.

"Ah, yes, ye' hear that music? That be him playing the violin," the taller woman said with a thick Irish brogue.

"Let's go." Gregore grabbed my coat sleeve and led me down the stairwell. He knocked on the metal door.

The door opened. A swarthy, muscled fellow with a thick, gold hoop through his nose guarded the entrance. His face suddenly brightened. "Gregore, you're back. Come in!" He opened the door wider and gestured for us to go inside, before closing the door with a heavy thud.

We stepped into a large, dimly-lit room, tastefully decorated in hues of deep maroon and black. Saturating the cool air, an earthy aroma mingled with the hazy curls of cigar and cigarette smoke. Dozens of patrons filled the plush conversational sofas and thickly upholstered chairs. Rows of glasses, goblets, and ashtrays sat on long tables in front of them. Dressed in only a sheer black gown accentuating her ample breasts, a female bartender poured cocktails at the well-stocked bar.

All eyes were cast upon the lone man with long black hair, sitting on a wooden stool at the center of the room. Playing a haunting tune on a violin under a single glowing spotlight, the man's pale face appeared poised in concentration as his nimble fingers quivered against taut strings.

Gregore leaned in and whispered, "That's Dominic."

We sank into the couch cushions. Gregore offered me a cigarette. I accepted. A young black waiter with spiky white hair, dressed in a revealing outfit made of the same sheer black fabric worn by the barkeep, appeared before us.

"What can I get you gents tonight?"

I raised a finger. "I'll have a whiskey and —"

"No, wait. Let me order for you," Gregore said, with a wily grin.

"Well, hello, Gregore," the waiter said, an impish glint in his dark eyes. "I didn't recognize you sitting there in the shadows."

"It's Tallon, is that right?" asked Gregore, leaning closer to the flickering candelabra.

Even through his dark complexion, the waiter blushed. "Right you *are*," he replied, singing the last word.

Gregore waggled his brows. "Tallon, get us both the house special."

The whites of Tallon's large eyes glowed. "Coming right up, sir." He turned on his toes and headed toward the bar.

Dominic finished the haunting piece, and the spotlight above him abruptly went dark. Guests erupted with cheers and applause. I watched as he carefully set the bow and violin into a weathered leather case, then glanced at our table, making eye contact with Gregore.

Dominic snagged our waiter as he passed by and said something to him, before setting the case in the corner and walking toward our table.

"Gregore. Good to see you again," said Dominic. "Is this the friend you mentioned?"

Dominic's azure gaze swept over me. Immediately, I could see what Gregore had talked about. Indeed, the man was handsome and just as he had described.

Gregore announced, "Dominic Voltaire, this is Derek Rudliff."

We shook hands, and Dominic took a seat across from us in the plush chair. "Rudliff. I feel I've heard this name before, long ago," he said, cupping his square chin. "Where, I can't remember."

The waiter arrived with chilled sterling goblets. "This is on the house. Compliments of Dominic."

Dominic dipped his head in a nod.

I took an ample swallow of the "house special" Gregore had ordered.

Both Dominic and Gregore watched as I tasted the cool liquid. The drink felt especially smooth against my tongue, the taste fruity, like a punch, but an earthy quality lingered that I couldn't quite place.

"Am I missing something?" I asked, my gaze shifting between the two men, trying to decipher their impish grins.

"Good?" Dominic asked. "Hits the spot, doesn't it?"

"Delicious." I downed more and licked my lips. Frowning, I said, "I taste a mixture of … what is it?"

Gregore's eyes darkened. "I wanted to tell you about it earlier, but I thought I would surprise you."

The waiter approached and whispered into Dominic's ear. Dominic rose. "Excuse me a moment, gentleman. I have a business matter I must tend to."

Warmth slowly spread through my veins. "Surprise me with what?"

"The drink," said Gregore. "It's what we've been missing. It's what we've been waiting for. It's the key that opens the door so that we can live securely among mortals."

I had no idea what the hell he was talking about. "Speak up, Gregore. What key? Stop with the riddles."

"Yes, yes, you're right." He leaned in closer. "Look inside the goblet."

I looked inside my silver chalice, but I still had no idea where Gregore was leading.

"The ingredients you taste — the mixture flowing in your veins right about now, warming you, is a potent combination of herbs: deadly nightshade, devil's dung, and some others mixed with blood. Human blood."

I would have imagined that drinking such a concoction in my human form might disgust me. It did not. In fact, the drink tasted better than anything I'd had in a very long time. Heat surged across my torso, slithering along my limbs, exciting me in ways I could not readily put into words.

Gregore laughed. "I know. It's amazing, isn't it?"

"I don't understand. Enlighten me, Gregore. Why those particular herbs? Why human blood?"

"Years ago, these *Others* learned how to stop uncontrollable shifts, like during heated sex and uncontrollable rage."

I pondered his words. "But you must admit, sometimes we don't mind the shift during sex with our kind. Some say they prefer it."

Gregore frowned. "And for those that wish to risk shifting, they can. The drink is not formulated for them. But it *is* made for us, Derek. This crazy concoction we're drinking gives us free will to change when we *choose*. This drink would allow us to have sex with mortals — without fear of uncontrolled shifting and taking lives. Don't you see? If we grow angry, hateful, frustrated, we can control it by the help of this drink. Lord knows I've gotten in trouble more times than I can count, and you remember what happened to Franz?"

I snorted. "Of course I remember."

Flickers of candlelight danced in Gregore's eyes. "It's a magic potion. Protection for our kind."

For our kind. I contemplated his words.

Gregore sighed. "Look, you've been a saint for far too long. You've resisted temptation more times than I can count — am I right? Do not forget, I have seen the many times you have turned down the fairer sex."

I scoffed and waved my hand. "That's been my choice, and you *know* why."

"What I know is that you are a king who's been granted a gift —"

"A gift?" I asked. "Have you lost your mind?"

Gregore scanned the room before turning his insistent gaze back to me. "Hear me out. Yes, a gift. A gift that will allow your beloved Ersule to rejoin you once again and very soon. Until then, you are a free *Were* with needs of his own."

Gregore was right. I had enjoyed women, mortals and *Weres* alike, but only on rare occasions. Believing my piety was a noble gesture, my needs had gone unsatisfied on many lonely nights.

Silently, I took in his words while brooding over my goblet. I thought back to the frightening predicaments my pack had encountered over the centuries.

But a simple blood and herb concoction as a remedy?

It seemed too good to be true. I looked around at the diverse group of *Others* gathered, leading to more questions.

I leaned forward. "Nothing can avoid the lunar shift of the full moon — correct?"

Gregore nodded. "No, you're right. No *Were* can be spared from the lunar pull, but we know when the full moon will occur. This allows us to control our environment rather than our surroundings controlling us. In fact, Dominic says the parties here are amazing and the punch flows from fabulous ice sculptures —"

"What about rage? We cannot predict when and where something might enrage us — what then? Without the drink, we could shift and then what?"

"Which is why this protective drink is so brilliant." He drew closer. "They sell it here. You can actually buy it, take it home, even carry it with you in a flask."

"Like a drug," I said flatly.

"It *is* a drug, my King, a drug that will change our existence."

I wouldn't readily admit it, but my interest had piqued to a new high. "Where do they get the blood, and how long does it last in our bodies?"

"Oh, that." He waved his fingers. "Connections in the morgue — easy if you know the right people. It's fine as long as it's fresh or kept frozen."

"And the other part? How long does the effect last?"

Gregore sucked in his cheeks and his eyes widened. "Well, now *that* is much trickier to predict. Dominic says it usually lasts about twelve hours. But everyone is different, and you have to work with it a few times."

"And how do you know when the effect has worn off?"

"That's easy for a man." He glanced at my crotch. "You won't feel like you do right about now."

The liquid snaked through my veins, satisfying me with

hypnotic warmth, narrowing in on all my pleasure points.

Jesus.

Gregore reached for a bottle of Bacardi sitting on the table. He poured the rum into our goblets. Waggling his brows, he said, "The punch is even better with booze." He held up his goblet. "To our new life."

I hesitated a moment, then joined in the toast and poured the spiked drink down my gullet.

Dominic returned and took his seat. "I assume you told him."

Gregore smiled. "Most of it."

Dominic raised a jet-black brow. "Not everything?"

"Told me what?" I asked. Somehow, I didn't care. All I knew was I felt alive.

A small band had set up where Dominic had played the violin. With the click of the drumsticks, the spotlight above them lit, and they began playing. With or without partners, patrons shot up from their seats and shook what they had to the rhythm.

A man with wide, pale green eyes and a large pointy nose strutted with a raven-haired female whose pale skin glowed like thin white parchment held above a flickering flame. A stout male dwarf wearing a flowing black cape danced with a spindly woman three times his height.

Gregore glared at me. "Fascinating to watch, aren't they?"

I nodded. "I have the feeling there's more variety than I ever imagined."

Dominic tapped my wrist and gestured toward the pointy-nosed fellow I'd been watching moments earlier. "That's Jasper. Watch him."

Jasper moved and swayed in flowing form, raising and lowering his arms. As if on cue, he suddenly spun his head completely around.

"What the devil?" I muttered.

Dominic smiled and lit a cigarette. "He's Raptor."

Damn. He did look like a bird. I cast my gaze toward the pale woman Jasper danced with.

"And her?"

"Garden variety Vamp. I've known her for centuries."

Gregore stood and stared down at me. "Come on — let's dance."

"I think I'll sit tight." I tapped the passing waiter. "I'll have another."

"Coming right up," Tallon sang.

Dominic slid his hand over mine, smiling. "It's very potent. Be careful until you know your dosage. And just so you know, it's quite something when a mortal drinks of the powerful mix. You know that feeling you have drinking the cocktail? How it narrows in right to your cock? Mortals are sexually insatiable after drinking of the liquid and apparently quite fertile."

I hadn't thought about mortals imbibing the liquid. "Can they overdose on it?"

"Only if they're lucky." Gregore bit on his bottom lip and smiled like a scamp. "No, seriously. It's not like that."

Dominic rose from the chair. "Come on, Gregore, you can dance with me."

Dominic snubbed out his cigarette and snapped his fingers to the beat before following Gregore to the dance floor. I tapped my toe to the rhythm, the heated beat pulsing through my veins.

Tallon set the chilled drink before me. "Mmm, look at you, starting on your second. Big plans tonight?"

I poured a hefty shot of rum into the goblet. "Not particularly."

"You tellin' me you're going waste it. For shame!" He smiled wryly and walked away, swinging his thin hips.

The second drink went down my throat faster than the first. I was just about to light a cigarette when tawny fingers plucked it from my mouth. Before I had time to object, a wiry- haired brunette yanked me up by my hand, dragging me toward the dance floor.

The *Others* danced, fully immersed in the music, limbs flowing, hips swaying, asses rubbing and bumping against groins. The stiffness of conventional dance was clearly not an option at The Blue Moon Lounge. I spotted Dominic and Gregore dancing in the middle of the crowd.

"What's your name?" the woman asked me.

"Derek. And yours?"

"Jessamine. You're new here, aren't you?"

I tried to loosen my muscles. "Is it that obvious?"

Her dark eyes narrowed. "Come on now, give me some grinding."

I coughed. "Excuse me?"

She slipped behind me, rubbing her ample breasts slowly against my back, and then circling me while gazing through half-closed lids, like those of a purring cat.

"Like this," she said, lifting her corkscrew hair above her shoulders. She turned and rubbed her firm ass against my pelvis, slowly at first, then faster, joining the rhythm of the steel drum.

My cock instantly stood at full attention.

She looked over her shoulder, smiling at me. "Just like that, honey. Now give me some sugar."

Everyone danced, grinding away, and before I knew it, I was fully engaged. The blood cocktail had unlocked the reservations I'd placed upon myself so long ago, the deep fear of being discovered a *Were* among judgmental mortals. A sense of liberty flowed through my veins with each grind of her pulsating hips. I danced like I'd never danced before, sensual movements, entangled arms, pelvises mashing against each other until sweat dripped from every pore of my body.

Jessamine moved in closer and guided my hands on her swaying hips. Her gaze narrowed. "What are you?" she asked.

"How do you mean?"

"Are you *Warlock, Were* — perhaps a *Vamp*?" She tiled her chin, assessing me closely. "No, definitely *not* Vampire. Too much warmth to you, honey."

"What are you?" I asked.

Her full lips curved seductively. She turned, grinding her muscular ass against my pelvis again. Dear God. I'd had about all I could take, or I'd explode for sure.

"What I *am* is yours for one night," she said, turning to face me again.

Words eluded me.

"Come with me." She grabbed my hand, and before I knew it, I was being led up a set of narrow interior steps.

I followed her through a long hallway on the top floor of the building, passing numbered apartments along each side.

She stopped, reached above a doorjamb, and retrieved a key.

"In here," she whispered.

Jessamine unlocked the door and drew me by the sleeve inside a small, candlelit room. No sooner had the door closed, she slammed me up against the wall. She splayed her hands across my chest, her cinnamon face a mere inch from mine.

She brushed her lips across my neck and whispered, "I'll give you what you *crave*. I'll give you what you *need*." A warm hand slid over my erect shaft.

Enough games. The potent blood cocktail flowing through my veins merged with my instinctual urge to slip my cock inside the willing female. I grabbed her ass in both hands and dug my fingertips into the enviable mounds.

Her teeth grazed my throat. I quickly unhooked my trousers, letting them fall in a pile to the floor. She unbuttoned my shirt, and I slid out of it faster than I ever thought possible. I glanced around the room. Her apartment, I presumed.

She kissed my bare chest, ran her hands across my shoulders. "You *want* this, Derek. You *need* this."

Something in the tone of her voice made my desire for her grow tenfold. I searched her eyes. "*What are you?*"

Her long lashed lifted from her cheeks. "You shall see. Don't be afraid."

I carried her to the bed across the small room and lay on top of her. I slid my hands underneath her dress and inched my fingers up her bare thighs until I found her warm core. Moist, ready, and very willing.

I slid into her like a rabbit into a greased hole. I rode that woman like the Greek god Phaeton driving his father's sun chariot across the sky, like almighty Zeus battling the Titans, grunting like a Neanderthal. I showed that woman no mercy, nor did she ask for any. My insides churned, muscles tightening, my body ready to explode like a violent eruption of Mount Vesuvius, and then ...

I hoisted up on outstretched arms and looked into Jessamine's face. She opened her eyes, and my heart stopped dead in my chest.

Lying beneath me was Ersule.

"Such an animal you are tonight," she breathed in my wife's sweet voice of long ago. She wrapped her legs firmly around my waist and grabbed my buttocks, pulling me in deeper.

God help me!

I had already crossed over the edge and could not pull out. I reared up, my face straining as I came inside her. "My God!" I choked out, "*What did you say?*"

With trembling fingers I smoothed the dark hair covering her brow and gazed into the familiar emerald green eyes. Stinging tears suddenly blinded me. I quickly rubbed the moisture away. "Ersule. Oh, my God in heaven. *Ersule.*" I hugged her and buried my face in her hair and neck, searching for the familiar scent.

" 'Tis only you I love," the voice said, trailing away.

But the sweet intoxicating scent of my beloved wife was not there.

And it never had been.

I rose up with balled fists and beat the bed, barely missing Jessamine's face.

"Why?" I shouted. "*Why* did you do this to me? How in God's name can you appear beneath my loins as my dead wife?" I rolled away and covered my face in my hands. "What are you — some evil God-damned *witch*?"

Glaring at me, Jessamine bolted from the bed, her feet hitting the floor with a mighty thud. "Ha! You're angry with *me*?" She picked up a hairbrush and waved it at me. "It is *you* that beckoned her from within *me*."

Had I lost my mind, gone stark raving mad like a lunatic straight from the depths of hell?

I shot up from the bed and paced the room, darting wildly, trying to make sense of what had just happened. Was it the drink? Had I imagined it? Was it possible I had just made love to Ersule?

Jessamine stuck her bottom lip out and sank into the bed. I marched straight toward her and grabbed her shoulders. "Woman, you *must* give me answers. I will not leave here until you do so."

Her face twisted. "What the hell do you expect of me?"

I tried to keep the rising anger from my voice, for Jessamine appeared as bewildered as I. "I will ask you this only once again before I grow irate. *What. Are. You?*"

She signed. "You men. You want your cake and to eat it, too." She swatted my hand. "I'm a Mestaclocan."

"What? What the hell is *that*?"

"A Mestaclocan? I'm a *Changeling*. Lord, don't you know anything?"

She tugged at her skirts, smoothing out the thin fabric, clearly irritated by my interrogation.

"I'm like you, but I alter into whatever a person most desires. I *thought* I was helping by giving you what you desired more than anything in the world."

The ache inside my chest swelled. I raked my hands through my damp hair and sighed heavily. "What the hell have I done?"

Pity softened Jessamine's dark eyes. "Look. You've done nothing wrong. I saw you moping at the table, looking downright miserable, if you ask me. I thought we were doing each other a favor."

I closed my eyes so tight they throbbed as I tried to recapture the sight of Ersule lying beneath me.

God. It had been her. I know it!

I could barely form the question. "Jessamine, is it possible that part of her was here — *really* here?"

She sighed and patted my arm. "If that's what you wanted, then yes, it's possible."

My stomach twisted in knots so taut I thought I would vomit.

"Don't pity yourself," Jessamine said in a wistful tone. "Imagine what it's like for me. Only once in my life was *I* the woman a man most desired in his heart during the heat of passion. Only once, and it was very long ago."

I listened to Jessamine's words, but I barely heard what she said. I dressed and opened the door. Upon hearing voices, I pressed against the door. A young couple approached, laughing, slipping into a nearby room and shutting the door behind them.

Thankfully, they had not detected my presence. Inebriated and coarse-natured, I had no desire to speak to anyone, nor did I wish to return to the boisterous crowd downstairs. I shook my head, trying to discern whether I were utterly drunk, fiercely ill, or completely insane. All I knew was I felt *empty*.

I exited the building, retrieved my horse and buggy, and headed toward the hotel. Listening to the steady beat of clomping hooves echoing through the quiet street, I took solace in the calm of darkness.

Following my senses, made keener by the cocktail, I lifted my chin and inhaled deeply. Ersule's sweet scent filled the cool air, strong as ever. Her words to me at the park reverberated inside my skull. "I see you in my dreams. ... I see you in my dreams. ... I see you in my dreams."

Such torturous words from a child!

I smacked the buggy whip, urging the horse to a faster clip. I slapped again and again. I tilted my nose higher, allowing her heady fragrance to blast into my nostrils. Before I knew it, I had seized the leather reins, turned hard, and nearly flipped the buggy in my haste to make the unexpected detour.

Dizzying determination flooded my mind. Even if I were courting my own disaster, I would not be derailed from what beckoned me.

I approached the block where I knew the little girl known as Erin resided. I tethered my horse, lowered the brim of my hat, and walked quickly around the corner. I closed my eyes, letting the aroma stream into my head, begging for the answer I desperately craved. I inhaled again, still haunted by her words to me at the park.

Her scent led me to a simple, brick row home. A white rocking chair next to a potted bush adorned the small covered porch. I slowly stepped up to the darkened entrance and sat on the brick steps. I bent over and planted my face in my hands.

God help me.

What had I unleashed? All this time, I had resisted the temptation to seek Erin. But with the awakening of Ersule tonight, even if only fabricated within my tormented, drunken mind, her scent drew me in like sweet honey to a bee. I couldn't turn back even if I wanted to.

I'm here. Now what?

I rubbed my whiskered chin and swore under my breath. *Lord.* I knew *exactly* where she laid sleeping. Only a small barrier of mortared brick separated us.

I stood, and the moment I touched my fingers to the brick wall, my hand quivered. I could *feel* her sleeping only feet away; *hear* her serene, slumbering breaths resonating like the harp of an angel. I stepped back and slammed balled fists to my ears to silence the sweet sounds, threatening my sanity.

But it was within my own head the haunting noises originated.

I marched to the side window, only feet away. Peering in, my warm breath instantly fogged the pane. I wiped the vapor with my sleeve and gazed through the glass. My chest tightened. Before me, Erin lay sleeping, tucked in her bedding surrounded by the soft glow of candlelight.

Gripping knots of guilt seized my belly. I leaned over, struggling for breath. I needed to know that my long years of waiting had meaning — *had purpose*. If only I had a sign. One small signal and I could wait forever. But slipping inside the bedroom of a sleeping child? *Lunacy!*

Facing heavenward, I closed my eyes, begging that her window would be locked tight, sealed away from my madness.

It was not.

Ever so gently, I inched the window open. I slipped one leg inside, then my head and torso, followed by the other leg. Lest she wake from the chill, I quietly closed the window.

The pale walls topped with a paisley border narrowed the moment I intruded. She was lying in a small bed among lightly-colored quilts and pastel pillows. On her night table sat a pitcher and an empty glass, along with two books, *Alice's Adventures in Wonderland* and *Kinder- und Hausmärchen*, authored by the Brothers Grimm.

Dear Lord, did she read German?

I sat in the corner chair staring at her beautiful sleeping form, inhaling her sweet scent. I watched as her small fingers twitched in her sleep, as her eyes moved slowly beneath soft lids framed by lashes of black lace. I stared, mesmerized by the sound of her rhythmical breathing, watching the gentle movement of her small chest rising and falling in peaceful slumber. She licked her rosy lips and rolled to her side, toward me.

My breath seized in my chest. *Get out now!*

I placed my hands upon the chair arm to rise — to slip out silently — when she mumbled. I froze in place, my body perched in the chair like a giant gargoyle.

"I knew it," she murmured.

What does she know?

"I knew it," she repeated, dreamily.

My heart hammered against my chest, and the tall ceiling closed in above my head, threatening to squeeze the life out of me. Slowly, *cautiously*, I rose up, tiptoed back to the window, and inched the frame open.

Light suddenly filled the small space below her shut door, followed by the sound of approaching footsteps.

Christ!

I scrambled so quickly my shoe hit the windowsill. I hurled the rest of my body through the open window and landed with a heavy thud below. I shot up to my feet and pressed my fingers to the glass to lower the window. That's when I heard her sweet voice say, "Come back to me. Come back to me, Derek."

Chapter Twelve

Everett, Washington

Erin entered the darkened house. The ticking of the grandfather clock echoed across the hardwood floors, making her head throb all the more. She removed her shoes and left them on the braided entry rug.

Moonlight slanted through the stained-glass window, lighting her way toward the staircase. She tiptoed up the steps. The stairway suddenly creaked, and light flooded the crack at the bottom of Maggie's bedroom door.

Erin hurried the last steps, her stocking feet moving so fast along the polished flooring, she slid past her bedroom door. She groped for the doorknob threatening to pass her reach, darted into her room, and shut the door.

"Miss Erin?" Maggie called.

She couldn't feign sleep. Maggie knew better. "Um, yes?"

"May I come in a moment?"

"Just a second." Before opening the door, Erin licked the tip of her finger and tucked loose tendrils back into her tousled chignon.

"Maggie," Erin said, holding the door open, silently cursing the heat racing to her cheeks.

The servant cocked her head, her observant eyes narrowing. "I wanted to speak with you before your father did," she said, sidestepping Erin and entering the bedroom.

Erin shut the door and turned around to face her. "What about?"

"Mr. Frederick Dimsdale. He came here tonight looking for you, and he and your father got to talking."

"What were they talking about *this* time?" She folded her arms across her chest in an attempt to subdue Maggie's cool, measured gaze.

"I try not to meddle in your life, you know that, yes?"

Erin frowned. "Yes, but what's the urgency —"

"What I'm trying to say is, normally I'm not one to interfere in your life."

The back of Erin's head pounded, and the thought of coming up with a plausible story for her father by morning, explaining her late return, made her feel like retching. "Maggie, I'm tired. I need to go to bed. Perhaps we can discuss this in the morning?"

"Dear, sit down. Mr. Dimsdale came here in a mighty huff tonight. He was abrupt with me, which isn't like him, so I stood in the hallway and listened to his conversation with your father."

Erin sat on the bed. "So you eavesdropped?"

Maggie pursed her lips. "Well, yes, I did. Mr. Dimsdale reeked of whiskey and Lord knows what else, and I didn't know what to expect."

Erin rolled her eyes. "Go on."

"Wobbling and swaying, Mr. Dimsdale entered the house insisting I fetch your father, which I did. I heard him tell Mr. Richland that he had seen you leave in a carriage with a man. I couldn't make out every word, but I think he knew the man's name. I tried to hear more of the heated conversation, but your father shut the door to his study. After that, I only got bits and pieces. The last thing I heard your father say as he bid him goodbye at the door was that Mr. Dimsdale needed to 'sleep it off,' and your father reassured him he would indeed speak with you in the morning. I thought it fair

I gave you some warning."

Lord. Erin's mind raced. She could handle Father's displeasure. She'd grown accustomed to that, but Frederick's spying on her was another matter.

"It's not my place, Miss. I know that. I'm not your mother, God rest her lovely soul, but I do hope you know what you're doing. Mr. Dimsdale has nothing but the best intentions —"

Erin snorted louder than she'd expected. "Best intentions? You must be joking. A man spying on a woman he claims to be fond of is *not* well intentioned."

Had Erin been home when Frederick came to the house stinking drunk, demanding to speak to her father about *her*, she would have slapped his face beet-red. Both her father and Frederick constantly injected their old-fashioned rules into her contemporary beliefs, never once asking what she wanted in life. The ridiculous bullying was going to stop. It was time they respected her wishes, her dreams, her aspirations.

Erin's head pounded with throbbing pain. "I appreciate your concern, Maggie. I'll deal with it tomorrow. Thank you for the warning."

Maggie patted Erin's arm. "I have faith in you, child."

"I'm glad someone around here does."

ERIN yawned and stretched her arms over her head, welcoming the morning sun flooding the bedroom window. The cotton nightgown scraped across her nipples, still tender from the ravishing the night before.

Lord. She rubbed the throbbing bump on the back of her head, recalling the bizarre evening with Derek in more detail. The disturbing vision she had seen while in the bathtub with him had seemed so real. After the unsettling images faded minutes later, there was no way she could have brushed them aside and made love. Her clumsy fall knocking her out cold only made matters worse.

Waking in Derek's bed with those soulful eyes of his framed with lines of concern, only confused her more, and she didn't have the heart to press him about the name he had called out just before she hit the floor. *Ersule.* Somehow, she already knew the lovely name belonged to his deceased wife.

Everything about Derek intrigued her. He was different from other men — fashionable, contemporary, but wise and old-fashioned, too. A sense of fluency and ease filled the air when she was near him, a comforting familiarity that carried far beyond their physical attraction. The heated, peculiar night with him at the costume party, the sexual play in the bathtub just last night — Derek knew exactly how to please her.

Erin thought back to her intimate awakening while away at college. She had assumed her English Literature professor's modest style of lovemaking was likely as good as it got for any woman. It wasn't until she had made passionate love with Derek that she realized what she had been missing all along. Had the professor not disappeared from the face of the Earth, perhaps she would still be pining away for his affections, unaware that the rat was actually married with three children.

The image of Derek, stark naked, smiling, standing above her next to the bathtub, flashed through her mind. She sighed. Too bad the disturbing visions intervened when they did.

Determined to keep focused, Erin shook the image from her head and rose from bed. *Voting day.* So many women had worked tirelessly in the last months, gaining support from male family members and friends. Hopefully, all the effort would pay off. While dressing, she heard Frederick talking with her father downstairs.

Her stomach dropped to her toes. She rushed to the door and pinned her ear against the wood.

"Well, my boy, I do wish you luck," her father said. "Between the two of us, we'll put an end to this."

"And you certainly know how much I care for her," Frederick replied.

"I do, my boy. I'll send Maggie upstairs to get her. I believe she's up. I heard footsteps in her room."

Erin quickly brushed her hair and twisted the mass into a tidy chignon. She raised her chin, pinned her mother's cameo on her blouse, and smoothed the sleeves.

"Miss Erin?" called Maggie. "Your father and Mr. Dimsdale are downstairs. They wish to speak with you."

"All right. Inform them I'll be down in a moment."

Erin brushed loose powder along her nose and cheeks, erasing the rosy hue produced by her intimate thoughts of Derek moments earlier. She smoothed her skirts and inhaled a deep cleansing breath. There was no way around it; she had just been summoned to the lion's den.

She took slow, measured steps down the staircase and entered the bright dining room. Maggie had set out a plate of biscuits, jam, and eggs. Rather than greet the two men in the parlor, whose eyes followed her every move, she took a seat in her dining chair. If she didn't get some food in her stomach, she'd get sick.

Her father marched into the dining room with Frederick on his heels. "Ah, there you are. Frederick's here to see you."

Frederick cleared his throat. "Good morning, Erin. I was hoping —"

"Would you men like some coffee?" Maggie asked.

"Uh, yes, thank you," said Frederick, promptly taking a seat

in the dining chair next to Erin. Edward sat at the head of the table.

Maggie quickly returned with the coffee pot. Erin noticed the older woman's hands trembled as she poured the steamy liquid into cups.

Erin smoothed the jam on her biscuit and took a healthy bite, followed by a sip of coffee.

"So, Erin." Frederick scooted closer and lowered his voice. "I was thinking perhaps you and I could get away today."

Erin frowned. "That's impossible. I have work to do. You know it's an important day."

"Oh, yes, the vote. Well, your father has seen fit —"

Edward leaned forward. "What Frederick is trying to say is I have given you the day off. I think — *we* think — perhaps you should take some time away and go enjoy yourself for a change. You've been terribly busy these last days."

There they go again. The two of them planning her day the same way they plotted her entire life. The wedge of biscuit she'd just swallowed felt heavy as a brick inside her stomach. She took a long drink of coffee, tossed the linen napkin on the table, and glared at both of them. "What do you want me to say? I've already told you what I'm doing today."

"There's no need to be sour, Erin. I took that into account. I have David monitoring the polling. I thought perhaps you could write an article, if the women get the vote, that is."

If the women get the vote. He and Frederick would prefer women never got the right to vote. *Heathens — both of them.*

"You're my employer, Father. Is that what you want — a story *if* women get the vote?"

Edward's round cheeks burned red. "Well, yes, that's what I had planned." He waved his fingers. "But a story either way is fine."

Frederick slid his hand over hers. "Dear, I was hoping to take you out today for a ride in my new buggy. Perhaps have a lovely dinner —"

Erin freed her hand. "I don't feel like an outing today. In fact, if I've been dismissed from working today I think I'd rather return to my room."

"That's rude, Erin," her father said. "Frederick has come to see you, and your attitude is most unladylike."

"Unladylike?" She rose from her chair. "It's too early in the morning for this nonsense. If you invited Frederick, then perhaps the two of you can spend the day together."

"Erin!" Edward rose. "Honestly, I don't know what to do about you anymore." He sighed and left the room.

Frederick raised his hands. "Hold on. Hold on, now." He twisted the ends of his bristly mustache to gleaming points. "Erin, please, calm down. We should talk." He guided her by the elbow to the parlor. "Come now."

His patronizing tone made the contents of her stomach instantly curdle. She inhaled deeply, trying to squelch her rising anger. Avoiding his gaze, she fanned out her skirt, and sat on the couch. "What did you need to talk to me about?"

Frederick slid next to her. "I'm not here to upset you. Honest, I'm not."

His tranquil tenor took her by surprise. She lifted her lashes from her heated cheeks and met his gaze.

His brown eyes softened. "Please don't be angry with your father. He means well, surely you know that."

Her shoulders curled forward. It was true. Her father loved her, and ever since Mother's passing, he had grown particularly overprotective. "I ... I know he does."

He reached for her hand. "Despite my inapt misgivings at times, I, too, want what's best for you. You know that, right?"

She frowned and tilted her chin. "Yes, I suppose. But surely you must know how much it infuriates me when the two of you close ranks on me."

A smile spread beneath his mustache. "I'm sorry if I've given you that impression. It's just that ... it's just that your father and I, well ... " He sucked in his cheeks and released her hand.

"Well, what?"

"Well, what I'm trying to say, perhaps not as eloquently as I had hoped, is that your father and I are alike. Both of us care deeply for you and want what's best for you. I was hoping to do this later in the day, but … " His eyes stayed fixed upon hers as he rummaged through his trouser pocket.

Erin met his longing gaze with a questioning frown. "What are you doing?"

"Ah." Having found what he was looking for, he smiled and dropped to one knee. "Erin —"

"Oh, God." She shot to her feet. "Oh, Lord in heaven, Frederick, what are you doing?"

Frederick's mouth twisted into an awkward smile. "Erin, I was wondering, hoping, really, if you would … " He cleared his throat. "As I was saying … " He opened a small burgundy box.

Erin flopped on the couch and cupped a hand over her mouth.

"I would be honored if you would agree to be my wife."

The brilliant diamond solitaire gleamed in the sunlight glinting through the damask drapes. She gazed into Frederick's longing eyes. He was her friend, but their friendship was often strained by his possessive, unyielding nature. Did he truly believe the two of them would make a compatible couple? "I don't know what to say."

He plucked the ring from the delicate box, rose up from his knee, and sat next to her on the couch. "Well, I was hoping you would say yes, my dear."

Her mind raced as fast as the beat of her fluttering heart. "I — it's just that … "

His eyes prodded her for an answer.

Erin cast her gaze toward her meddling father's shadow, hovering outside the parlor doorway. "Frederick." She took his hand in hers.

He inched in closer. "Say it, Erin. Say yes, and you'll make me the happiest man on earth. You know in your heart that we would make a marvelous couple."

She bit down on her bottom lip and squeezed his hand. "I enjoy making you happy, Fredrick, but … "

His eyebrows arched high. "But?"

"I'm sorry. I cannot marry you."

The muscles along his jawline pulsed as he wedged the ring into the case and shut the velvet box with a snap of his finger. He shot to his feet and paced to the large picture window. "It's because of Rudliff, isn't it?"

Her entire body stiffened. "This has nothing to do with Der — Mr. Rudliff." She joined Frederick at the window and placed a hand on his shoulder.

He jerked at her touch and turned away.

Erin sighed and spun him around to face her. "Honestly, Frederick, do you truly believe in your heart you and I would make a happy home? I cannot thank you enough for your thoughtful fondness, but I'm sorry, my affections for you do not go beyond friendship."

Frederick's dark eyes narrowed, simmering with anger. "You know, I should have expected this. Ever since you banded together in those women's groups, you've changed, and not for the better I might add, little lady."

Anger seared her cheeks. "This is *exactly* why we can't be together." She tilted her chin high and turned away from him on her heels.

He seized her arm. "Face it, Erin. That's not the reason —"

"It is most certainly the reason!"

He leaned in, his face only inches from hers. "It's your ridiculous infatuation with Derek Rudliff. Let's be honest, my dear. I saw you yesterday." He pointed a firm finger in her face. "I saw *you* get in his carriage and enter into *his* house."

"You've been spying on me," she hissed between pursed lips.

He rolled his eyes and turned away. "Ever since I saw that look in your eyes after you met him at the cemetery, I knew something was up between you two. I went to your father with my concerns. We both agreed it was best to make an honest woman of you before you humiliate yourself further."

She swatted his hand from her arm. "Oh, how *very* noble of you, Frederick. You came here and asked me to marry you to save me from myself? Is that right?"

His eyes narrowed to slits. "You don't know him, Erin, and —"

"Ha! And you do?" she said, challenging his seething gaze.

He leaned forward and whispered, "I know a lot more about him than you do, my dear."

She laced her fingers together in an attempt to stop their shaking. "I don't believe you. Go home, Frederick."

He seized her shoulders, nearly knocking her from her feet. "I know he'll hurt you. He's not the man you think he is. What do you know about that red-headed woman we saw him with at the cemetery?"

She planted her feet firmly on the floor and stared into Frederick's angry eyes prodding her for an immediate answer. "Her? She's an old friend and new in town. Now, unhand me, you fool."

Frederick snorted and dropped his arms limply to his sides. "Is that what Rudliff told you? Perhaps you should venture downtown and check out the brothel on Chestnut, my dear."

She frowned. "What the *hell* are you talking about?"

He gasped, his mouth twisting in disgust. "My Lord. Now you curse like a dockhand, too."

Erin marched to the entry and opened the front door. "I've had enough of this nonsense. It's best you leave."

Frederick clicked his tongue, a wry smile on his thin lips. "Like I said, my dear, you might wish to venture downtown, chaperoned of course, and see for yourself the new madam in town. Seems Rudliff's 'old friend' Regine Delacour is quite the businesswoman."

"I … I don't believe you. Have some dignity, Frederick." She grabbed hold of the knob to slam the door in his arrogant face.

Frederick moved quickly, wedging himself in the doorway. "It's not just you I've been keeping a watchful eye upon. It's Rudliff, too. Not only is his *friend* Madame Delacour a trollop, he owns the building and set her up in the business himself."

Her father darted into the room. "I'm sorry, but I couldn't help but overhear —"

Erin's jaw dropped. "Overhear! You've been hovering like a ghoul outside the doorway ever since you left the room." She shook her head in attempt to flush her fury. "Both of you are really too much. I have to get out of here." She grabbed her coat, hastened past Frederick, and marched down the porch.

"Erin, wait," her father called.

"Where are you going without a hat or umbrella?" Frederick called. "Have you gone daft?"

Chapter Thirteen

New York

A package arrived from my lawyer. Inside were financial ledgers, journals, and letters. According to a neatly penned missive, the elderly Mr. Watt had recently passed away. Having no family of his own, the old man had left his entire share of the business to me, and the company name changed to Rudliff Land and Timber.

The company had grown considerably under the elder business owner's previous tenure. Inside the journal, one of Mr. Watt's last penned entries written during his recent visit to Washington State caught my eye.

"Lush and green and sitting between pristine forests of evergreen mountains to the North and East, the waters of Everett, Washington, are the perfect transport vehicle for lumber."

I'd been mulling leaving New York ever since my shameful behavior that led me into Erin's bedroom that pitiful night. With the business clearly marked for growth in the West and solely at my discretion now, it was clear I needed to make a decision.

But the idea of parting from Erin until she reached the attainable age of twenty-three invaded my thoughts by day and haunted my dreams at night.

Could I truly move farther away from her young spirit, even for a few years? After returning from The Blue Moon Lounge one evening, I hatched a plan.

I stood outside the Richland home, hoping Erin's father would exit. Minutes turned into hours. Finally, the door opened. I tugged the brim of my hat over my brows and bent low, pretending I had just stopped in place to adjust my shoe.

A stout man wrangling a large leather satchel glanced over his shoulder and said, "Inform Mrs. Richland I won't be home for dinner tonight." Then the door promptly shut behind him.

I kept a respectable pace behind the man, allowing unwary pedestrians to fill the space between us. Finally, he walked into the building of *The New York Herald.*

The New York Herald, I mused.

One late afternoon the following week, I waited outside the newspaper building. Once Mr. Richland exited, I trailed him to a nearby pub. He sat with a handsomely dressed group of younger men. I ordered a beer and listened in on their conversation from a nearby table. Erin's father knew his wife was ill. Consumption, I deduced, judging by his description, and he was genuinely unhappy living in New York.

Unhappy in New York. I downed my beer and wandered the streets for hours.

On the second evening, I shadowed the unsuspecting Mr. Richland to the very same pub. This time, I heard one of his friends ask him a poignant question.

"What is it you long for, Edward?" the younger man asked.

Edward paused for a moment, drank the rest of his foamy beer, and said, "I wish to be my own man."

I wish to be my own man. Something in his words nagged me, haunted me. I leaned in, listening closely, shoving aside the dawning realization that his bleak feelings mirrored my own.

"I've wanted to leave here for so very long," Edward said with a sigh. "Yes, I want to be my own newspaper man — maybe out West."

Ideas flooded my mind so fast I couldn't keep up. I purchased a large piece of land overlooking Port Gardner Bay in Everett, Washington. Soon thereafter, I sent Edward Richland an innocuous advertisement for property at an irresistible price that would make the perfect location for a new city newspaper.

Erin's father had taken the bait. As I began the lengthy preparations for my move to Washington, the plan was suddenly derailed when I learned Edward's wife had passed away in Washington and Erin had returned by herself to New York to attend school at Barnard College.

I watched Erin grow into a mirror image of my lovely Ersule. Each time I cast my gaze upon her sweet face, I died again and again.

When school was in session, I would watch her from a safe distance as she walked to and from college with her schoolbooks, often with young, fanciful women by her side. As time passed, young men with lust-filled eyes began escorting her, strolling arm-in-arm with my beloved.

One night while sitting with Gregore and Dominic at The Blue Moon, I couldn't help but feel the two were keeping something from me.

Curious, I scanned their solemn faces and asked, "All right. What's going on?"

Gregore gnawed on his bottom lip and stared at me for what felt like an eternity. Finally, he said, "I saw Erin today in the park."

I was delighted to hear any news concerning her, but the trepidation within his soulful eyes gave me heed. "You did?"

"Tallon!" Dominic called, gesturing to the waiter for another round of blood cocktails.

Gregore flinched at the booming sound of Dominic's voice. Looking directly at me he said, "Vamps. They're *so* dramatic."

"What's going on?" I asked, suddenly aware of the unease between the two of them.

Gregore sighed and looked at Dominic. "You know I can't keep such a thing from him."

Dominic shrugged and took a big swig from the bottle of rum on the table.

"What?" I asked.

Tallon brought the round of cocktails on a silver tray and set them on the table. "Anything else, gentlemen?"

Gregore's eyes stayed fixed upon mine. "I saw Erin in the park … with a man."

Tallon froze in place, his eyes like bright orbs. "Uh oh."

Dominic's fangs protruded in a flash. "*Leave!*"

The waiter promptly scurried to the next table.

I smiled at the spectacle, though my heart missed a few beats. "Is that all? She's a student, Gregore. Of course she has male friends."

He slowly shook his head. "No. This was not the case, my King."

"Ah, ah," Dominic interjected said with a frown. "You forget, Gregore, there is no aristocracy at The Blue Moon. We are equal here. *Never* forget that."

"Yes, yes. I'm sorry." Gregore's gaze snapped back to me. "This man was older. More mature. Something didn't feel right, so I watched. They sat huddled together, his hand on hers. Then they kissed and rather passionately, I might add."

I poured a hefty measure of rum into my chilled goblet. Silently, I took in what he had just revealed, all while the spiked blood cocktail bled into my veins like molten lava. "Well, I'm … I'm sure there's an explanation."

My mind raced. Up until now, it had never occurred to me I might have a true rival before Erin reached the ripe age of twenty-three.

"You see," Gregore said to Dominic. "I told you he wouldn't tear your lovely lounge to pieces."

No, I wasn't going to tear The Blue Moon into pieces, but I

sure as hell felt like I could the way my blood suddenly heated as though ready to boil.

I raised my chin. "Tell me. What else did you see?"

Gregore leaned in. "I watched for a time. They parted ways after an intimate embrace."

The Caribbean-style band began to play, and Gregore's face instantly lit up. "Oh, let's dance," he said to Dominic.

I sighed heavily, brooding over my cocktail, contemplating my next move as the two headed for the crowded dance floor.

I went to Barnard College and stated I wished to grant the institution a sizeable donation. An hour into the tour of the school, I saw Erin sitting in the front row of a classroom, writing feverishly on paper as the professor spoke. Later in the day, I sat outside, waiting for her to leave.

Erin exited the building wearing an eager smile, her glossy hair pulled back. The indulgent wind loosened her tidy chignon, sending tendrils wisping across her ivory neck.

My breath hitched. How I longed to press my nose against that lovely throat and breathe in her heavenly scent.

I followed a safe distance behind as she strode in a different direction than usual. She entered an apartment building, and I was left outside wondering with whom she might be visiting.

Two cigars later, she exited with the handsome professor I had seen standing in front of her in the classroom earlier. I tugged the brim of my hat over my brow and yanked up my frock collar.

The pair walked past me, laughing and looking adoringly at one another. My heart sank at the sight of her gleaming eyes and rosy cheeks filled with enthusiasm. I froze, unable to follow them, but I needed not, for they ducked into a hotel a half-block north.

I placed one numb foot in front of the other and made my way to the three-story hotel entrance.

My God. I could only imagine one reason the two of them would enter a hotel together.

I entered the revolving glass door, my heart hammering like thunder. After picking up the newspaper sitting on the entry table, I took a seat in the lobby.

"Good afternoon, Mr. and Mrs. Johnson," said the hotelier to the couple. "Nice to see you again."

Again? I peered above the opened newspaper I held between stiffening fingers.

The doughy man behind the counter extended a key. "Room 112."

Erin offered the man a modest nod, a rosy hue flushing her cheeks.

Once the two left, I approached the gentleman at the counter and asked for a room on the first floor.

He ran his rotund fingers down the ledger. "All I have left on the first floor are rooms 102, 105, and 111."

My heart jumped. Naturally, I accepted room 111.

Not wishing to be seen by the couple, I waited another ten minutes before venturing toward my assigned room. Once inside, I paced the floor, unable to get a grip upon my bounding pulse. Finally, I sat in the chair next to the bed and listened.

Nothing.

I shook my head violently and shot up from the chair. *What the hell am I doing?*

I marched to the door and grabbed the brass doorknob. Just then, muffled voices and laughter, coming from behind the wall, filled the silence.

My stomach twisted, and bile slowly rose in my throat as the noise gave way to obvious sounds of lovemaking.

My hands turned to clenched fists. I stepped backwards and sat on the bed. Mere inches separated me from the two lovers behind the thin wall. I froze, listening to their jagged breaths and moans of desire. I closed my eyes, hearing her hastened breathing as visions of Ersule lying beneath me years ago imprinted upon my eyelids.

Willing my fists to open, I placed my hand against the wall. I could *smell* Ersule's freshly washed hair smelling of sweet rose, could *feel* her soft flesh under my once callused hands, could *hear* her soft whimpers of desire as I plunged her sweet depths.

I opened my eyes. Staying in this room any longer would only lead me to madness.

With my heart so heavy I could barely move my feet, I left the hotel to find solace among my kind at The Blue Moon Lounge.

The following day, I inquired about the professor. Evidently, while the handsome young professor was bedding my beloved, he was married with three young children in tow. My anger swelled into blinding rage. And for the first time in more than three hundred years, I gazed at the darkening sky above, impatient, vengeful, and eager for the kill.

Chapter Fourteen

Everett, Washington

Erin tromped up Grand Avenue and stood outside Derek's house in the cold, pouring rain. Knees shaking, teeth clicking, she wondered whether the man would even be home this time of day.

She walked up the steps and knocked on the door. After what felt like an eternity, the large door opened.

"Good afternoon, Miss Richland." Mrs. Schauss's penetrating gaze assessed her from head to toe. "May I help you?"

"I'm here to see Mr. Rudliff."

The servant's dramatically arched brows knitted together. "I see." She fingered the cameo pinned at her throat. "And do you have an appointment?"

"Um, no, I'm sorry I don't. May I please come in to warm up? I'm terribly cold and wet and —"

The sound of a door slamming shut from inside the house echoed across the tall ceiling.

The servant flinched. "Master Rudliff is terribly busy. Perhaps you can return —"

"Mrs. Schauss," said a firm voice. "Show Miss Richland to the parlor, *now*."

The servant nodded and gestured for Erin to enter. After the elder woman hung the drenched coat, she cast her gaze to the floor and whispered, "Follow me."

Erin followed her into the enormous parlor.

"Wait here, Miss Richland," she said, turning quickly to leave.

Erin stepped forward. "Excuse me, Mrs. Schauss. May I have a towel to dry my hair?"

Derek entered the room. Upon seeing Erin, he turned toward his servant, his gaze seething. "Get Miss Richland a towel and some warm tea immediately."

Mrs. Schauss turned on her toes and fled, clearly avoiding further reproach.

Derek rushed toward Erin and draped his arm across her shoulders. "My God, you're soaked." He searched her eyes.

Erin turned from his piercing gaze and stiffened her back. "I … need to talk to you, Mr. Rudliff. It cannot wait."

Frowning, he stepped back and thrust his hands into his trouser pockets. "Mr. Rudliff, is it? I take it this must be a business visit."

Mrs. Schauss entered wearing her familiar scowl and handed Erin a towel before darting from the room.

"Thank you," Erin called to the fleeing woman dressed in dreary black. She dabbed the length of her fallen hair hanging in long wet ropes to her waist.

Derek tilted his chin. "What's happened? Are you all right?"

She sighed heavily and flopped on the divan, undaunted by her wet skirt soaking through the silken sofa fabric. She hung her head. "I wasn't sure where I should go."

Derek slipped in by her side. "Look at me," he whispered, tipping her chin up to meet his gaze.

Drawn in by his calming voice and the bottomless blue eyes gazing into hers, she couldn't look away.

"You've come to the right place," he said. "You're always welcome here." He moved to slip his arm around her.

What had she come here for again? *Questions. Yes, questions.*

She ripped her gaze from the mesmerizing stare threatening her resolve. "I have to speak with you. I must ask you some important questions."

His eyebrows jumped. "Now? Look at you. You're absolutely drenched. I insist you allow me to have Mrs. Schauss get you some dry clothes first, and I won't hear another word until then, deal?"

Derek was right. Miserably cold and wet, her teeth clicked like castanets. "Deal."

He ran his hands through his hair and sighed. "Besides, I have some urgent business I must finish up in the library. Mrs. Schauss will help you until I return."

The servant led her down the long hallway. As they passed the corridor of rooms, Erin could hear Derek in the library speaking in hushed, agitated tones. She tried to make out the conversation, but the only word she heard besides cursing was "trouble."

Mrs. Schauss escorted her into a room at the rear of the house. "Inside the armoire is an assortment of clothing. I'll bring you hot tea or cocoa. Which do you prefer?"

Erin pondered the choice. "Tea sounds good."

"Tea, it is," the woman said, pausing in the doorway. Finally, she exited with a sigh and shut the door behind her.

Something about the older woman sent a quiver racing up Erin's backbone. Shivering, she glanced around the well-appointed bedroom. A scrolled, four-poster bed stood at the center of the room, draped with an elegant cream-colored lace canopy top. Tall leaded windowpanes filled the rear wall, allowing a dramatic view of the gleaming bay below. She opened the armoire and dressed in a white chenille robe. Within minutes, Mrs. Schauss returned with the hot tea.

Erin sipped the steamy liquid, the tea gliding down her throat, instantly warming her belly. Footsteps sounded along the long hallway.

"This is *all* I will do for you. Nothing more," hissed Derek.

Erin cocked her head, listening closely to what sounded like the shuffling of papers.

"Oh, you shall do more," said a female voice, "a lot more. Goodbye."

Erin raided the armoire. Instantly, she was drawn to the lovely lavender dress hanging inside. Matching satin slippers sat on the shelf below. After dressing and finishing her tea, she ventured into the parlor where Derek sat reading the *Everett Messenger*.

"These murders around here are horrific," he said, glancing at her over the paper. His eyes widened, and she heard the breath catch inside his throat. He lowered the newspaper and stood. "My Lord. You look lovely."

She tilted her chin high, ignoring his lengthy appraisal. "Yes, the murders are horrible. It's been difficult writing about them and talking with frightened citizens. I've even had nightmares about the incidents."

Derek nodded. "I can imagine." His eyebrows rose. "I must say, I certainly like these stories you've been writing on the women's vote. You must be pleased." He patted the divan. "Come, let's sit."

Seeing him standing there, beckoning her, looking devilishly handsome, warmed her chilled body straight to the core. She sat, allowing ample space between them. He instantly inched closer and set down the newspaper.

"Talk to me," he said, in a voice as smooth as warmed honey. "Why did you walk all the way here in the pouring rain?"

She gazed into his expressive eyes. Everything that had been churning away inside her came flowing out as though her mouth had a mind all its own. "I had an argument with my father and Frederick. I had to get out of there, Derek, and the only place I thought about going was here … to you."

"*Shhh.*" He pulled her against his chest. "Calm yourself, now."

The steady rhythm of his pounding heart hummed a tune against her ear, and that invisible energy she'd felt with him before passed between them yet again. Steady. Strong. Seductive.

"How's your head?"

Had he just asked her a question? "What?"

"The bump on your head? You haven't forgotten —"

"Oh, that." She rubbed the lump at the back of her skull. "No, it's fine now. It gave me a terrible headache, but that's all."

She shook her head in an attempt to gather her wits. Why did the man have such an effect on her, a way of making her forget why she came to see him in the first place?

She pulled from his embrace. "Derek, wait. I feel so distracted. I really must speak with you about an urgent matter."

His gaze narrowed. "I can see you're upset. I'll answer your questions, but first I want you to inform your father you'll return home in a few hours. You don't want to alarm him, do you?"

"I don't care what he wants — or Frederick — for that matter," she said. "I'm so sick of the two of them, I could spit." She shot up. "I can't stand it anymore, and I'm not going back today. I may never return, and you can't make me —"

He darted up and pulled her into an embrace. "Surely, you know how much I would love for you to stay with me here. But you'll hate me for it later," he whispered, smoothing her damp hair with warm hands. "I won't sit back and watch your reputation shattered. I insist you allow me to get you a hotel room —"

"No. No hotel." She pulled away from his arms and stared evenly into his eyes. "Please, Derek."

He searched her eyes and sighed. "All right, no hotel, but I absolutely insist you inform your father that you're safe."

She bit down on her bottom lip. "Yes, you're right." The walls of the room moved in slow waves. She smoothed the lavender dress and sat on the divan. The long walk to his house, icy-cold fingers of rain raking across her face, the warmth of the hot tea — had she ever been this exhausted?

He slipped in next to her and said, "Now, tell me you didn't traipse here in the pouring rain just to interview me for the paper."

His deep voice lulled her weary mind, reminiscent of a sweet dream from long ago. She cleared her throat, determined to speak with him before exhaustion destroyed her nerve. "No, not an interview. I have much more personal questions I must ask."

He cocked his head. "Really? Perhaps that too can wait until later, after you inform your father —"

"No." she glared at him, trying to keep calm and composed as she rose from the divan and took a seat in the chair opposite him. "Now."

A single brow arched. He sat back and rested splayed hands on his thighs. "This *must* be serious."

"I … " She paused, choosing her words carefully. "Do you agree there is something between us? I must know, or I have no right to demand answers to the questions I have come to ask."

His eyes narrowed, darkening to indigo slits. "Do you really need to ask me that?"

Her heart skipped a beat, then resumed with a heavy thud against her breasts.

Derek leaned forward, his eyes following her every move.

She blushed at the intensity of the heated gaze aimed at the snug bodice of the dress. She angled her chin. "Yes, well, I have heard rumors about you."

He snorted. "I take it you mean the rumors originating from your so called 'friend,' Frederick Dimsdale — am I correct?"

She frowned. "Do you know him?"

He shot up from the couch. "The man has been following me all over the city for days and asking questions. I must say, I don't think he cares much for me, and the feeling is most certainly mutual."

He paced the room.

"He's told me there is more to your involvement with Madame Delacour," she said. "Much more."

Derek turned, his gaze narrowing. "Pray tell, Erin, what else has he told you?"

Feeling as though she could wilt from the heated eyes staring her down, she yanked her gaze from his and said, "Well, he told me that she is, well, that she is a madam of a bawdy house, and that you own the building in which she conducts her sordid business." There, she'd said it. She looked up.

The small lines around Derek's eyes deepened, and the muscles in his jaw pulsated. "I won't lie to you about this, Erin. You mean too much to me."

Erin rose and joined him at the window. "You say you care for me. Please, tell me, Derek. What is it between you and Madame Delacour? I must know."

Silence filled the room as he gazed out into the distance. Finally, he lowered his head and whispered, "Honestly, I don't even know where to begin."

The gloomy light of outdoors bathed his face with gray, making him look a decade older. A stabbing pain pierced her ribs. She moved in, wedging herself between him and the window. "What is it? *Talk to me.*"

He raked his hands through his hair and sighed heavily. "The vile woman is blackmailing me."

She gasped. "Blackmailing you? With what?"

Slowly, he met her gaze. "Yes, she's a parlor madam. I've known the woman for ages, Erin, and I've hated her for many, many years. Now she's threatened me."

She frowned and shook her head. "But I don't understand. Don't stop, Derek. Tell me — I wish to know more."

There was something about Regine Delacour she had not

trusted from the very first moment she'd laid eyes on the lovely red-head. Having a worthy reason to despise the French Madame excited her in a perverse and most unchristian manner.

Derek pulled her into his arms. "My lovely Erin. God, how I want you … and only you. You must believe me."

The heated touch of his hands sliding along the small of her back comforted her. But she had come for answers. She stiffened in his arms. "Tell me, Derek."

He smoothed her hair; lean, gentle fingers combing damp tangles as he spoke. "She has a son." He sighed heavily. "A bastard child from a night that never should have happened."

Her throat turned bone dry. She swallowed hard and gazed up. "Are you telling me what I *think* you're telling me?"

"I wish I could say the child is not mine." He lowered his head. "God, how I had hoped he was not mine."

She frowned and slid from his embrace. "Illegitimate children are born all the time. Everyone knows these things can, and do, happen. What is she blackmailing you with?"

His gaze snapped to hers. "You name it. My business … and you."

"Me? *Why?* What does she know about me?"

"I've told her absolutely nothing about us, Erin. But she knows how I feel about you." He turned away, his hands clenched in tight fists. "The woman is a witch, I tell you, and when she threatened to go to you and explain —"

Erin grabbed his arm. "Let me get this straight. You set that vile woman up in her disgusting business because of me?"

He eyed her firm grasp upon his arm. "I … I didn't know." He moved from her clutches and slowly paced the room. "It's complicated. I wasn't thinking clearly. Hell, she told me she wished to open a French bakery. Stupidly, I believed her. I needed a tenant anyway. I had no idea she would be up to her old tricks again. While

I was out of town, she set up a saloon with a parlor above."

Erin sighed dramatically, her mind racing in all directions.

"I wanted to throw her out, but she threatened me. I couldn't bear the thought of losing you."

Erin moved in and planted her feet in front of him. "Look at me."

He lowered his gaze to meet hers. "What?"

"You do realize it was in your building where the mauling and murder occurred?"

He closed his eyes and slowly shook his head. "I know. God help me, I do, and I hope they catch the evil person responsible for the wicked crime."

Erin's heart cleaved into a million pieces as she listened to Derek, his voice wracked with pain, clearly tortured by secrets threatening to unravel his life and their new relationship. He cared so deeply for her that he would have allowed Regine Delacour anything she desired just to keep her quiet. And as she watched him now, wounded, suffering, spilling his secrets, her true feelings for him became clearer.

She was falling in love with Derek Rudliff.

Derek reached for her, his bottomless gaze searching her moist eyes. "I'm so sorry if I've caused you pain. You see, your friend Frederick was right to a certain degree, but I assure you, he doesn't have all the facts." He cupped her chin in his palm. "Now you see how much I care for you. Please tell me you feel the same way. I need to know."

Her heart thumped wildly against her chest. Dare she tell him how she thought of him by day and dreamed of his touch at night? How her body responded so naturally to his, it was as though it were part of her own?

As if he'd read her mind, he drew her to his chest and kissed her.

She slid from his lips and whispered against his cheek, "And who is Ersule?"

His breath caught in his throat. "I'm … I'm so sorry. I didn't mean to call you by the name of my deceased wife. It was merely instinct. I —"

"No." she placed her finger to his lips. "Don't speak of it."

What a little fool. Of course it was his deceased wife, and she had suspected as much. She should have simply disregarded the innocent mistake, when in a moment of panic, he had called out his wife's name. But part of her had wanted to hurt him, make him share the ache ripping through her heart now.

Humiliated, she lowered her gaze. "Perhaps it is I who should apologize."

"You're still chilled, my dear," he whispered against her flushed cheek. "Would you like a lovely bath in the tub?"

His warm breath caressed her earlobe, and she instantly felt powerless against his seductive suggestion. "A hot bath sounds divine."

"I'll fill it myself." He kissed her passionately, his body melding against hers, teasing her with the promise of more. "I'll meet you in the bathroom in twenty minutes."

Erin listened to the ticking clock in the bedroom counting down the twenty minutes. She slipped out of the dress. Wearing only the chenille bathrobe, she stepped out the door and padded down the hall.

When she opened the bathroom door, at least a dozen flickering candles greeted her. She slipped out of the robe and sank into the large tub filled with water so steamy the mirrors and window were completely fogged. On a small table next to her sat a bottle of rose bath oil. She poured a generous dollop into the water and swished it about.

"May I come in?" asked Derek from behind the door.

She smiled and sank deeper into the tub, allowing only her head to poke out. "You may."

Dressed in a pitch-black silken robe, he entered and locked the door with an echoing click behind him.

Her gaze wandered over the length of his handsome, naked body as he untied his robe and let it drop into a pool of slick fabric on the marble floor. He sank into the water and pulled her against him in an embrace. Despite the hot water, the feel of his firm body against hers sent fiery sparks racing up her backbone.

The rose oil slickened every inch of their bodies. She suddenly flinched, recalling the frightening vision that had sent her scurrying from the bath in a panicked flurry before.

"Are you all right? You're shaking."

"I'm fine. Just a momentary chill."

His hands leisurely slid along the slippery curve of her waist. "You arouse me to the point of distraction, woman," he whispered said against her throat. He grazed her neck, the tip of his tongue lingering against her racing pulse point.

Determined to shake off the eerie vision threatening to resurface, she pulled him deeper into the water.

"My, my, Miss Richland," he said.

She slid on top of him, her wet hair fanned out, floating on the surface of the water, framing their bodies like a shroud. She nuzzled the wet mat of curled hair on his chest, brushing against her cheeks, and kissed his muscled torso.

Firm hands glided along the sides of her breasts, the curve of her hips, moving over her buttocks, stopping to grip the round mounds and pull her firmly against his body.

Derek slid her up the length of his body until her mouth reached his. He kissed her, deeply, passionately, his hands massaging the tops of her legs, her bottom, a slick finger slipping between her silken thighs. His finger curved into the crevasse of her buttocks.

"Your skin feels like silk," he said, his voice, deep, throaty, and seductive. "The things I want to do to you … "

His firm manhood pressed against her belly. The heated bathwater penetrated her skin, flooding her veins with yearning, heating her straight through to her core.

She reached down and gently grabbed hold of his slick shaft. He moaned, and his muscles tensed, his firm legs and torso tightening until he trembled. She massaged him, taking her time as she explored the smooth mass. His thighs grew rock hard beneath her as he pressed his feet firmly against the foot of the bathtub.

His breathing quickened, and she sensed his desire gathering like an approaching storm. He grabbed her bottom, pulling her closer, his long arms reaching until his fingers found the silky hairs of her moist cleft.

The moment his finger penetrated her, she grew warmer. Her buttocks tightened, and a throaty moan of pleasure escaped her lips. She circled his erect nipple with her tongue.

"My God, woman," he breathed.

Erin gazed into his smoldering eyes. He turned her around, pressing her back to his chest. He reached around the front, one hand sliding up her silken stomach, capturing a breast. The other spread her thighs, his fingers slipping into her moistened warmth, pausing to finger her wet bud.

Resting her head against his broad chest, she moaned, and the disturbing vision threatened to surface again. "Derek," she whispered. "I … "

"Hush, my angel," he whispered said softly, from somewhere distant and unreachable.

A finger slipped inside her, slickening her, fragrant oils smoothing the way. Her nipples beaded like pearls between his fingers. Growing desire pulled from somewhere deep within her pelvis. Breathless with yearning, she turned her head from side to side, her cheeks pressing against his muscled chest; all willpower to halt obliterated, as waves of unfulfilled passion grew unbearable.

She gasped the moment he spread her wider, his hand moving faster, and just before she felt her insides explode, he seized her jaw, forcing her cheek firmly against his shoulder, his mouth coming down hard upon her throat.

"Oh, Derek, I … "

Jagged breaths caressed her neck. "You what, my love?"

My love. His haunting voice, resonant of an old dream, made her shudder. Rhythmic waves rose, cresting in moist surges of desire against his experienced hands.

She arched as his mouth came down upon her neck once again, nibbling, grazing her sensitive throat with his teeth, his body tense with desire.

Growls of pleasure and heated passion hummed against her neck, sending her plunging over the edge. Her body pulsated with an exquisite climax, vibrating streams of warmth enveloping her entire body like a quivering veil.

"You what, my love?" he asked again.

He rose from the bath and drew her breathless, trembling body into his arms.

Her eyelids flew open. "Are we stopping?"

A devilish smile spread beneath his mustache. He stood her up on legs that felt ready to collapse. After wrapping her in a towel, he led her by the hand to his candlelit bedroom.

The towel fell to the floor as she flopped on her back against the cool sheets, trying to capture measured breath. The glowing candlelight flickered, yellow flames hissing and rising as he slid above her, his strong arms cradling her neck. Their dark, naked shadows moved along the walls and high ceiling, looking like menacing night creatures on the hunt.

He gazed into her eyes, his firm chest pressed against her

breasts. Slowly, gently, he slid his hand between her legs, fingering the soft flesh of her inner thigh. Instantly, the steady smolder of arousal began anew.

"Derek," she whispered. "You torture me with pleasure."

"Woman, you torture me more than you'll ever know. Look into my eyes," he said in a deep tone that caught her off guard.

A solitary finger slipped inside her. She gasped.

"Look at me," he repeated, firmly.

She did as he commanded, gazing deep, deeper, *deeper*, slipping into the fathomless depths of indigo, as he removed his finger and slid it around her slick pearl.

His fingers did things she never knew were possible, "Oh, Derek," she moaned, as his fingers withdrew. "I want you, all of you."

Gazing into her eyes, he lifted his hips and plunged inside her heated depths. Over and over, deeper and faster, he drove her to the very edge of release. Gasping with yearning, she barely heard his demand.

"Wrap your legs around me," he breathed against her cheek.

Erin lifted her legs and wrapped them around his waist. He plunged deeper and dug his fingertips into her tender buttocks. He increased pace, rubbing along her sensitive pearl. She arched as the tide within her swelled, cresting, and just as waves of pleasure collided, Derek's body stiffened, and his buttocks grew rock hard against her hands as she pulled him deeper.

Breathless, she watched the dancing candlelight licking the bedroom walls as their moans of ecstasy echoed across the high-beamed ceiling while they rode the waves together.

Chapter Fifteen

New York

Dominic worked the large crowd squeezed into The Blue Moon Lounge, there to celebrate his milestone birthday. I surveyed the handsome Vamp. *One thousand years old.* In mortal years, Dominic appeared thirty-five, at most.

Gregore's gaze followed mine. He leaned across the table and said, "Look at Dominic, that devil Vamp, heading to the dance floor. Not a care in the world. I think I might be jealous of him."

I frowned. "Jealous? How so?"

Gregore snorted. "Because he has the best of all worlds. Just watch him."

I focused on Dominic, nose to nose with a particularly lovely wench, his hands digging into her buttocks as they danced.

"Sexually, he enjoys women, prefers them, actually, but they weaken him. It's the blood of viral men that strengthen him."

Charlotte plucked a thin cigarette from her jeweled handbag. "You two were correct. This truly is a grand affair."

"Indeed, my dear," Edgar said, striking a match and holding it out for her. "It appears America has much to offer us."

I smiled, thankful to finally have my cherished pack members back in the fold where they belonged.

Tallon glided by. "I'll be back in a flash with another round."

I watched as *Others* of every shape and size danced in the middle of the room. Clearly showing off, Jasper swayed excitedly in front of a group of seductive witches, waving his arms and swiveling his head. Jessamine caught my eye and gestured toward the dancing crowd. I smiled and shook my head. She shrugged and grabbed Franz as he strode past her.

Tallon headed toward our table with chilled cocktails.

"This round is on me," said Dominic as he approached our table.

Gregore patted the soft cushion. "Sit for a spell, birthday boy. You must be exhausted."

Dominic sat, his penetrating blue eyes narrowing as he scanned our faces. "This room is exciting, but I guarantee the patrons on the second floor are having a wickedly good time."

Gregore dragged on a cigarette and blew out a perfectly formed smoky ring. Gazing at me with a glint in his coffee-brown eyes, he said, "Dominic's an especially naughty *Vamp* tonight."

Dominic grinned and stared at me. "You sure you're not up for a roguish night of debauchery, Derek?"

I swallowed the cocktail warming my lifeless soul and slowly shook my head.

Edgar leaned closer. "The mortals were a divine treat, Dominic. Very festive, indeed. I must say, Charlotte and I haven't partaken of such hedonistic activities in many decades."

Charlotte's tongue darted out and moistened her bottom lip. "He's right. What can I say?"

For weeks, the upcoming party had been the talk of the city among our kind. After lengthy negotiations, Dominic had managed to procure New York's most desirable male and female prostitutes. Insisting the luscious mortals modify their usual repertoire, it had cost the lounge owner a pretty penny. He explained that they were to drink their fill of the house specialty cocktail, followed by allowing the Blue Moon patrons whatever they sexually desired.

A woman wearing a sheer white dress, sporting nothing underneath except fiery-red pubic hair, sauntered from table to table offering sugary delicacies.

"Gentleman?" She held out the skillfully decorated pastries on a sterling platter.

My mouth watered. I chose an almond croissant drizzled with dark chocolate.

"Compliments from the owner," she said.

"Help yourself, fiends," said Dominic. "These sinful treasures are a birthday gift from a friend of mine."

The dark chocolate melted against my tongue. I glanced around the large room. Ever since Erin had left for Washington State, it seemed as though my beating heart had stopped dead and withered to black ash. No matter how brief the moment, I welcomed the delicious croissant managing to warm my cold soul.

Gregore shot up. "Let's dance."

The small lines around Dominic's eyes crinkled with amusement at Gregore's inexorable passion for dance. "Let's go."

Others poured in through the metal door, filling every square inch of the lounge. After drinking my fill of cocktail, the stimulating scents of the boisterous immortal crowd filled my head until I thought it would explode. The nagging bulge inside my trousers led me to ponder whether perhaps I, too, should consider partaking of the wicked festivities filling the rooms on the second floor.

A familiar aroma blasted into my nostrils. Instantly, bile rose in my throat, and my heart hammered against my vest. I rubbed my neck trying to smooth the tiny hairs rising along my nape. I inhaled deeply and surveyed the room.

There.

I rose from the chair and cleared my throat. "Excuse me," I said to Edgar and Charlotte, trying my best to hide the rising alarm flooding my veins.

Charlotte tapped my hand. "Oh, tell me you're not leaving this fine party."

Edgar piped up. "Let the man be, my dear. Of course he's not leaving, right, Derek? Derek?"

Her back faced me, and the air instantly chilled as I slowly approached the group of females conversing in the rear corner of the room.

"Oh, my," said a fair-haired woman with narrow predatory eyes.

Regine stiffened her spine and spun around. "And who do we have here?" she asked, a look of false innocence drawn upon her pale face. "Why, Derek Rudliff, how long *has* it been?"

I willed hostile words to form in my throat. Instead, my mouth hung wide open.

"Quite the grand soirée, don't you agree, *chérie?*"

I grabbed her elbow. "Excuse us," I muttered to the group.

"Why, Derek, you only needed to ask —"

"Shut up and come with me."

Her feet barely hit the floor as I hurried her toward the darkened stairway corridor.

"My heavens, *chérie*. You always were a royal pain in the ass, and I do mean that quite literally."

I stopped in my tracks and spun around. Regine slammed into my chest and gasped. I dug my fingers into her shoulders. "Why the hell is it everywhere I go, you manage to follow?"

Regine's brown eyes flashed with flecks of illuminating golden candlelight. She snorted dramatically. "You flatter yourself."

"Do I?" My fingers curled, nails digging hard into her collarbone. "Tell me now," I said between clenched teeth.

Her seething gaze narrowed. "Let go of me before I scream for Dominic." She pulled from my firm grasp.

"You know Dominic?"

She adjusted her gown and looked at me as though I were insane. "But of course."

I sighed and raked my hands through my hair. "Enlighten me, Regine. Just how long have you been in New York?"

She fluttered her lashes. "Long enough to firmly establish my new business. You've probably heard of *Bonbonniere Sweet Shoppe*, yes?"

Indeed, I had read about the place. Owned by a group of "innovative females from Europe," the new establishment flaunting delicious French pastries had been covered many times within the gourmet section of the local newspapers.

"I hope you shared in the sweet delicacies I provided for the party tonight."

Suddenly, the croissant sitting inside my stomach turned into a boulder, and the loud lounge music screamed inside my head, hindering my thoughts. A woman peered around the corner, watching us. I couldn't think straight. I had seen her before, but where? I caught her eye, and in a flash, she was gone.

I rubbed my temples and glared at Regine. "Woman, I want you gone."

Her red eyebrows arched high. "You want what?" I'm sure I didn't hear you correctly. It sounded as though you said —"

"Dammit! You heard me. I want you gone, Regine. I know you're only here to torment me."

She inched forward. "You're a fool, Derek," she said. "You were *always* a fool. I'll have you know it was Rudolpho who insisted we move to New York. You remember him, yes? *Your son?* Do you still imagine he doesn't exist?"

Looking at Regine made my skin crawl. The room. The music. Everything. I had to get the hell out of there, and fast. I turned to walk away, but she grabbed my arm, stopping me.

"You will do nothing to jeopardize my plans, my business, or our son. Do you understand?"

My fingers curled into fists. I wanted to hit her. I wanted to strike her hard and wipe that arrogant grin from her face. Rather than cause a commotion, I settled for a threatening, throaty growl.

She cocked her head and smiled in a way that caused my chest to tighten. "I know you have the power of your pack behind you now. I, too, have mine. Let me just give you fair warning, Derek. If you dare stand in the way of Rudolpho becoming King, I'll inform the authorities of a trail leading straight to a missing college professor."

Dear God. I swallowed hard.

Queen Regine Delacour tilted her chin high. "Of course, that trail would lead to a certain young female who happened to discover her handsome professor was actually a philandering adulterer." She leaned in, her lips inches from mine. "Do we understand one another?"

Adieu! Adieu! thy plaintive anthem fades
Past the near meadows, over the still stream,
Up the hill-side; and now 'tis buried deep
In the next valley-glades:
Was it a vision, or a waking dream?
Fled is that music: — Do I wake or sleep?

— John Keats, "Ode to a Nightingale"

Part Three
The Reaping

Chapter Sixteen

Everett, Washington

Holding Erin, breathing in her freshly washed hair smelling of rose, feeling her warm, ripe body next to mine, I knew Regine had spoken the truth in the library.

Good God.

At first I had doubted the Alpha *She*, assuming she sought any excuse to destroy the woman I loved out of jealousy and spite. But the signs were there, just as the evil *She* queen had claimed. Now I lay wondering: would the child Erin unwittingly carried within her womb be mortal or *Were*?

Queen Regine Delacour had said she would fight to the death to see Rudolpho as King, not the child I conceived with another woman. And I had come too far to let the wicked bitch destroy all I had worked for.

All I had longed for.

Clearly, protecting Erin and our unborn child from Regine was paramount.

Hundreds of years had passed since I had taken Ersule's life, and my dream of spending eternity with her was finally within my greedy grasp. But what would I gain once Erin professed her love for me? What would I acquire once I inflicted the mortal wound upon her slender throat? Would I have my meek, submissive Ersule, or my fiery, independent Erin?

And what would become of our unborn child?

My gut curled as I tried to wrap my mind around the persistent contemplation threatening rational thought. Ersule resided somewhere within Erin's mortal body.

And I was deeply in love with both of them.

Sweet Ersule of my past had emerged into the modern world as Erin Richland, a young lady with her own dreams and aspirations, a strong woman with her own rules in life. And declaring her love to a man simply because he had bedded her was clearly *not* one of those rules. The sheer weight of forbidden, unattainable love hovered like a dark angel whispering over my shoulder.

The day I had longed for drew near — I could feel it. Just as Koenig had prophesied, Erin was drawn to me like a bee to honey, and at twenty-three, she was mature, ripe, a passionate woman giving herself to me willingly.

I had played by the rules, and yet, tonight, a nagging question lingered. Would Erin give herself freely if she knew I would follow her proclamation of love by sinking my teeth into the slender column of her ivory throat?

I doubted it.

Earlier, I had tugged her chin to one side, pressing it firmly against my bare shoulder. I had grazed upon her smooth neck, felt her bounding pulse quivering against my persistent lips and tongue. The wolf inside had beckoned, clawing like a wild beast trapped inside my gut, threatening to emerge.

Torture.

As we made love, I had cleverly hidden my torment as my pulse coursed like fire through my veins, and the sheer willpower to resist shifting and inflicting the premature mortal wound had nearly pushed me to the brink of insanity.

But I had managed restraint, managed to keep control, for I

knew if I had dared draw a solitary drop of Erin's sweet blood before she declared her love, my long-held dream of eternal life together would have vanished in the blink of an eye.

"Erin, wake up." I brushed my lips across her tousled raven mane and whispered, "You must send word home."

She moaned sleepily. "What time is it?"

"After six o'clock."

She slowly sat, and I watched as the sheet slipped low, brushing against her nipples as the satiny fabric slid to her waist.

She bit down on her bottom lip. "Yes, you're right."

Her agile ivory fingers loosened small tangles in her ebony mane. She rose and retrieved the chenille robe.

"I'm just so tired." She sighed.

"I'll instruct Franz to deliver the message to your house. But are you sure you don't wish a hotel room —"

Her gaze snapped to mine. "No, no hotel room. I want to spend the whole night with you."

Pale light reflected in her eyes as she turned toward the rising silver moon glowing through the towering bedroom window. Accepting the fact that she wished to be with me the entire night, my heart soared. "As you wish, darling." I sat up and stretched. "What are your plans for tomorrow?"

"I'll be writing about the election." She frowned. "Why?"

"Can you take time away from the office? I have a surprise I think you would enjoy."

She sank on the bed and inched close to me. Smiling she asked, "Business or pleasure?"

I cupped her chin. "Both."

"Hmm. You have me quite intrigued."

Against the glowing firelight in the hearth, her eyes sparkled like emerald gems. I drew her to my chest. "Nothing pleases me more than to intrigue you, my dear."

I awoke in the dead of night with a start. I slid from Erin's arms encircling my waist as she slept, dressed quickly, and ventured to the front windows. A shadowy figure stood across the street.

Enough.

I opened the door and marched down the porch steps toward the figure swaying beneath the glowing street lamp.

"You!" the man screeched, waving his flask so violently that liquid spilled down the front of his crumpled trousers.

"Go home," I growled.

He teetered toward me. "You've ruined everything for me, Rudliff. *Everything*," he shouted.

"Good God, Frederick. Have some dignity."

Marching cockeyed, he advanced toward me and said, "Don't you talk to me about dignity, you — *Oomph!*"

I caught the wretch as he tripped over his own feet and fell forward.

"Unhand me!" he bellowed, plucking at the lapels of his wrinkled jacket.

I did just as Frederick Dimsdale requested and let the wretch fall like a sack of potatoes to the ground. He managed to haul himself up on all fours, then proceeded to bawl in heaving sobs at my feet.

"I know she's here. I just know it. *I love her*," he said, wailing at my feet. "Don't you see? She's mine. You hear me, Rudliff?"

Over the past several weeks, it had become obvious Frederick Dimsdale was determined to lure Erin into his heart and into his bed. I rolled my eyes heavenward. *Christ Almighty.* The man was a disgrace.

"I'll see you dead, Rudliff. Do you hear me? *Dead*, before I'll let you have her."

I'd had enough of the lout's spying and lame attempts to come between Erin and me. I left him in his puddle of misery and contempt and went inside to wake Franz.

I touched Franz's shoulder, and he sat up like a shot.

"What? What is it, King?"

"There's a drunken fool out front. I'll help you load him into the carriage. I want you to haul his inebriated carcass down to Madame Delacour's."

Franz flashed a crooked smile. "Madame Delacour's parlor, huh?"

I rummaged through my trousers. "Absolutely. Here's a hundred dollars. Make sure he gets his money's worth."

Franz's steely eyes widened. "A hundred dollars. Damn, you want the man to die?"

I snorted and smiled. "No, not death. This one just needs to be knocked off his high horse."

We loaded the semi-conscious Frederick Dimsdale into the carriage and plopped his hat on his head.

"Oh, and Franz," I said, "make sure you give the ol' boy a good tug or two of the cocktail before handing him over to Madame Delacour."

Franz nodded and quietly urged the horses forward down the darkened, deserted street.

I undressed and crawled back into bed.

Erin stirred and dreamily said, "I thought I heard voices."

I pulled her body against mine. "It's nothing, darling. Go back to sleep."

She moaned and snuggled closer. "I had a dream," she said in a sleepy, faraway voice.

"Was it a good dream?" I whispered in her ear.

She rubbed her eyes. "It was very good. I was a young girl running barefoot in a wheat field under the bright sun. I stopped when I saw something lying on the ground up ahead. I placed my hand above my brow to shield the blinding sun. Regardless of my trepidation, something urged me forward. I sprinted as fast as my bare feet would carry me. When I arrived, I saw a boy, a handsome young man, really, lying on the ground. He looked up at me with the most beautiful blue eyes I had ever seen. It was you, Derek. It was a much younger version of you."

God in heaven. She dreams Ersule's memories.

Erin lifted her face to mine, but I quickly pulled her close, lest she witness the tears welling in my eyes.

"Go back to sleep, my angel. Rest yourself," I managed to choke out.

I lay awake the entire night, holding her in my arms, listening to her soft sounds of sleep, watching her chest rise and fall with each slumbering breath, just as I had done when she was a wee young girl in New York.

Chapter Seventeen

Waking to the peaceful light of day, wrapped securely within his warm arms, Erin could not deny the obvious any longer. She had fallen deeply in love with the mysterious man who had somehow managed to topple her sensible world.

"You awake?" Derek whispered.

She rolled over and faced Derek's soulful gaze. "I am, and I'm wondering what it is you have planned for us today."

He smoothed a stand of her hair between his fingers. "If you don't have to rush into work today, I'd like to take you some place special after breakfast." He tugged on a long tasseled rope hanging near his bedside.

"What's that?"

He smiled. "You'll see."

Within minutes, Hannah's voice called from behind the door announcing breakfast was waiting outside the bedroom door.

Erin trailed a finger along the silky mass of curls on his chest. "My, my. What service. Is this something you do every morning? Breakfast in bed?"

"Good Lord, woman. No." Derek rose and donned his robe. "I wish I could, though." He opened the door, wheeled in a rolling cart, and placed two cane chairs at each end. "This I arranged with Hannah late last night."

Gazing at the plates smothered in eggs, ham, biscuits, and gravy, she all but salivated with hunger. "I can't believe how famished I am this morning."

Derek's eyes paled as he surveyed her. "Eat, my dear. The damp chill of winter is in the air these days. You need to stay healthy."

Erin frowned. "Heavens. I've always been healthy as a horse all my life, chill or no chill."

"Be that as it may —"

A knock rattled the bedroom door.

Derek sighed. "Yes, what is it?"

The long pause coming from behind the door filled the large bedroom. Finally, a voice laced with melancholy announced, "Franz has informed me that the horses are hitched to the carriage, sir."

"We'll be there shortly, Mrs. Schauss," Derek said.

Erin squished her nose. "She seems even more sinister than your man Franz. Have you ever thought of hiring cheerful staff?"

Derek choked on his coffee and smiled. "You know, that's rather funny. Hannah, my cook — you met her — she's cheery."

"That's true. Seriously, though. Franz scowls like a ghoul, and Mrs. Schauss, well, I don't know what her —"

Derek raised his hand. "That's just it, my dear, you don't know. Mrs. Schauss, and I, well, let's just say we go back a long way with one another."

His gaze snapped from hers in a flash. Erin knew when to leave well-enough alone. Perhaps his current staff had been in his employ when he was married to his wife. Further, maybe they viewed her presence as a lame replacement for someone they had once cared about.

Brushing the troubling thought aside, she sipped her coffee, wondering if there was any word on the women's vote from the day before. Normally, she would be rushing off to work, hot on the heels of the city's biggest stories. But after the heated argument with her father and Frederick, followed by the night of passionate lovemaking with Derek, her restless curiosity felt tethered by her conflicted heart.

Franz met them out front and opened the door to the carriage. Erin scooted in and tucked the ends of the cumbersome coat under her bottom. Turning to Derek, she said, "This huge coat you've insisted I wear today tells me we must be going somewhere outdoors."

Derek scooted in next to her and slid a hand over hers. "You're right."

She stroked the smooth fur on the garment. "What is this thing made from anyway — wolves?"

"Wolves?" Derek snorted and shook his head. "No, I can assure you it's *not* made from the fur of wolves. The coat you're wearing, my dear, is made from one-hundred-percent sheared beaver fur."

Erin dropped her chin to her chest, examining the fur more closely. "Beaver. Hmm. You don't say."

Once the carriage drove outside of the city limits, they headed toward east, toward the forest. Muddy water from recent rains filled the numerous potholes along the way, making the lengthy trip exceedingly bumpy.

She squeezed Derek's arm. "You're taking me to one of your logging camps, am I right?"

"You're a perceptive little thing, aren't you? You're correct. You asked me for a story. I think you should see another place I like to call home."

The earthy aroma of moist soil laced with evergreen drifted up her nose. She breathed in deeply, letting the cool, fresh air linger inside her lungs. Tall green canopies darkened the narrow road the deeper into the forest they rode. Sword ferns and wet, lichen-covered rocks dotted the earth between huge tree trunks, and pinecones lay scattered amid brilliant hues of jade moss woven in a low bed of fog.

Sunshine illuminated a clearing directly ahead. The coachman wound along the muddy path, stopping when they reached the sunny patch. He descended the carriage, unhinged the horses, and tethered the handsome beasts to a weathered, gray stump.

Derek exited the coach and extended a hand toward Erin. "This is as far as we can go in the carriage."

Glancing at the surroundings, she said, "I have absolutely no idea where we are."

"We're near one of my logging camps. This one in particular is special to me."

She surveyed the lush surroundings, inhaling the cool air hinting of distant wood fires. "It certainly is beautiful out here." She looped her arm within Derek's. "What is it that makes this particular area so special, other than the obvious beauty?"

"Here you be, sir," said Franz, holding out a wicker basket.

Derek grabbed the carrier and waggled his eyebrows. "First, my dear, we're going on a picnic."

"What? A picnic — in this cold?"

"You didn't think I had you wear that huge beaver coat without a damn good reason, did you? Come on."

He grasped her gloved hand, and they walked in the ray of sunshine illuminating a path, stopping when they came upon a rustic log cabin with gray smoke swelling from a stone chimney.

"Who are we going to see?"

He smiled and squeezed her hand. "This little place happens to be mine."

A narrow, river rock pathway led to a small covered porch. Derek opened the door and gestured for her to go inside.

After looking at the cabin from the outside, Erin was surprised how much bigger it truly was inside. A smoldering wood fire graced the stone hearth, creating a cozy atmosphere within the rustic bungalow.

Derek leaned in. "The cabin is comfortable, but I should warn you, there's no indoor plumbing."

She hung the massive coat on an iron hook and meandered down the hallway, poking her head into each of the small bedrooms. "It's really quite cute." She glanced at the hearth and frowned. "Who lit the fire?"

"Gregore. You remember him from the party, yes?" he asked, busily opening the picnic basket and setting out the food. "Hannah makes the best fried chicken and potato salad this side of the Mississippi."

"Gregore. He was the man dressed as a monk?"

"That's him. He's here from time to time and helps watch over the place for me."

Derek rummaged through a drawer and brought back knives and forks. "Have a seat, my dear."

Erin studied Derek's handsome face. He appeared especially calm and comfortable. The forest, the cabin, the hissing wood fire in the hearth — it seemed a more natural environment for him than his palatial home on Grand Avenue.

Derek moistened his bottom lip and spread a linen napkin on his lap. "I have an idea. Suppose after we eat, instead of walking, if you're up to riding horseback, we can venture up the road and see the men working at camp. You'll have a good idea of what goes on around here — for the newspaper."

She smiled. "I may have spent my early years in New York, but once I came to Everett it was though I'd been born to ride a horse all my life. Sounds wonderful, Mr. Rudliff."

While they finished their meal, Franz saddled the horses. Derek eased Erin up onto the smaller gelding, and he climbed on the larger steed.

After slowly venturing along a sun-filled trail, they made a sharp turn onto a narrow path enveloped by thick green canopies of hemlock, cedar, and fir, blocking out the bright light. The sudden damp chill sliced her cheeks. She gazed up at the treetops that appeared to ascend into the heavens.

"Derek. How tall are these trees? Some appear to go straight to the stars."

"The tallest we've taken down was well over four-hundred feet tall. A mighty Douglas fir about four-hundred-and-fifty years old."

"Amazing," she murmured.

The soft sound of trickling water resonated from somewhere nearby. They followed the path leading to a clearing. Thick gray stumps and stubs of timber, as far as she could see, dotted the landscape. She swallowed a gasp. Having just come out from under the towering lacy green canopy moments earlier, the land before her now appeared ravaged and desolate. As they headed farther, shouts and the steady buzz of hissing machinery grew louder, echoing across the hills.

Several men tending a fire in front of a row of wooden bunkhouses came into view. A slovenly woman hung wet laundry on a weather-beaten rope secured between trees, nodding her head as they rode passed.

Derek tipped his hat. "Ma'am," he said. "Gentlemen."

"Good afternoon, sir," the men said.

As they drew closer to the increasing noise, dozens of brawny, thick-chested men with muscles all but bursting from their woolen shirts came into view. Some sharpened axes while others held giant, toothy saws.

Derek explained the noise she was hearing came from the "steam donkey" up ahead. Operating the machine required the services of several men. The choker-setter attached the cable to a log; a donkey-puncher tended the steam engine, and a spool-tender guided the whizzing line over the spool with a short stick. Erin murmured each job, hoping to commit his words and imagery to memory for when she wrote her article later.

An especially tall young lad the men called "Little Timber" was what Derek referred to as "the whistle-punk." His job was to communicate the choker-setter's position among the logs to the steam-whistle on the donkey engine. When the choker-setter secured the line, the whistle- punk tugged his wire as a signal to the engineer, letting him know the log was ready to be hauled in. As soon as one log was yarded, it was removed from the line. Horses then hauled the line back from the donkey engine to the waiting choker-setter and the next log.

They rode deeper and stopped. Derek thrust his arm back, gesturing for her to hold back. "Stay right where you are, and watch this."

Shouts rang out. Derek identified the two men as "fallers." One fellow shouted, "Down the hill!" and men quickly scattered like fleeing rats. She looked up at a massive tree quivering and swaying just before it fell like a mighty beast on the sodden earth in a monstrous, deafening thud, causing the very ground to tremble. Then as quickly as the men had dispersed to get away, they scrambled toward the fallen tree, and the process started anew.

This was the first time she had ever set foot in a logging camp, and the process of getting wood from the forest to the mills was far more complicated than she had ever imagined. "I had no idea. I've heard these men worked hard, but I had no idea how hard."

Derek turned, his piercing eyes locked upon her gaze. "Which is why I wanted to bring you here. I have three other camps, as well, but my cabin here reminds me of my humble beginnings."

Erin winced. Her back had begun to ache from sitting upright on the saddle so long.

"Are you tired, dear?" He looked up at the sky. "Perhaps we should return to the cabin and rest the horses a while before I have Franz hitch them for the return home before dark."

"Derek! Miss Richland!"

Erin turned to see the man she recognized as Gregore jogging up the path toward them.

"Ah, Gregore," said Derek. "Another fine job having the cabin ready for my arrival. When do you go back to the city?"

"I'm due at the morgue tomorrow."

Derek leaned toward Erin and frowned playfully. "And you think Franz is sinister. Gregore works part-time at the City Morgue."

Erin scrunched her nose and smiled. "Oh, my."

"What?" Gregore asked defensively. "Someone has to do the job."

Derek smiled. "I know, I know, and you're a good man."

Gregore grabbed the reins of Erin's horse. "Let's get these beasts hitched."

She dismounted, and Derek and Gregore tethered the horses to a post. Up ahead, a cluster of burly men stood in a circle, cursing and shouting at one another.

"What's that all about?" asked Erin.

Derek jutted his chin out, gesturing toward the boisterous group. "I believe I have some business to tend to. I'll be back in a few minutes. Won't take but a moment."

Erin watched as Derek strode toward the group of men and began talking to the group. She wondered if he had said something about her, because they all glanced in her direction at once.

"So, Derek says you're here to see the logging camps," said Gregore. "Are we going to be in the newspaper and terribly famous?"

She laughed. "I don't know about *famous*."

He removed his hat and scratched his scalp. "Say, what did you ever find out about the murders at the cemetery and that poor girl downtown? Sure is a shame to have such a thing happening in our little part of the world. Did I hear a large wolf was seen in the city, too?"

"That's what they say." Erin lowered her gaze. "It's the most awful thing. I'm not sure we'll ever really know exactly what happened to that unfortunate girl."

"But I heard there was a witness —"

"Ah." Derek patted Gregore's back. "I think that business situation is taken care of."

Gregore's gaze snapped to Erin then back to Derek in a flash. "Oh, all right, then. I'll bid you two farewell." He plopped his hat on his head at a rakish tilt and stuffed a smoldering corncob pipe in his mouth. "Nice talking to you, Miss Richland. And good work on those stories you've been writing on the women's vote." He sauntered toward the other men, still hovering in a small circle.

She tilted her head, smiling, watching Gregore leave. "I like him."

Derek's eyes followed hers. "I do, too. Gregore's a character. The man should have been in the theatre."

They rode leisurely back to the cabin. Upon entering the door, Erin removed her boots and plopped on the sofa with a long sigh.

Derek frowned. "You look exhausted. Would you like to lie on a bed and relax?"

She sprawled out, using a cushioned arm as a pillow. "No, I'm fine here," she said, her voice trailing away with the nagging need for a nap. "I don't know why I'm so tired."

He knelt by her side and swept up loose strands of hair that had fallen across her cheeks. "You rest, then."

ERIN woke to voices outside. She rose up, peered out the cabin window, and saw Franz and Derek, their brows knitted together in angry frowns. She wrapped a wool blanket across her shoulders and listened.

"It must have been those massive potholes. Damn thing is split to hell," said Franz.

"Well, that's just *perfect*," Derek sneered. "I'm not taking her all the way home on horseback, that's for sure."

"I'll try to get this fixed by tonight, but I'm not sure —"

"Christ Almighty!" Derek thrust his hands into his coat pockets and started for the cabin door. "Do what you can, Franz. We need to get her out of here."

Derek burst through the cabin door. She sat up tall and tugged the wool blanket to her chest. "Did I hear something about the carriage wheel?"

He stood frozen, the lines on his face deepening as he shut the door behind him. "I thought you were asleep. What else did you hear?"

The question caught her off guard. She narrowed her eyes, studying him. "Well, nothing. I just woke up. Why?"

He waved his handed dismissively. "Oh, no reason."

"Are we stuck here — for the night?"

Derek bit down on his bottom lip, and the muscles along his jawline pulsed. "Franz will try his best to repair the carriage, but we might be stuck here for a bit longer than I had planned."

Thank heavens she had sent the note to her father. Not that he would be any less worried. But with him under the assumption that she was staying at Delia's to "cool off," at least he wouldn't be calling the sheriff or sending out a search party.

Derek rocked on his feet, frowning, gazing out the window as the dying sun dissolved in the evening sky. The orange sphere dipped low, glowing like fire between the thick tree trunks and hills. It was impossible to know what he was thinking, but he appeared lost in thought, bewildered, alone, as though he had forgotten she was even there.

From the small window, she saw Franz walking up the path with a mallet thrust over his shoulder. He knelt by the carriage and began banging away unmercifully. In between the pounding and thumping, he cursed up a storm rivaling even the roughest longshoreman, kicking at the injured wheel for added emphasis.

Derek turned and said, "Will you be all right here by yourself for just a bit?"

"Of course." She wove her finger through the loop on his trousers. "Take as long as you need. If I get hungry there's plenty of leftover chicken."

His gaze turned to the burning embers of the fire. He opened the door and returned with an armload of split firewood. He placed two logs on the fire and set the remainder in the copper caldron next to the hearth.

"Stay inside," he said. "There should be enough warmth from the fresh logs. Toss a few more in there if you get cold." He lit two lanterns. After placing one by her side on the small end table, he grabbed the other and said, "I'll be back shortly."

Erin smiled. "I know how to keep a fire going. Don't worry."

A hasty peck on her forehead replaced the passionate goodbye kiss she had expected, before he headed out the door. She watched as he marched down the darkening path with the lantern lighting his way, his frame disappearing to nothingness as the bleeding sun gave way to the rising silver moon.

Stacks of old magazines, books, and papers filled the cabin's niches, keeping her occupied. Wind whirled outside, and a biting draft blew gusts of cold air beneath the front door.

Outside, the gleaming moon glistened above the arcing treetops, casting claw-like shadows scraping across the windowpane.

She surveyed her surroundings. Tea, perhaps. She rummaged around the tiny kitchen. One by one, she found the necessary items. A spoon. A cup. A kettle to boil water on the fire. A tea ball and tea in an old tin. She scanned the room. But what about water?

That's right. No water.

Derek had mentioned there was no indoor plumbing. She

remembered seeing a water jug inside the carriage.

She sank on the couch on her knees and gazed out the window. Franz was nowhere to be seen, and the carriage sat perched off the path at the edge of the forest. She stared at the large garment hanging by the door, debating wearing the massive beaver coat for such a short distance. Perhaps she could simply wrap the wool blanket across her shoulders, hightail it down the path to the carriage, grab the water, and rush back. Then she'd have tea in no time.

Crisp maple leaves blew inside, whirling like orange tops across the wooden floor the moment she opened the door. She stepped outside, yanking the brass knob forcefully to shut the cabin door. A powerful gust nearly ripped the blanket from her clutches, and the fiery lantern she carried wobbled precariously.

Hmm. Racing to the carriage would be out of the question. She trod carefully, steadily, keeping the lantern from flailing about in the biting wind. Sidestepping puddles and mud, she made her way to the side of the carriage. She opened the door, extended the lantern, and grabbed the water.

After tying the wool blanket around her waist, she grabbed the lantern and jug of water and closed the door with a heavy sway of her hip. She narrowed her gaze, trying to focus in the near darkness.

A rushing blast of icy air whirled through the forest, howling like a wounded animal caught in the arcing treetops. Birds squawked wildly as they fled their perilous roosts groaning with imminent warning.

A towering branch high above her head snapped, and she heard the harsh scrape and whirl as it raced toward her.

Shrieking, she jumped away, just before a massive, splintered branch crashed to the ground with a shuttering thud.

Heated blood ripped through her veins, and her heart pounded so fiercely she thought it would leap from her chest. Willing her numb feet to move, she inhaled deeply and exhaled in slow, shallow breaths. To her left, a shadowy figure darted across the path in a flash. Within seconds, another figure scurried past her, disappearing behind a thick trunk to her right.

She held out the lantern. The flame vibrated in tune with her shaky hand. "Who … who's there?"

The only reply came from a screeching owl above. She inched her feet forward, toward the cabin. One step, two, three —

A large figure moved swiftly across her hazy line of vision about twenty feet away.

"Dear God in heaven," she whispered. The lantern wobbled in her hands as she angled it forward at arm's length. "Just get me back to the cabin, and I promise I'll —"

At the sound of crunching leaves and snapping twigs on the forest floor, she stiffened. She stared straight ahead at the cabin, then glanced back and faced the disabled carriage. Gauging the distance, she figured she stood about halfway between the two.

The smell of wood smoke billowing from the chimney beckoned a reprieve. All at once, she made a mad dash for the cabin.

Though her feet flew forward as fast as humanly possible, she felt as though her body were moving in a slow wave.

To her right, something with glowing amber eyes crouched low and paced toward her. To her left, another creature with the same glowing eyes moved in.

Oh, my God. Oh, my God.

She froze and dropped the water jug. Slowly, she stepped backwards, one foot behind the other. With each shaky step, the creatures slowly advanced toward her, side-by-side, mere yards away from where she stood. Moving into view, the beasts hunkered lower.

Moonlight angled across the path, illuminating large, protruding snouts and bared teeth. Bristled fur glistened, and their wild scent seeped into her nostrils.

Cautiously, never taking her eyes off the beasts, she stepped backwards until her back hit the side of the carriage. She extended her arm, slanting the trembling flame toward the two creatures. "Get. Go away," she croaked.

Trying not to blink, she focused on their thick paws and curled nails gripping the earth, as though ready to pounce at any moment. Illuminated gray vapor rose from their nostrils, drifting like fog in the stiff breeze.

Her heart hammered, thundering in her ears, the pounding force rising into her neck, threatening to strangle her.

One of the beasts growled and bared its massive, ivory fangs. The other snarled in return. In unison, they slowly advanced toward her.

Dear God. Oh, Lord in heaven. Don't let me die. Please don't let me die.

The creatures roared and sprang into the air, lunging straight for her.

She screamed and hit one in the face with the lantern. The other snapped wildly at the wool blanket draped around her waist. The lantern fell to the moist earth, and the flame extinguished in a single blue flash. A sheath of clouds veiled the moonlight. In an instant, darkness consumed the area.

"Derek! Help!" she shrieked. The harrowing sounds of her terror echoed across the forest as the beasts tore at her clothes, ripping the protective blanket to shreds.

Her fingernails snapped painfully as she scraped and groped her hands along the carriage door. Gripping the handle, she flung the door open and scrambled inside, tugging the door behind her.

"No! Get away!" Screaming like a ghoul into the night, she tugged and pulled, but the door was caught on the larger beast's throat. Trapped against the carriage door, the massive head and jaws snapped violently. In one swift movement, she kicked the creature in the mouth.

The animal retreated with a yelp, and she slammed the door

shut. She hadn't time to catch her breath before the second beast slammed into the carriage, scratching the door in a frenzy of grinding claws against metal.

The first injured beast shook off her kick with a single shake of its massive head, then leapt onto the outside bench. Clawing and chewing, it shredded the exterior in its frantic attempt to reach her.

Pure terror numbed her throat. She couldn't swallow.

Or scream.

Or cry for help.

Unblinking, she focused on the sliver of moonlight emerging through the towering treetops, illuminating the large glistening fangs as the beasts ripped at the carriage. The taste of bile stuck in her throat with the frightening realization. Soon they would break the glass, and she would be torn to shreds within their mighty jaws.

And she would never have had the chance to tell Derek she loved him.

She gulped in jagged breaths, trying to calm her racing heart, threatening to leap out of her mouth. Suddenly, a massive gust of wind rattled the carriage, threatening to topple it over. She sank in the seat, covering her face with trembling hands.

Then, just as swiftly as the howling wind had ascended, it was gone, replaced by a deep chorus resounding in the distance. Animals howled, feral sounds resonating in unison through the immense dark woods.

Had the two beasts retreated?

Breathless and weak as a newborn kitten, she slowly rose up, wiped the vapor from the window, and peered outside.

Crack!

The window shattered, and glass shards embedded in her hands and wrists. She hurled her body to the opposite side as a massive furred head with drooling fangs and glowing amber eyes bounded inside the broken window.

She saw another creature bounding toward the carriage with

amazing speed. In a flash, the beast tore into her furred attacker and dragged it outside the shattered window.

Wild animal scents blasted into her skull as she watched the beasts rolling in balls of bristly fur outside the carriage.

Dizzy and nauseated, she squeezed her eyes so tightly shut, stars danced against her eyelids. A deep growl sliced through the darkness, followed by a high-pitched yelp, then another.

The familiar scent of bayberry laced with evergreen wafted into the shattered carriage window and straight into her brain.

A stone hearth. Wine. Making love.

She opened her eyes and stared at the large, blue-eyed wolf standing triumphantly over the injured beasts lying near its massive paws.

Fangs, fur, blue eyes.
Blue eyes.
His blue eyes.
Dear God.

Chapter Eighteen

I tossed the newspaper on the table and reached for my coffee. *Christ in heaven. Another murder on Chestnut Avenue.* And judging by the article Erin had written, she was still determined to get to the bottom of the twisted mess, no matter the danger.

I rose from the chair and gazed at the rough sea below. Weeks had passed since the frightful night in the woods, the night Regine and her hideous son — *my evil, twisted son* — nearly took Erin's life. The night Erin had looked into my *Were* eyes after I saved her life. Then she lost consciousness. At that very moment, my animal heart had stopped dead.

All these years, I had prayed for the rebirth of Ersule, confident her unwavering love would rise above earthly bounds. But Erin's clear refusal to see me now gnawed inside my empty soul, my once hopeful heart having turned into lifeless ash with each missive she returned.

That terrifying night in the woods haunted me. The blood oozing from her small open wounds that night had called to me, urging me forward with the promise of more.

The promise of eternal bonding.

The unexpected knock at the front door yanked the breath from my chest.

Mrs. Schauss tidied her unadorned bun of white hair and

smoothed her apron. She sighed and slowly plodded past me.

I avoided her mournful eyes. What, pray tell, was she feeling? If I felt dead inside, surely the older woman did, too, though it was hard to discern with her, for her stoic German bloodline rarely allowed her to express emotion.

Suddenly inhaling the familiar scent, my heart momentarily stopped dead.

I heard a sharp inhale of breath from the servant upon her opening the door. "Why, good morning, Miss."

I froze in mid-step.

The door opened further, and in walked Erin. My heart bounded to life with a single, massive punch against my chest.

"Please come in," Mrs. Schauss said with a sudden air of liveliness. "Have a seat in the parlor, Miss Richland, and I'll get Master Rudliff."

I stood in the hallway, paralyzed with uncertainty and trepidation.

The servant smiled as she approached me. Sensing my anxiety, she opened her arms and hugged me.

"She's here. She's back, Derek. You must act soon. I beg of you."

I nodded and gathered my wits before heading toward the parlor. To an awaiting Ersule. To an awaiting Erin.

My God.

The moment I entered the room, Erin's chin angled upward with obvious determination.

Though common sense warned me to keep my distance and give her space, my heart said otherwise. I advanced toward her far too fast.

She gasped and twisted away.

I took a step back and inhaled deeply. "Miss Richland."

She slowly turned and gazed at me with green eyes radiating

emotion I had never seen before. I remembered what Koenig had said so long ago. "She will be drawn to you for reasons she does not understand."

Confidence guided my feet forward. I gazed down at her, willing myself not to pull her into my arms and kiss her. "I've missed you, Erin."

She gazed into my eyes, but only for a moment. She turned on her toes and walked toward the sofa and sat. "I'm here on personal business."

I smiled and ventured toward the couch. "Personal? I like the sound of that."

"Yes. I need your help with Frederick."

She avoided my gaze as I stood like a gargoyle poised above her and thrust my hands in the pockets of my woolen trousers. "Frederick Dimsdale?" I asked, my voice rising. "I read that he's in jail. Why on earth would I help him?"

She sighed dramatically. "Because he's innocent. And according to him, he's only in there because of you. Frederick is a hypocrite, I know, and his vile interest in Madame Delacour's parlor, well … " Her voice trailed away with the rising flush upon her cheeks. "Let me just say, while I know he's a rat, I truly don't believe he's capable of murder."

I sat next to her, my gaze narrowing. "I read your article in the newspaper about this new murder he's accused of — truly horrific."

She inched away and folded her trembling fingers in a pile on her lap, the bloodied scratches on her hands and wrists now nothing more than faded scars. "Well, Frederick is many things, but he's not a murderer."

"Did he send you here to plead on his miserable behalf?"

Her eye color dulled to unpolished jade. "No. Not exactly."

She might be pleading on behalf of the Dimsdale lout, but I sensed she was truly here for *me*. I leaned forward and whispered.

"Then why exactly are you here, Erin?"

She rose from the sofa, her shoulders wilting, and shook her head as though flushing cobwebs from her mind.

Without thinking, I bolted up and pulled her into an embrace. "Erin, sweet Erin," I whispered against her ear. "Talk to me."

She melded against my chest. I smoothed her ebony hair. "Talk to me," I repeated. "Why are you *really* here?"

She gazed into my eyes. "I'm angry. I'm confused. I'm so many things right now that I can't think straight anymore."

She pulled away and turned her back to me. Instantly, my heart hammered, squeezing the breath from my lungs. She turned on her heels and faced me with a menacing gaze, but moist tears softened the intended intensity.

"That night. The night in the woods. I must know. I don't understand."

Her eyes narrowed, brows knitting together as she attempted to stare deeply into my eyes. She stepped forward, her gaze locked upon mine.

I froze.

"Who are you, Derek?" She took another step until she stood mere inches away. "Who are you *really*?"

For years, I had imagined dozens of possible confrontations with her, but the scenario before me now was not one of them.

"Your voice. Your touch." She gently tugged my chin, forcing me to look at her. "Those blue eyes."

Panic gripped my gut. "I thought you needed my help with Dimsdale," I managed to croak out.

As if a spell had suddenly been broken, she blinked repeatedly and dropped her arm to her side. "Oh, yes, that." She rubbed her temples, and her face paled. "Pardon me, Mr. Rudliff, could I get a cup of hot tea? Perhaps some toast?"

Her posture wavered. I gripped her elbow and led her to the

sofa. "Are you ill, my dear?" I asked, though I suspected what truly ailed her.

She leaned her head against the sofa back. I rang the bell on the side table, signaling for help from the staff.

Mrs. Schauss entered, and upon seeing Erin, her eyes grew wide.

I gave the servant a reassuring nod. "Please get Miss Richland some hot tea and toast."

With a swift nod in reply, Mrs. Schauss scurried toward the kitchen.

My gaze swept over Erin. Did she know she was with child? *My child?* Was that why she was here?

"Perhaps I should return home. My father is expecting me shortly. Ever since that night in the woods, well, he's not been himself."

My anger swelled as I recalled the night of the attack. Erin's frightened eyes. Her loss of consciousness. The mad dash in the ratty supply buggy to get her swiftly home. Her father's hostile, threatening words to me at the front door of his home.

I enclosed her hand with mine and asked, "Your father has not been unkind to you, has he?"

Erin covered her mouth with a shaky hand. "I'm sorry. A touch of dyspepsia. I could really use that tea and toast now."

Mrs. Schauss entered with hot tea and rye toast and placed the items on the coffee table in front of Erin. "Perhaps this will help," she said, laying a linen napkin on Erin's lap before departing.

Erin sipped the tea and took a bite of the crisp buttered toast. She winced. "I don't know why, but nothing tastes the same to me anymore."

She didn't know.

I gestured for her to eat more. "As you were saying — your father?"

"He was so angry that night. He's barely spoken to me since, and Maggie skulks around the house, muttering below her breath, avoiding both of us. Father visits Frederick in jail and listens to his tale of woe. Thanks to Frederick, he, too, suspects you're somehow behind the mess." A crimson hue stained her pale cheeks. "Frederick is beside himself. He can't remember the night in detail, but I overheard father saying he had been found 'buck-naked' and 'covered in blood'."

I couldn't conceal the growing smirk on my face. I quickly pulled her into my arms. "You don't say."

She lifted her face to mine. "God help me, Derek, I've tried to stay away. Truly I have, but … "

I dipped my head and kissed her lips tasting of chamomile tea and sweet honey. "But?"

She wrapped her arms around my neck and whispered against my cheek, "Try as I may, I cannot keep away from you, my love."

My love.

She had said, "*My love.*"

My stomach fluttered. Something didn't feel right. I was one step closer to Ersule, of fulfilling the dream I had longed for, yet I couldn't imagine Ersule, my wife of long ago, the love of my life, coming back to me and Erin's spirited soul taken from me at the same time. I loved both women; one body, two minds, two souls.

She nuzzled my neck. "Do you hear me, Derek?" she whispered again. "I love —"

The abrupt knock at the front door caused us both to flinch.

"*Derek.* Derek, you in there? Mrs. Schauss, open the damn door!"

"What the devil?" I bolted up and opened the door.

"I'm just *beside* myself!" Gregore said, marching inside. "The murders, trouble at the morgue —"

"Gregore," I said, signaling him with my eyes, "you remember Miss Richland."

He looked past my shoulder at Erin, who rose from the sofa

with a puzzled look upon her face.

He instantly strode past me and clasped her hand. "Miss Richland, I was so worried about you after the vicious wolf attack."

"I'm fine now, thank you," she said. "But what is this about the murders — the morgue?"

If there was one thing I knew about Erin it was that nothing caught her attention faster than a sensational story for the newspaper, or the chance to break the murder cases plaguing Everett.

Gregore released her hand and glanced at me before turning quickly back to Erin. "I'm sure I know less than you, Miss Richland. I've been reading your articles in the paper."

Erin's gaze narrowed. "I'm assuming you're talking about the murdered prostitute just this past week, yes?"

"Yes, yes," said Gregore hesitantly. "That and the voting results, of course." He winked. "I knew you women would get the vote. Congratulations."

Undeterred, she stepped closer to Gregore. "What is this about the morgue? I've heard nothing about suspicious events there. As I recall, you're employed there, correct?"

Gregore quickly glanced at me before saying, "I, well —"

I stepped forward. "Such dreary talk, you two. What is it you came here for, Gregore?"

Gregore sighed, clearly thankful for the reprieve.

"Derek, I must discuss some urgent business matters in private." He smiled crookedly at Erin. "I'm sure you understand, Miss Richland."

I led Erin back to the couch. "Please, my dear. Have a seat and finish your tea. This should take only a moment or two."

Erin pinched my side playfully, out of view of Gregore.

Mrs. Schauss sauntered through the hallway with a dusting feather, whistling a ditty.

"Mrs. Schauss, please get Miss Richland more tea."

She smiled. "Yes, sir."

Erin sighed and reached for her teacup. "I'll be fine here, you two. Run along."

Gregore followed on my heels to the library. I shut the door behind us. "What the hell is going on?"

Gregore raked unsteady fingers through his thick hair and sighed. "Everything is going on, that's what." He turned away and faced the wall of dusty hardbound books towering from floor to ceiling. "We have to get out of here, Derek. The sooner the better."

I marched forward, grabbed his shoulders, and spun him around to face me. "What are you talking about?"

Gregore broke into guttural sobs.

I drew him close. "Christ, Gregore. Tell me what's wrong."

He pulled from my embrace and stared at me, unblinking, fear radiating within his moist gaze.

"This morning my employer discovered my stash of strained blood. He found the tins of herbs and the ledgers. He hasn't put two and two together yet, but he knows I've been up to something. Christ Almighty, Derek. I've been draining the dead and falsifying documents for my own greedy purposes. I've made a mint on the cocktail, but he's on to me. All of this along with the recent murders, well, I'm sure a scandal of monumental proportions is sure to break soon."

"Oh, God." I winced and turned away, my mind racing.

"Oh, God, is right, King. I've done the best I could covering our messes. Same with Franz and Edgar doing their part, but we've stayed too long. We *must* leave Everett."

With his feet planted firmly in front of me, he gazed up with misted, poignant eyes. "This city is far too small. We can't get away with the same things we did in New York. You said we could leave once, well, you know."

"Yes, I know," I said more abruptly than intended.

My mind sprinted. Erin had been within a mere tick of declaring her love for me, the avowal I'd been waiting centuries for. Now this disturbing news arrived with a terrified Gregore.

"How close are you?" Gregore asked in a small, hesitant voice. "Has she?"

I waved my hand. "Don't worry about it. I have it handled." But the more I grumbled, the less confident I became. With Regine and Rudolpho determined to fulfill their devious plan, and time being of the essence more than ever, my plans would need to change.

Chapter Nineteen

She shouldn't have scooted out on Derek without so much as a goodbye, but the longer Erin sat in his parlor, the more her stomach had twisted into nauseous knots. What she couldn't shake now was Mrs. Schauss's odd reaction when the older woman had caught her slipping out the front door.

"Please don't go. Please don't, Miss," she had said, blocking the exit.

And when Erin firmly asked the older woman to step aside, the servant's eyes misted with tears.

"So strange," Erin muttered, gazing out her office window. She sighed and sank into the chair at her desk. Flipping through the pages of her calendar, another wave of dizzying nausea hit. She stared at today's date. Her hand moved in a flurry of fingertips back and forth along the calendar, examining the dates more closely.

She yanked her hand back and groaned. "Oh, *nooooooo.*" She'd not only missed her monthly once, she'd missed it twice, and she'd been far too busy of late to even notice.

And now the daily episodes of nausea.

"Good afternoon, you," David said, walking into her office and promptly taking a seat on the chair opposite her. "You see your father yet?"

Had he just asked her a question? Erin tore her gaze from the calendar. "What?"

David leaned in and crossed his lanky legs at the ankles. "Oh, my. A party last night get the better of you? You look awful."

She narrowed her eyes. "Thank you very much. I need your nasty comments like I need a hole in the head." She shoved her chair back, paced to the window, and folded her arms across her chest.

The grating sound of scraping chair legs along the hardwood floor filled the office. She turned and saw David advancing toward her.

He froze, clearly measuring her seething gaze.

"Lord above, Erin. I'm sorry. It's just that, well, it's just that you look different somehow — extra tired perhaps. Truly, I'm sorry. I didn't mean to offend you."

She really wasn't offended, but his timing stank. She sighed and nodded. "I know. I'm sorry for biting your head off."

Her father hurried past the open office door in flash of woolen trousers and suspenders, grumbling something about "incompetent idiots."

"What was it you were saying about my father?"

David rolled his eyes. "He's on a tear to get to the bottom of the latest murder, and there's been some chatter about trouble at the morgue. Course, the hunters sent into the logging camp to find the bloodthirsty wolves that attacked you turned up nothing, either."

The morgue. Was that what Gregore had been talking about when he entered Derek's house?

She frowned and waved her hand. "Father's been impossible lately. It's best to avoid him as much as possible these days. Trust me, I know firsthand."

As she walked home, Erin drew in the fresh air whirling across the bay. Angry steel-gray clouds above threatened a downpour. The thought of returning home another evening to a disappointed

Maggie gave her pause, and she slowed her pace. On second thought, perhaps she'd drop by the florist shop to see if Delia were there and available for dinner at a restaurant.

"Whoa, there, now," she heard a familiar voice say.

She turned to see Derek's irritable driver, Franz, tugging on leather reins, guiding the horses to the side of the street. The moment the carriage came to a complete stop, Derek exited the carriage door and was by her side in a flash. She gazed at his face, etched with lines of concern.

"Erin. My God, woman. Are you all right?"

She had never been happier to see anyone in her life. Caught off guard, she stared into his eyes in awkward silence as pelts of rain dropped from the charcoal sky, landing in loud flops upon her coat.

"Come," Derek said, leading her by the arm to his carriage. He guided her inside just as the sky broke open in a deluge of showers. He adjusted the cushioned seat and tossed his hat to the side.

Sparking blue eyes suddenly paled to blue-gray as he gazed at her with an expression she couldn't place. Sadness? Sorrow? A sudden stab of guilt for leaving him earlier pierced her ribs.

A warm hand slid over hers. "Have dinner with me, please. At my home."

Without hesitation, she murmured, "Yes, of course."

Derek rapped the carriage top, and the driver urged the horses forward.

"You left me without a word, Erin. *Again.*" His tone was smooth, yet firm. Heat radiated from his body, warming the chilly air.

She jutted her chin out. "I wasn't feeling well."

He inched closer and looped his arm within hers. "And are you feeling better now?"

Actually, she was much better and hungry for the first time today. She nodded.

He gazed out the window and sighed. "I've just returned from freeing your Mr. Dimsdale from jail."

Erin frowned. "You did? But how?"

"I have my ways."

Of course he had his ways. He was Derek Rudliff, and nothing about him surprised her anymore. She cleared her throat in an attempt to rid the nagging realization. No doubt, it wouldn't be long before Frederick showed up on her doorstep with lame excuses for his immoral behavior, begging for her forgiveness.

The steady beat of the iron-hoofed horses matched the rhythm of her heart. Sitting beside Derek, his warm body next to hers, soothed the growing agitation that had plagued her for most of the day.

She gazed out the window. If her life wasn't complicated enough already, the realization today that she was carrying a child, *Derek's child*, was a prickly reminder. Instinctively, she placed her hand upon her small belly.

A fierce rush of wind ripped across the bay with a mighty howl. The carriage shook and shimmied. Tossed like a ragdoll, she shrieked as she was thrown against Derek's hard chest.

He steadied her shoulders and pulled her close. "There now. It's just an angry gust, my love."

She stared out the window, smiling. *My love. He loves me, just as I love him.*

The driver urged the horses to a faster clip. Naked branches passed by the carriage window, twisting, bending and snapping like the bony fingers of skeletons. Franz soothed the wary horses with calming words as the beasts sidestepped the dangerous terrain.

The carriage stopped in front of Derek's home. The driver released the carriage door, popped open an umbrella, and handed it to Derek. He helped her exit the carriage, and the two whisked up the path to the covered front porch.

"It's really coming down now, and the wind is a beast," Derek said, opening the front door.

She stepped inside, and the heavenly aromas of prepared food made her empty stomach rumble with hunger.

"Come." Derek removed her coat and bonnet, hung them in the entry armoire, and led her down the hall to the dining room. "Hannah has prepared a meal fit for a famished carnivore."

While the statement initially gave her pause, she realized what he'd meant. On the long dining table sat a beef roast, a stuffed turkey, and a large ham adorned with glazed cherries, pineapple, and cloves. The size of the shiny china plates paled in comparison to the massive meat dishes perched on large sterling platters. Off to the side, roasted sweet potatoes, glazed turnips, and steamed green beans sat in shiny porcelain bowls. Freshly baked rolls and crocks of creamy butter completed the lovely setting.

Derek smiled. "I hope you're hungry." He inched out a dining chair. "Please, sit and enjoy this meal with me."

The hanging chandelier above the table flickered. Erin smiled and sat. "I think we might lose power."

"Not to worry." He gestured for Hannah, who stood watching outside the doorway. She scurried to his side. "Light the candelabras. Miss Richland and I may be dining by candlelight this evening."

Hannah nodded and left the room. Again, the wind howled, and the massive hanging light above winked in reply.

Erin moaned unintentionally as Derek dug into the roasted meats and filled her plate. The divine aromas made her salivate with such hunger.

After filling both of their plates, he smiled and said, "Shall we dig in?"

Hannah returned with long wooden matches and lit the candelabras on the mahogany sideboard, then placed one at the center of the dining table.

Erin watched as the firelight accentuated the piercing blue gaze following his servant's every move. She tried to ignore the tingle traveling the length of her spine by clearing her throat and declaring, "This meal looks delicious, Hannah."

"Thank you kindly, Miss Richland." Hannah left the room and joined Mrs. Schauss, who stood watching from the darkened hallway, her arms crossed against her chest.

Erin gasped as another howl of wind clipped the eaves outside, and the electricity went out in a flash.

Derek slid his hand over hers. "You're not frightened, are you?"

"No," she replied automatically, though the tingle up her backbone jarred once again.

Mrs. Schauss entered the room with two filled goblets. "Your beverages," she said after placing the chalices above each place setting, next to the water glasses.

Erin glanced inside the cup. "Is this the punch from the party? The recipe handed down to you from long ago?"

" 'Tis," Derek said, evenly. His gaze narrowed as she lifted the chilled goblet to her lips, the small lines etched in his face growing more pronounced.

Erin paused, thinking about the baby growing inside her. "Does the punch contain spirits? I can't recall."

Derek's gaze snapped away from her lips, his eyes deepening to indigo. With a tenor as smooth as silk, he said, "There's absolutely nothing in that beverage that will harm you, Erin."

She watched as he lifted his goblet and drank the crimson beverage, his lips curving against the silver chalice and the hollow of his throat wavering with each swallow. The more she watched him drink, the thirstier she became.

She placed the goblet to her lips. One sip, two, three. Warmth spread from her mouth to her chest, seeping slowly into her limbs, instantly countering the icy fingers trailing along her spine.

Harsh gusts of wind shook the outside eaves, and seagulls squawked frantically as pelts of rain splattered like large inkblots against the leaded glass windows beside her.

Heat spread through her torso, warmth widening along the curves of her waist, settling with a pull deep within her pelvis. "The taste is ethereal. The drink is cold, yet the warmth it radiates is similar to drinking a glass of sherry."

"Indeed," he whispered, gazing at her over the rim of his chalice.

She ate every morsel on her plate, but Derek had merely picked at his food, appearing, at times, too preoccupied to eat. After she set her napkin on the table, Derek stood and claimed both of their goblets.

He cleared his throat. "Let's adjourn to the sitting room, shall we?"

His deep voice resonated like the calm before a fierce storm, serene, composed, yet authoritative, demanding attention.

As though her feet had life all their own, Erin followed behind him. She cast her gaze to his broad shoulders spanning the back of his maroon-colored vest and the dark blond hair grazing the stiff collar on his white cotton shirt. Flaming candlelit sconces hissed and flared with each advancing step along the darkened hallway. As she watched him stroll in front of her, the punch spread seductively through her body, warming her in all the right places.

They passed his bedroom, glowing with lit candles and burning orange embers of a dying fire set within the stone hearth.

Tiny sparks of heat spread up her calves and thighs, settling within her privates. Before contemplating, she stopped in place and said, "In here."

She heard his sharp inhale of breath. Turning, he glanced at the bedroom, then at her. His gaze narrowed. "Are you sure?"

She reached for a goblet in his hand.

He handed her the fuller of the two.

He laced his fingers with hers and led her into the shadowy bedroom. As if the wooden door knew the moment they had entered, it slowly closed shut behind them.

Erin's eyes widened. "How —"

"Just the breeze blowing through the seals along the windows," he said, before setting his goblet on the night table.

Erin stared into Derek's eyes, absorbing the flickers of candlelight dancing in their depths. She took another swallow of punch, and another, then set the goblet next to his.

He took a step forward, gazing into her eyes with an intensity she'd never seen before. Invisible inches stood between them, yet an imperceptible force gathered in the middle. Heat radiated from his body, like liquid fingers penetrating her clothing, finding its way to her plush core.

He squeezed her hand. "Woman, I want you so bad I can taste you."

His words melted any remaining resolve left within her. There was nothing in the world she wanted more than to make love with Derek.

He clutched her by the neck and drew her close. "You *are* mine, do you hear me?"

Her breath shuddered within her chest. "I ... I do," she whispered.

Deftly, he lifted her into his arms and laid her on the silky bedding. "Mine," he repeated.

Standing beside the bed, he towered above her. Slowly, he unbuttoned his vest, his gaze locked upon hers. He draped the garment over the velvet bedroom chair. Following his lead, she began unbuttoning the front of her dress.

"No. Allow me the pleasure of undressing you," he said, his voice growing deeper with each measured word.

He removed his cotton shirt, revealing a pale, broad chest matted with darker hair. Her yearning for him instantly grew fierce. Her breasts burned, the corset binding and pinching with each deep breath.

He sat beside her on the bed and cupped her chin, angling her face upward toward his approaching lips. He kissed her tenderly, gently coaxing her mouth open with the tip of his tongue. His hand found way to the long row of satin-covered buttons running the length of her dress.

With the release of each button, a warm finger trailed along the sensitive skin between her breasts. The blast of cooler air instantly made her nipples strain beneath the binding undergarments.

Slowly, he moved to the bottom of the bed and removed her shoes, followed by each stocking, his fingers snaking along the curves of her calves.

Silently, she cursed the pinching corset squeezing her breath. She reached for her stays, but his hand was instantly on hers, and she heard the breath catch deep within his throat.

He leaned over her. "No." He licked his bottom lip. "I will do it."

Derek slid the dress from her shoulders and gently pulled it down and over her bare feet. Moisture beaded across her neck and chest, and the sensitive space between her thighs slickened. He touched her in such an acquainted way she fought the urge to shudder with each glide of his warm hands across her sensitive skin.

He stood and draped her dress over his discarded garments on the chair. Looming over her near-naked body like an effigy, he said, "Stand."

The demanding tone of his deep voice made her instantly feel vulnerable. Instinctively, she covered her chest with splayed hands. "What?"

A single eyebrow rose above his smoldering gaze. "Stand so that I may undress you *entirely*."

She hesitated, his words drawing her into the blue depths of his commanding eyes, calling her on an indefinable level.

In a flash, he bent and pulled her to her feet. The sheer force of his power made her dizzy and the moisture between her legs intensify.

Firm hands slid from her bare shoulders across her concealed breasts. Her corset throbbed and pinched until she thought she would suffocate. She lifted her lashes from her heated cheeks and whispered, "Do it."

A low throaty growl of pleasure rose from his throat. Strong, agile fingers untied the dainty satin ribbon resting above the long row of eyehooks. One by one, he unfastened them all, down to her navel.

She stood before him in only her sheer drawers, gulping for air, watching how the glowing amber candlelight licked the bedroom walls with each new breath she drew.

He draped the corset over her dress on the chair, his gaze never drifting from her body. He stepped forward and placed his hand upon her neck, as if to draw her into a kiss. Instead, his hand lingered, a thumb pressing firmly upon the side of her throat.

Her pulse beat violently against his fingertip, and the desire for him to make love to her right then and there was so strong she knew she'd surely go insane if he pulled away now.

She covered his hand with her own. "Kiss me, Derek. Kiss me now."

As though forced from a dream, his gaze snapped to hers. He moaned and lowered his lips to hers.

Erin closed her eyes, but the flickering images of capricious candlelight skipping across the bedroom walls remained behind her eyelids. The heat roaming through her body intensified, as though moist sparks of fire had ignited every nerve ending in her pleasure zones.

He slid his hand down the curve of her waist, a solitary finger toying with the elastic band of her undergarment. The moment his hand slipped into her drawers, her legs turned to jelly.

He moaned as his finger dipped into her moist cleft. "My God, woman," he groaned. He bent low and tugged her drawers to the ground in one fluid move.

She held onto his shoulders as she stepped out of the sheer garment. Sprawling out across the silken coverlet, she said, "Make love to me, Derek."

He quickly removed his trousers and drawers and moved above her, his arms extended out. Though inches separated them, the warmth of his body penetrated every small pore of her skin.

He gazed into her eyes, the dim lighting accentuating the small lines traversing his forehead. He lowered, and a hand instantly slid between her thighs.

She inhaled in jagged breaths, scarcely able to contain the unbearable yearning pulsing within her core.

A solitary finger slid around her slick pearl, and in a single thrust that yanked the breath from her lungs, he slipped a finger inside her. Then two.

She wrapped her arms around his neck and breathed, "I want you so much. I need you. I need you *now*."

His moustache grazed her neck. "I've waited for this."

"Me, too, my darling."

He kissed her neck, pausing at the pulse pounding in the hollow of her throat. "I've waited so very long."

His words barely registered as he moved lower, out of her shadowy view and lifted her legs. She bit down on her lips, barely able to contain the desire swelling within.

The flick of his tongue against her small bud sent a wild current of pleasure tearing through her pelvis. Her thighs shook uncontrollably in his firm hands. She arched her back when he followed a second flick with a deep plunge of his tongue. In and out and all around, his mouth did things she never imagined possible.

He licked and sucked and used his fingers all at the same time, driving her into frenzied passion, left limp, yet tense, gasping for air, thirsty for release. "Oh, Derek, the things you do to me," she breathed.

He slowly rose up, lowered himself over her, and slid his shaft inside her with a single slick plunge. He gazed into her eyes and grasped her wrists above her head.

The way he moved within her, it was as though he knew every inch of her body and how she would physically respond to his increasing rhythm, making sure to strike her sensitive pearl with each slick stroke.

Still inside her, he paused and nuzzled her neck. "I love you," he said in a low throaty growl.

She throbbed with need, her insides swelling and growing moister. "Don't stop, Derek, she whispered. "Take me."

Warm lips suckled her neck, each kiss more urgent than the last. "Do you love me?" he asked.

Her head spun as he dove deeper, and his nails dug into her wrists. Sensations of both pain and pleasure added to her arousal. "I'm yours, Derek, you know I am."

His fingernails dug deeper. He plunged again. "Tell me you love me," he said against her neck. His tongue darted out, tracing a line across her throat.

His breathing intensified as he plunged faster, sending her so close to the edge of ultimate desire she had to bite her lip to keep from crying out.

"Say it," he demanded.

"I do, Derek," she said, reaching the brink of ecstasy, not caring one morsel that she had bitten her lip so hard she could taste blood. He moved faster and faster until everything went blinding white. She moaned and breathed and tried to yank her wrists free, but he held them like a vise grip. "I love you, Derek. I'll love you … for all eternity."

Chapter Twenty

Her words came at me in slow motion. *I love you, Derek … for all eternity.*

I plunged into her sweet depths, nipping and tasting her supple neck, my arousal for her near the brink of climax. "I love you," I whispered in return against her throat. "I'll always love you, Erin."

Erin.

Dear God in heaven. I had just told Erin that I loved her. And I'd meant every word. I truly had fallen for this modern woman who, for years, had turned my life upside down during my attempts to lure Ersule into my greedy trap. I adored the headstrong woman who resembled my wife in every physical way possible, but was really nothing like her, at all.

I released her wrists and slowed my pace, trying to keep my wits.

Dammit!

Perhaps it hadn't been such a good idea to have Mrs. Schauss fill my goblet with burgundy wine rather than the numbing blood cocktail. The moment was close at hand, but my mind was nowhere near rational or ready for deductive reasoning. Feeling Erin's beating cord of blood against my urgent tongue, the taste of her, dear God, I could sense the wolf inside me beckoning escape.

Please, not just yet. I need to think!

Erin, the woman beneath me, her body writhing with pleasure, her essence, *her soul,* all meant the world to me.

The world.

Oh God.

If I proceeded with my devious plan, what would become of her? Would my submissive Ersule return with absolutely no hint of my spirited Erin? Would the vivacious woman known to the contemporary world of today merely *vanish?*

I rose up on my hands and stared at Erin. Beautiful, willful Erin. What if this was all a mistake, an error of monumental proportions?

"Derek," she breathed, her cheeks flushing with intense desire in the glowing amber candlelight.

I groaned involuntarily. "My love." I winced, forcing the vile beast clawing inside my belly to remain trapped. I clenched my jaw and gritted my teeth. If I climaxed now, I could lose all control. If only I could delay the shift while I gathered my thoughts.

I reached for her goblet on the night table and drank. *Two swallows. Not nearly enough.* My fingers trembled as I set the chalice down.

She grasped my chin and angled it toward the candlelight. Her gaze narrowed as she assessed me closely. "Your eyes are wildly blue tonight."

Soft hands drew my shaft back inside her. I wanted to scream as I gazed at the moon mocking me from the bedroom window. I shivered, for the scene before me felt all too familiar.

I plunged again. And again. And again.

Erin closed her eyes and pulled me into a deep kiss as her body gave way to rising passion.

Blood. Dear God, I tasted blood. Ersule's blood. Erin's blood.

I clutched a thick strand of her hair and wrapped it around my hand, tasting the succulent drops upon her tongue as I drove deep inside her silky depths. I moved faster, unable to pull away even if she begged me to stop. Her soft, primal whimpers of pleasure called, and I growled, my arousal at the brink of no return.

She moaned, clearly provoked by the intensity of my desire.

"*Derek*," she murmured. "Such an animal you are tonight."

The moment she uttered those familiar words, I froze.

Her eyelids flew open. Frowning, she looked at me, unblinking, and I watched as trepidation rose within the emerald stare.

Suddenly, her eyes paled, grew faraway, dazed, as though she were trying to remember an uncomfortable vision.

Her rising unease and my instinctual need to claim her only fueled my growing desperation. I yanked her wrists above her head, digging my nails into her soft flesh, demanding the beast inside me remain hidden. I turned from her gaze, unable to look into her inquisitive eyes any longer.

Instantly, the wolf inside sensed the physical power I had over the small creature and seized my moment of weakness.

I released her wrists and shoved her thigh, attempting to flip her onto her stomach. Erin resisted my forceful maneuver to no avail, and just as our eyes met, flames of terror rose within her emerald stare.

She cried out, "What are you doing?"

I moaned like a wounded beast and spilled my seed within her moist depths. Panting and breathless, my gaze snapped to the rising moon through the window, my ears tuned to the howling chorus of my small awaiting pack, who'd endured much and for so many years to ensure our survival.

Though terror radiated within her moist eyes, something paralleling pity resided, too.

She quickly sat up. With a firm hand, she gripped my tense jaw and forced my face to hers. With the visceral changes threatening to consume me, I could shift in a flash. I forced my gaze away from hers and faced the luminous moonlight slanting through the window.

"Look at me," she whispered so softly it could have been the gentle song of a mourning dove. " 'Tis only you I love. Come back to me. Come back to me, Derek."

My heart stopped dead.

Erin's hands fell limp to her sides. She scooted to the edge of the bed. I gripped her shoulders. "What did you say?"

She looked at me as though I'd gone mad.

"I … I didn't say anything, or at least I don't think I did." She rubbed her temples. "I feel so strange. So *very* strange." She scrunched her eyes tightly shut. "I'm remembering something. Something from long ago, I think, and fear looms each time I edge toward recollection." She grabbed my hand. "Feel my heart."

I placed my hand upon her chest. Her heart beat like that of a trapped hare awaiting slaughter, blood pounding, pounding, pounding.

"Visions like nightmares," she said, lifting her gaze, "and only when I'm with you."

My jaw tightened with pain, the first sign of the inevitable shift. I cleared my throat, watching the firelight claw the bedroom walls.

"I see a fire in a stone hearth," she whispered. She cast her gaze toward the fireplace. "Much like the one in this very room. I'm drinking from a tankard. I see … "

She flinched, and I felt her heart stop only to resume with a monstrous thud against my hand.

She gazed up at me, terror flooding her eyes. "I see you. I see *you*, Derek!"

In a flurry of naked flesh, she tossed my hand aside, rose from the bed, and snatched her clothing.

I rose. "Wait, please. Let me explain —"

"I cannot. I'm so frightened."

She staggered. I reached for her and gripped her shoulders to steady her gait. "Perhaps you should sit —"

"No!" She swatted my hand and jerked away. "Ouch! What's that — on your hand?"

I looked at my palms and saw nothing unusual. Then I turned

my hands over. Several bristled hairs had already thrust forth across my knuckles.

She gasped.

I quickly reached out for her.

"Don't touch me!" she shouted, slowly backing away.

Desperation fueled the beast. My jaw tightened until it throbbed. I groaned as the steady shift began its merciless course.

Her eyes widened with fear. "It's you. In my visions, in my dreams. It's *always* been you!"

I had risked everything, *everything* on this moment, and the thought of being with neither woman was like a metal spike thrust straight through my dark heart. I couldn't let Erin go.

I *would not* let her go.

"Erin, my love." I extended my hand toward her. "I must explain —"

In a flash, she reached in her dress pocket and withdrew a sheathed knife with a polished wooden handle. She yanked the covering from the shiny blade, her eyes fixed steadily upon mine. Trembling hands pointed the dagger toward me. "Stay away," she shouted. "I mean it!"

I held up my hands. "What are you doing?" My breath caught in my throat at the sound of my deepening voice. The small swallows of cocktail had slowed the shift, but I knew it would soon wear off.

"I've carried this ever since the wolves attacked me. Don't come near me, Derek." She cocked her head and listened to the feral chorus outside. She bundled her clothes in her arms and slowly stepped backwards, toward the bedroom door. "Keep away!"

Candlelight flashed against the dagger blade. She opened the door, her eyes locked upon mine, then slammed it shut behind her. I heard her run along the hallway and close a door. The click of the metal lock echoed off the hardwood floors.

I grabbed my trousers and saw more blades of dark golden hair had sprung across my knuckles.

Christ!

I stepped into my trousers and opened the bedroom door. At the end of the long hallway, Erin opened the bathroom door standing in bare feet, wearing her dress and carrying her undergarments and shoes. She saw me, shrieked, and fled toward the front door.

My gut turned to knots of desperation. I bolted after her. A door opened in the hallway, and Hannah stepped out. I ran into her with a loud thud, nearly knocking the servant over.

Hannah wobbled, her eyes wide with fright. "Sweet Jesus, Master Derek," she said, tugging at her crocheted nightcap.

Lord. The only mortal servant in the household. She'd never understand this twisted mess. I gripped her shoulders. "Stand aside, woman."

Her chubby feet padded backwards. "Oh, yes, sir."

Erin unlocked the front door and escaped outside. I sprinted after her, stopping at the entry, trying to get a lock on which direction she had headed. Light snow had begun to fall, and the whipping wind clawed my face with icy fingers.

Dammit! I snatched my boots sitting in the entry and thrust them over my bare feet.

My throat tightened, and my heart pounded so fiercely I feared it could flee from my chest. I retrieved my coat from the iron hook and ran down the front porch. My gaze darted to the right, the left. Wet snowflakes plopped on my face and eyelids, obscuring my view.

I heard her voice and turned.

There.

Up ahead stood Erin, talking to the driver as she stepped inside the open buggy. The driver cracked the whip with a mighty snap, and off they sped down the snow-dusted street. It only took a moment before my senses picked up the evil scent left in their fleeing wake.

Chapter Twenty-One

"But how did you know I was here?"

"For heaven's sake, Erin. Where else would you be? You've been out of your mind carrying on with this man, without a rational thought in your head for some time now. I was on my way to fetch you before you compromised yourself further."

As they sped down the icy streets, Erin swallowed hard and looked back. Best she could tell, Derek hadn't followed her. A sudden, painful emptiness rivaling her fear swept over her.

The buggy made a turn northward. Erin frowned. "Aren't you taking me straight home?"

Brown eyes narrowed to slits. "Don't you think that would be the first place he'd look for you?"

"Yes, I suppose you're right," she murmured.

With a heavy sigh, Erin put on her socks and shoes and gazed at the falling snowflakes. She needed time to think before she could discuss what had unfolded with Derek.

Dear God in heaven.

And just what *had* happened? She had made love with Derek, given her body and heart to him, and she had felt his unwavering love in return.

But the penetrating visions and nightmares could no longer be ignored.

Somewhere in those horrible apparitions lurked Derek. Each time before, she had been able to push the frightening vision away.

Recalling the intensity of his blue eyes while they had made love, she shivered at the implication. Little doubt remained. The eyes that had gazed at her with such love and longing moments ago were identical to the wild blue eyes she had seen in her visions … and the night of the wolf attack.

The horses slowed to a trot as they neared the lyrical sound of lapping water. Flurries fell in splats across her forehead. Up until that moment, pure fear had kept her warm, but now she was icy cold to the touch. She rummaged under the seat and pulled out a wool blanket.

"This wind bites me to the core," she said, draping the blanket over her head and clutching it tightly shut with both near-frozen hands.

They rode silently in the quiet cold of night. She gazed upward, watching the dark, snowy clouds spread out like an opaque fog, obscuring the silvery moon. A chorus of howls and wails echoed in the distance, sending a charge straight up her backbone.

The buggy slowed and finally stopped. Erin narrowed her gaze, trying to focus amid the darkness consuming the area. She could make out nothing other than the soft glow of water up ahead. Puzzled, she frowned. "But why are we stopping here? We're in the middle of nowhere."

"I want to pull the top up on the buggy."

Erin rolled her eyes. "Yes, of course. That's a good idea."

The charcoal sky released the last white snowflakes with a gust of icy air, and a sliver of moonlight angled across the water, illuminating their surroundings.

They were near the water's edge, next to the train tracks. The odors of moldering wood crates, rusted crab traps, and old fishing nets permeated the air. She glanced around. "Good heavens, why are we here?"

"Get out of the buggy."

Erin's teeth chattered. "No. I don't want to. It's cold, and this place is disgusting. Now let's get out of here and go someplace warm. I need to think before heading home."

"I said, get out of the buggy. *Now.*"

Erin frowned. "What's gotten into you?"

The woman snorted and pulled something from her pocket. A flicker of moonlight illuminated the barrel of a pistol pointed squarely at Erin's chest.

She stared at the servant. "What the … have you gone mad?"

"Get out now, or I'll drag you out myself," Maggie said.

Erin slowly reached inside her dress pocket, searching for the knife.

Maggie waved the pistol. "Put your hands up, Missy. Right where I can see them."

Erin raised her empty hands. The blanket slipped from her shoulders, landing in a heavy woolen pool at her feet.

Seagulls squawked as they flew overhead, and small wooden boats anchored nearby bobbed against gentle waves. The wind carried earthy, salty scents of low tide, algae, and dead fish, making her stomach instantly curdle.

"Get down." Maggie ordered.

Flashing the servant a menacing glare, Erin stepped down to the rocky ground below. "What's going on here?"

"Put your hands up again where I can see them," she said, waving the gun. "You're as senseless as your mother was, aren't you?"

Erin raised her hands, confusion and anger piercing her ribs with each breath. "My mother?"

How could Maggie say such a mean-spirited remark about a woman she claimed to have loved like a sister? She stared, unblinking, at the gun held within Maggie's firm grasp. This wasn't the servant she had known her entire life. Not the plump woman who had tended each and every fever, skinned knee, and bruise when she was just a small girl. Clearly, the woman had gone mad.

Haunting howls and feral yips ricocheted off the high cliffs, the eerie sounds carried by the icy wind. Erin's fingertips tingled as a surge of blood blasted from her torso into her chilled limbs. She nodded slowly and spoke steadily. "Whatever you want, Maggie, it's yours, but we have to get out of here."

The servant laughed in a low throaty growl. "Whatever you want, it's yours," she mocked.

Erin scanned the desolate surroundings. "Why have you brought me here? Why the gun?"

Dark clouds slipped in front of the moon, and wild howls flooded the night, sending a cold current through her veins. Though frightened to the core, she summoned the courage to speak with authority. "I demand you explain yourself right now, Maggie."

The wind kicked up, and the shadowy clouds moved aside, allowing light to reflect over the water, illuminating the area.

The servant's eyes glowed. "That's what your mother said. 'Explain yourself, Maggie. You have some explaining to do, Maggie.' The woman simply knew too much to keep around any longer."

"*What?* What are you talking about? My mother died of consumption."

"Oh, she had consumption all right. Lasted longer than anyone thought possible. Put on this Earth to protect you, I'm sure." With each sentence, Maggie's voice grew deeper. "Your mother was on to me. Challenged me. I merely put an end to her misery."

Erin struggled for breath, recalling her mother's death in detail. "The death certificate stated she died of consumption."

"Yes, it does. It doesn't mention that she died with a little help from me in the way of lethal poison —"

"Stop!" Erin turned, fighting the sobs rising in her throat. Right before her mother had died, the doctor had said, "If I didn't know better, your mother would appear to be suffering from the effects of a poisonous toxin." But he had immediately followed his comment with a shrug, saying, "But of course she's been very ill for years. Your mother's time has come."

The sounds of the wild animals neared, claws clicking against the iron railroad tracks and wooden slats. Erin's heart hammered. She inhaled deep breaths and exhaled slowly, trying to remain in control.

"Put away the gun, Maggie. This is ridiculous. We have to get out of here." Over Maggie's shoulder, she caught sight of two shadowy figures coming toward them. "Help! Help me!"

Maggie held the pistol steadily within her grip and laughed. "Your cry for help falls on deaf ears, I assure you."

The couple walked leisurely toward them, clearly in no hurry to offer their assistance. Alongside a tall man, the woman's unmistakable flowing red hair glowed under the soft moonlight as they neared.

Through blinding tears, Erin glared at Maggie. "You're a horrible woman. I don't understand any of this! Why, Maggie? Why would you kill my mother?"

The servant slowly shook her head. "It was written in the stars a long time ago, child."

A paralyzing icy shiver rushed through her Erin's body as the pair advanced toward them. "Madame Delacour," she murmured.

"In the flesh," Regine said, stepping before her, a seductive smile spread across her lips. The man beside her grinned wickedly, and his golden brown eyes smoldered as his gaze wandered the length of Erin's quaking form. He looked like Derek, only different, sinister, eyes even wilder if that were possible.

Dizziness assaulted her. Maggie rushed forward and steadied her. "Stand straight, my dear. Don't you know royalty when you see it?"

Regine raised her chin and stared at Maggie. "You've done well, Charmaine."

Erin scrunched her nose and mouthed, *"Charmaine?"*

"Always at your service, my Queen." Maggie bowed dramatically, "And to you, my Prince." Maggie's eyes bored into Erin's. "Meet Prince Rudolpho. Soon to be *King* Rudolpho."

Sobering her instantly, heated anger rushed to Erin's cheeks as she stared at Regine Delacour. "Royalty? That's absurd. You're a madam — a prostitute!"

Rudolpho lurched forward and growled.

Erin gasped. "Stay away from me!"

Regine grabbed his arm. "Keep calm, Rudolpho. You'll have your turn with Miss Richland in just a moment." She cast her gaze toward Erin, appraising her from head to toe. "Feisty, isn't she, son?"

Rudolpho's eyes glowed like the dying embers of a smoldering fire. He licked his lips. "I prefer the meek, wayward lambs on Chestnut, but she'll certainly do."

With the subtlety of a lightning bolt, dawning comprehension smacked Erin between the eyes. It was Rudolpho who had murdered those poor fallen women down on Chestnut. Her face twisted with disgust as she surveyed the handsome, well-dressed man with the wild eyes described by Pearl.

Erin stepped forward and pointed a hard finger in his chest. "It was you!"

Rudolpho chuckled, clearly amused. *"Moi?"*

"Ever since the two of you arrived in Everett, the city has been turned upside down with … with —"

"With what?" Rudolpho tilted his head. "Maulings? Mayhem? Madness? The murders you so *brilliantly* wrote about in the newspaper?"

Erin lunged forward, teetering on the tips of her shoes. "How dare you mock me! You're no prince — you're pure evil!" Maggie yanked her back into place.

Rudolpho's expression turned grave, his attention clearly diverted. He lifted his nose high in the air and sniffed the breeze. "They near."

Regine rolled her eyes and put her hand on her hip. "Of course they near. That's what we want."

Regine's gaze snapped to Erin. "You're with child, Miss Richland. Are you aware of that?"

Erin turned from Regine's heated stare.

Regine Delacour turned on her heel. "Fine. There's no need for your confirmation. I've known you've been carrying Derek's child for quite some time."

Erin's eyes narrowed to slits as she surveyed the red-head. "What business is it of yours if I am?"

Regine gritted her teeth, her eyes blazing with anger. "Oh, it's very much my business." She patted her son on the back so hard he pitched forward and coughed. "And very much Rudolpho's business, as well. Between you and King Rudliff, I can't determine which one to kill first. You're both of equal threat now that you carry his child."

Had this woman lost her mind? Had all three of them gone stark raving mad? *King Rudliff?* What the hell was Regine talking about? Apparently, she held a bigger torch for Derek than she had originally thought.

Erin snorted. "*King?* Are you insane?"

Maggie lowered the gun and sighed. "My Queen, she hasn't a clue."

Regine's eyebrows rose high, and a flash of humor glinted in her eyes. "Is this so?" She slowly paced around Erin, hands clasped behind her back. "I suppose we'll just have to enlighten her, won't we, Charmaine?"

The howls and yips of the approaching beasts suddenly stopped dead, taking the foursome by surprise.

Before Erin had time to contemplate her move, she twisted and grabbed the gun from Maggie's hand. In a flash, she threw it as far as she could, letting out a sigh when she heard the splash in the water.

The moon illuminated the deep, angry lines spread across Maggie's face. "You should *not* have done that." She lifted her hand and formed a fist.

Erin flinched, waiting for the impact that never came. She opened her eye a sliver and saw Regine clutching Maggie's balled fist.

"Don't worry about that now, Charmaine. We have bigger problems."

Rudolpho slipped behind Erin and gripped her hands behind her back. The bones in her wrists rubbed together. She winced, fighting back the blinding pain in silence.

He leaned forward and inhaled deeply. "You smell divine," he whispered against her ear. His dry lips grazed the nape of her bare neck. "I imagine you'll taste just as sweet."

She thought she would pass out and fall straight to the ground in a limp heap, but he held her firmly in his clutches, keeping her upright.

"Help!" she managed to shriek. Suddenly, his large hand covered her mouth so tightly she couldn't bite down.

"Enough!" Rudolpho shouted.

His breath smelled like damp decaying earth. Instantly, her skin crawled.

She caught movement out of the corner of her eye. Dark shadows, high upon the cliff, moved swiftly down the bluff. Below, a pack of wolves, their haunches lowered, rushed like large rats along the tracks heading straight for the descending shadows.

Icy terror flooded her veins, and feral animal scents blasted into her nostrils, as the odor of wild creatures grew closer.

"Hold her tight!" Regine commanded.

There was no doubt about it. She was going to die if she didn't try something, *anything!*

Maggie leaned in. "I can see you thinking, Missy. You forget, I know you all too well."

Erin scowled at the older woman patting her down and rummaging through her dress pockets.

Maggie pulled out the sheathed knife and smiled. "Well, look what we've got here."

Erin's heart sank to her toes.

"Wait? What's that, coming down the bluff?" Rudolpho asked.

Regine turned, just as frightening yelps echoed into the night. Growls and yips and whines of pain ricocheted across the cliffs, reverberating in all directions.

Rudolpho raised his head and howled. Regine yipped in reply.

Erin froze, paralyzed with fear. She couldn't move now even if she tried.

In a flurry of movement, Rudolpho removed his hand from her mouth and roped her hands together, tying them in a tight bind behind her back.

She cried out, unable to hide the pain as the ropes dug into her flesh.

Maggie growled as though tortured. Rudolpho did the same, and Regine cried out in the night like an injured animal. Breathless with fear and near collapse, Erin watched in horror as the bodies of the morphing trio contorted and twisted, wild animal sounds coming from massive jaws glistening with saliva, as their clothes tore away, splitting like thin paper from their bodies.

Instinct to survive swelled from within, feet-first. Before she knew it, Erin took off running in her unfastened shoes, the binding ropes behind her back. She ran and ran, leaping over driftwood and dodging the slippery seaweed and barnacle-covered rocks dotting the darkened shoreline.

She glanced over her shoulder to see Maggie, Regine, and Rudolpho, each hunched on all four legs, their bodies covered in fur, as they sped toward the frightening sounds of wild animals fighting in a boisterous horde.

"Oh, God, oh, dear God in heaven," she prayed as she fled for her life. Her foot caught on the edge of a large piece of driftwood. She fell hard and hit her head and kneecap against the rocky shore.

Warm blood trickled down her temple. Stars danced before her, and stinging tears flooded her eyes. She wiggled and arched her back, trying to rise from the ground, but without the use of her hands for support, her injured knee collapsed beneath her.

She lay on the desolate beach, alone, terrified, hearing the horrifying sounds of wild animals in a vicious fight to the death.

If only Derek were here!

She blinked, and puddled tears streamed down her scraped cheeks. Ignoring the cutting pain, she rolled to her side, curled in a ball of injured flesh, and closed her eyes.

No doubt remained. Tonight she would die.

Chapter Twenty‑Two

I inhaled deeply, and the scent of Erin's fresh wounds blasted into my nostrils. I sprinted as fast as I could, determined to keep the emerging beast at bay. But hearing the harrowing sounds of my *Weres* fighting to the death with Queen Regine's formidable *Shes*, the more the animal inside me took hold.

Coarse hair burst forth, covering my hands. My jaw grew so tight I knew it was only a matter of time before I emerged a killer wolf.

I had to reach Erin, and fast.

Why hadn't I thought to drink of the cocktail before fleeing the house?

Wait.

I stopped in my tracks, tunneled through my coat pocket, and retrieved the flask. My fingers shook as I tried to unscrew the cap and pour the liquid into my mouth. *Drops. Only warm drops.* I tossed the flask into the wiry mounds of bramble bushes and tore after Erin.

I hurried down the bluff a safe distance north of the fighting near the tracks. The echoes and thuds of battling beasts bounded off cliffs, slicing through the darkness of night. Frightened birds squawked and screeched above, wings flapping hastily from sheltering roosts. Escaping vermin scurried near my feet in a frenzy of wavering brush clinging precariously to the bluff.

I jumped the rails at the base of the cliff and ran toward the shoreline. Odors of feral animal blood and gore permeated the moist air, baffling my senses, as I tried to detect Erin's exact location.

I stopped, closed my eyes, and lifted my nose high in the air.

My love, where are you?

I caught the aroma; the sweet, succulent scent that belonged to Ersule, and to Erin, mixed with the heady aroma of her fresh blood. A moan near the rocky shoreline caught my attention.

"Erin," I called.

A soft whimper replied.

A gunshot rang out high above the cliff, followed by loud bellows from an angry resident dressed in a bathrobe. The clashing beasts abruptly silenced.

Panic flooded my veins. *Christ. Hurry!*

Terror ripped through my heart with every rushing step. There, on the shoreline ahead, lay a wounded Erin.

I dashed forward, bent low, and cradled her neck with my morphing hands. "Erin," I murmured, though my voice had grown deep and gravely.

Her eyes opened a sliver. "Derek?"

Ropes bound her thin wrists. I fumbled like an eager child, and managed to untie the restraint.

"Maggie. She … "

"Shhh, my love. I know. I've been onto that woman ever since you arrived at my party wearing her grandmother's emerald combs."

"She … she took my knife. She held … a gun."

The sounds of clacking animal nails in flight tore into my skull. The noises drew closer, dozens of approaching wolves following on the heels of the other.

Fear, dread, and the instinctual need to survive the impending onslaught beckoned the wolf inside me.

My throat and jaw throbbed. Illuminated by the moon above, I kicked off my tightening boots as my clothes began tearing to pieces. I growled and hissed as mounds of smooth muscles under tufts of bristled golden hair burst forth.

Quickly, I scooped Erin into my arms.

"Take me away," she whispered before wilting into my arms.

Shiny hairpins reflecting the silver moonlight dropped on my feet, and her ebony hair tumbled, soft as silk against my muscled arm. Determined to keep her alive, I gently licked the bloody wound on her temple.

She stirred and whispered, "I'm dying, Derek."

"Hold tight, my love." Tears filled my eyes to brimming. Silently, I cursed every moment I had walked this earth. Cursed meeting Ersule. Cursed luring Erin into my wicked, devious, selfish trap. What kind of man was I? With the answer looming before me, ugly and as dark as the devil himself, I gnashed my growing teeth together.

I'm a man trapped between worlds of moral men and evil beasts.

Regine yipped franticly, rushing and nipping at Gregore's lean, furred legs, only inches behind him. The horde of wolves suddenly made a sharp turn and headed straight for us.

"Watch out, King!" yelped Edgar.

My eyes darted right, left — nothing for rapid shelter except a gathering of driftwood.

I lay Erin down and quickly arranged the pieces of wood. I placed her inside the sheltering area. "Stay still, my love."

I managed to place two more shielding pieces of wood above her small shelter before the first *She* lunged for my throat.

"Ahhhh!" I pounded her snout with my morphing paw and sent her hurling toward the water's edge. Fury mounted, and my limbs swelled into mounds of furred muscle, and my teeth grew into lethal blades jutting from my jawbone.

A second *She* lunged and bit into my arm, tearing away skin and fur. My cry of pain pierced the night sky.

Charlotte leaped into the air, her powerful jaws opened wide, and she tore into the *She* wolf.

I stood on all fours, haunches lowered, snarling, waiting for the next wicked *She* attack.

Gregore ran toward me, his tail and legs bloodied, with Regine snapping and biting mere inches from his muscled haunches. Tired and weak, he darted behind me as Regine and her son, *my son*, came in for the final kill.

Bristled hair rose tall along my back. With Gregore shielded behind me, I dug my thick nails into the dirt, holding my ground, and howled like the mighty King of Beasts I had truly become.

Regine, Rudolpho, and the trailing *Shes* stopped in their tracks, and everything went momentarily silent.

Queen Delacour panted, vapor rising from her large nostrils, her predatory eyes glowing.

My gaze snapped to Rudolpho, the man-beast who would become king of my clan upon my demise, the monster who would become king if the child carried within Erin's womb were slaughtered.

With every ounce of what was left physically human within me, I stared them down and growled, "You will not win!"

Regine lowered her mighty furred skull and slowly approached with Rudolpho by her side.

My weary *Were* clan tread forward and moved in next to me, their voracious eyes glowing in the darkness, feral loins poised for attack.

The queen's wounded, faithful followers lined up beside her, their large bared teeth glistening with fresh blood and gleaming sinew.

A rush of sea air carried the scent of Erin's injuries blasting into my nostrils.

And they smelled it, too.

Ravenous eyes instantly locked upon mine. In a flash, Regine lunged for me, and Rudolpho advanced at lightning speed toward Erin's small shelter.

I dodged Regine's swift advance and took off for Rudolpho. Regine followed, yipping as she shadowed my hindquarters. She was fast, incredibly fast, but my faithful white-furred *Were,* following on the queen's tail, was far faster.

Gregore sprang into action and fled toward Rudolpho, who scrambled like a demon on a mission straight from hell, pushing, tearing, and chewing the driftwood shelter leading straight to my beloved.

Erin screamed, and I saw the horrifying sight of Rudolpho's large head fully immersed within the enclosure and heard the grotesque sounds of his snapping jaws breaking the dark night.

Following on the heels of the faster white *Were* chasing Regine closer to the railroad tracks, Franz yipped wildly.

A *She* lunged for Gregore, and the two fought in a rolling ball of fur near the water's edge.

I attacked Rudolpho and bit hard into his shoulder, ripping fur and muscle from bone.

He yelped in a flash of pain. More determined than ever, he scratched and pawed violently at Erin.

Moonlight shimmered above the growing fog threatening to cover the area like a shroud. For a split second, my eyes locked with Erin's through the slats of the driftwood barrier.

"Come back to me, Derek," she said.

My God!

I tore into Rudolpho with everything I had, but he had managed to force his head deep within the shelter.

An agonizing scream of pain tore through the darkness, and the smell of Erin's deep wound permeated the air. I growled, ripped, and slashed, this time biting into Rudolpho's throat and not letting go. I forced his massive body to the ground and hovered over him.

Panting, bloodied, and wounded, he stared up at me, his glowing eyes seething with fury.

A sound both quiet and deafening arose from the small enclosure. At that exact moment, I knew that my evil, desperate son had inflicted a mortal wound on the woman I had vowed to love for all eternity.

A beam of light from the south came into view, followed by the clacking of an approaching train slicing the dark mantle of death. A massive shriek pierced the night as the roaring train passed.

I ripped into Rudolpho's chest with my jaws. He fought back with sharp, curled claws tearing into my legs. The clamor from the battling *Weres* stopped abruptly. Undaunted, Rudolpho and I fought to the death.

I wouldn't let go. *Not ever.* I needed his wounds to go especially deep. Deep enough for a true *Were* kill.

From somewhere behind me, Gregore called, "Queen Regine Delacour is dead."

Rudolpho growled and cried out, *"Nooooo!"*

His seething gaze snapped to mine, his glowing amber eyes simmering with hatred. "I was born to be king!" he spat. "Do you hear me? I must be king!"

The remaining *Shes* sniffed the air and fled, their yips of mourning and fear tearing across the night sky.

A steady flow of blood poured from the deep wounds I'd inflicted on Rudolpho's chest. Sensing the end of the madness lay near, I salivated, drool dripping from my mouth, landing lazily upon his muzzle.

Growing weaker, his body wilted, and his glowing eyes paled like the waning rays of the evening sun.

"Surely, you felt something for my mother all these years," he whispered. "You would not kill your own son, would you, Father?"

Father. My God.

My stomach knotted. Centuries ago, Ersule and I had longed to be parents. A daughter, a son, the gender of our child would never have mattered. But month after month, our hopes had dimmed to black. Now, my blood son lay begging for his life with haunting words.

At the moment of Queen Regine's death, Rudolpho had become king of his own *She* clan. But his dominant mother had raised him to be as malicious as she, demanding respect rather than earning it. Like her, he wanted it all, to rule the ancient bloodlines and spread evil. This murdering, man-beast was nothing I could ever have imagined in a son … or have ever wanted. His feeble attempt at binding us as father and son could never succeed, for he would destroy all that was true, dear, and worthy, dooming our small clan to extinction.

I recalled Koenig's words from long ago, *"You will know what to do. 'Tis in your blood."*

I forced my eyes from Rudolpho's and stared at the deep wound to his chest exposing his bloodied, beating heart. The injury would have been mortal to any man or beast, but not a strong, determined *Were.*

The image of Abraham leading his son, Isaac, to slaughter raced through my mind as I gazed down at him. This wicked son of mine would kill me, the woman I loved, and our child purely for his own gain. Unlike the biblical story, I knew no angel from heaven above would save Rudolpho's soul at the final hour.

I raked my nails along the shore where shells and smaller pieces of wood littered the rocky beach.

Rudolpho licked his chipped bloodied fangs. "You haven't the guts," he spat. "You're too much mortal and not enough beast!"

Anger heated my throat and stung the back of my eye sockets.

I blinked away the burn.

"You're weak!" he shouted, his eyes glowing fiery amber once again. "Do it, you coward. Do it — I dare you!"

I leaned, grabbed a splintered piece of driftwood with my large teeth, and held it firmly in my powerful jaws.

He spit in my face. "Do it, you coward!"

Wind whipped across the bay in a gust humming an ancient, primitive tune of survival. I held my breath and plunged the sharp end of the wood straight into the gaping wound, piercing his heart.

His wicked heart stopped beating for a moment, then resumed with a slow, steady, determined thud. His eyes slowly widened. "You are an evil beast, same as me. Never forget that. I will see you in hell, Father!"

"You first!" I snarled. I bent low and wedged the wood deeper.

Blood gurgled and dripped from Rudolpho's snout and mouth. His darkened heart skipped a beat, then two, then three.

As the black cloak of death slowly descended, I watched the fire within his hateful gaze slowly fade.

The sudden sound of quiet wounded my ears. I stared at Rudolpho — the lifeless, evil corpse that never should have walked the earth.

I rushed for Erin and tugged and tore at what was left of the small splintered shelter. I nuzzled her bloodied neck.

"Derek," she whispered. Her eyes closed, and she went limp.

My God, she would die a mortal death if I didn't do something quickly.

My eternal love for both Erin and Ersule gave me strength, guiding me forward. I licked and sucked the jagged gashes Rudolpho had inflicted upon her throat.

Humiliation filled my every pore knowing it was I who had caused such damage with my greedy quest for immortal love. But as I tasted her succulent blood, felt the warm liquid drip into my throat, my withered heart sprang to life. If Koenig had spoken the truth all those many years ago, my wife of so long ago would return to me. Piercing guilt gripped my belly, for I had fallen deeply in love with Erin, too.

Erin's heart ceased, and her body grew cold as I devoured the last drops of her sweet blood. Gazing at her motionless eyelids framed by ebony lashes, I willed myself not to crumble into a million pieces as I sat back on my haunches and waited.

And waited.

Hours later, she still lay motionless.

My panic grew with the lengthening shadows of late night. I cursed the moon and stars and anything I could mentally grasp in my rising anger. I nuzzled her icy-cold neck, her face, her nose.

Nothing.

All those years ago, I had tempted fate and made a sinful alliance between the living and the dead. Now my reason for breathing had vanished.

I pulled Erin's cold body close and curled next to her on the rocky shore. Even if I had to spend all of eternity burning in the fires of Hell, I was determined to die alongside my beloved before the break of dawn.

Chapter Twenty-Three

I gasped and opened my eyes.

A blanket of dense fog shrouded the bay as daylight broke. Angry as hell that I had survived the night, I bolted up in my human form, naked as a newborn baby, and tossed off the wool blanket.

Mrs. Schauss was crouched beside me, rubbing Erin's forehead.

"Anything?" I asked?"

She fastened the top button on her dark cloak and shook her head. "No."

What if this had all been for nothing? I dug the heels of my palms into my eyes. "My God, what have I done? What have I done, Mary?"

Mary Schauss rose and touched my chilled shoulder with her warmer hand. "You have done all you can, Derek. Now we must wait. You must have faith."

Faith. I'd carried the heavy weight of faith on my shoulders for over three hundred years. And where had my blind confidence taken me?

As I stared down at the pale, lifeless body of my beloved, I wanted to scream and shout and curse whoever fabricated the ridiculous virtue.

Faith? Faith was a lie.

Mary jutted her chin forward. "I brought your clothes. Over there on that rock."

Her voice pulled me from my dark hole of pity and self-loathing. "Thanks for covering me in the blanket. I saw how fast you sprinted last night. It was you who forced Regine onto the tracks of the approaching train, am I right?"

Nimble fingers brushed a fluttering strand of shock-white hair back into place. "You know there's nothing I wouldn't do for you … or my daughter."

It was true. It had *always* been true.

After discovering her daughter's body in the shallow grave in the meadow, the woman's deep sorrow had led her to edge of madness in the dead of night.

Guided by the aroma of fresh blood, Franz had found Mary Schauss kneeling at the creek bank, self-inflicted knife wounds to her wrists. Devastated, she sobbed and begged for the *Were* to finish her life so that she might join her beloved daughter — her only child — in heaven. Naturally, Franz obliged her desperate request, and we welcomed her within the pack.

After Ersule's rebirth, it had been especially hard on Mary as she watched me fall more in love with Erin with each passing year. And it was she who warned me that a shattered heart was sure to follow if I continued on the destructive path.

But I did fall in love with Erin. Hopelessly in love.

All these many years, Mary had prayed for the return of her charming daughter, Ersule. But unlike me, Mary's reserved nature had never allowed her the luxury of hope and optimism and, yes, *faith*.

Not until now.

As I breathed in the sea air, I sensed Ersule's presence nearby, as though she were whispering over my shoulder, reassuring me that the path I had taken had not been in vain.

Have faith.

I stood and wrapped the wool blanket around my waist, ready

to retrieve my clothes, when a small gurgle resonated from deep within Erin's throat. I gasped and choked out, "Did … did you hear that, Mary?" I dropped to my knees.

Mary stared, unblinking. "I most certainly did."

I brushed windswept hair from Erin's cheeks. By all appearances, the wound upon her neck looked to be healing.

Mary pointed. "Look!"

Erin's wounds grew smaller and smaller, then disappeared completely, and a pink hue rushed to her pale skin.

The air in my lungs sat heavy and stagnant. I was afraid to move or speak, for fear of breaking the spell of what appeared to be life emerging before my very eyes.

I heard a deep inhale of breath, and her rosy lips twitched. Erin slowly licked her parched lips and murmured, "Derek."

Mary crouched down, tears flooding her eyes. "Oh, my God in heaven."

My heart thumped so hard I thought it would explode. I brushed the tears from Erin's eyes and hovered over her. "It's me — it's *me*, my darling."

She stretched and yawned, as though waking from an especially long, peaceful slumber. I pulled her into my arms, tearing steaming down my chilled cheeks, trying desperately not to crush her smaller frame.

"Derek. I remember. I remember … " She stared at Mary, her eyes narrowing as though trying to recall who the woman might be.

Confusion blinded me, and my heart suddenly throbbed with pain. At that moment, I had absolutely no idea which woman I held in my arms.

Erin closed her eyes, "I remember. We had made love."

I'd made love to both Ersule and Erin the night of their deaths. I said, "Oh, my darling, yes. Yes, we made love."

A smile bowed her full lips. "We were in bed, a fire in the hearth.

I couldn't wait to tell you."

Tell me what? I held my breath.

She closed her eyes. "I'm so confused. Memories are flooding through my head from so far away and, yet, from just last night. My father must be worried sick about me." Her eyelids flew open wide, and she gazed up at me. "That night … in our cottage in Bedburg. I knew you were somewhere inside that … that creature."

The breath I'd been holding within my lungs came out in a sudden blast of relief. I wiped my eyes. *Dear God.* I could not have wished for anything more perfect.

I knew exactly who the woman I held in my arms was. She was the love of life, modern, headstrong Erin whom I had grown to love with my entire being, joined with Ersule's memories of our enduring love from centuries past.

I smoothed her ebony hair. "You said you never had the chance to tell me. Tell me what?"

"Mother knew before I did, didn't you?"

Mary smiled and wiped away her tears. "That I did, my darling girl."

Turing her face to me, I was struck by the beguiling smile that had melted my heart centuries earlier.

"I couldn't wait to tell you the wonderful news that I was finally with child, my love," she said. "Our child we had longed for."

Ersule had been with child the night I had viciously taken her life?

My God. And I had killed them both.

I fought back a rising sob. "I … I didn't know," I choked out. "I never would have —"

She pressed her finger to my lips. "Do not mourn, my love. When you told me not to answer to the Angel of Death, I did not."

She placed her hands on her small belly and gazed at me with eyes like sparkling emeralds.

"Alongside you, I have existed somewhere between the living and the dead, between dusk and dawn. Hope is not lost. Hope was never lost, my darling."

Hearing her words, my heart and soul had never felt so full.

She smiled. "I carry our child, Derek, and our dreams of eternal love await us."

Mary lifted her face to the straining sun breaking through the fog and murmured a prayer of gratitude.

My beloved tugged my chin and whispered in my ear. "I will love you for all eternity."

My heart soaring, I kissed her warm lips and whispered, "And I will love you, always and forever, my cherished queen."

The End

"Ode to a Nightingale"

My heart aches, and a drowsy numbness pains
My sense, as though of hemlock I had drunk,
Or emptied some dull opiate to the drains
One minute past, and Lethe-wards had sunk:
'Tis not through envy of thy happy lot,
But being too happy in thine happiness, -
That thou, light-winged Dryad of the trees,
In some melodious plot
Of beechen green and shadows numberless,
Singest of summer in full-throated ease.

O, for a draught of vintage! that hath been
Cool'd a long age in the deep-delved earth,
Tasting of Flora and the country green,
Dance, and Provençal song, and sunburnt mirth!
O for a beaker full of the warm South,
Full of the true, the blushful Hippocrene,
With beaded bubbles winking at the brim,
And purple-stained mouth;
That I might drink, and leave the world unseen,
And with thee fade away into the forest dim:

Fade far away, dissolve, and quite forget
What thou among the leaves hast never known,
The weariness, the fever, and the fret
Here, where men sit and hear each other groan;
Where palsy shakes a few, sad, last gray hairs,
Where youth grows pale, and spectre-thin, and dies;
Where but to think is to be full of sorrow
And leaden-eyed despairs,
Where Beauty cannot keep her lustrous eyes,

Or new Love pine at them beyond to-morrow.
          Away! away! for I will fly to thee,
          Not charioted by Bacchus and his pards,
          But on the viewless wings of Poesy,
          Though the dull brain perplexes and retards:
          Already with thee! tender is the night,
          And haply the Queen-Moon is on her throne,
              Cluster'd around by all her starry Fays;
                  But here there is no light,
          Save what from heaven is with the breezes blown
          Through verdurous glooms and winding mossy ways.

          I cannot see what flowers are at my feet,
          Nor what soft incense hangs upon the boughs,
          But, in embalmed darkness, guess each sweet
          Wherewith the seasonable month endows
          The grass, the thicket, and the fruit-tree wild;
          White hawthorn, and the pastoral eglantine;
              Fast fading violets cover'd up in leaves;
                  And mid-May's eldest child,
          The coming musk-rose, full of dewy wine,
          The murmurous haunt of flies on summer eves.

          Darkling I listen; and, for many a time
          I have been half in love with easeful Death,
          Call'd him soft names in many a mused rhyme,
          To take into the air my quiet breath;
          Now more than ever seems it rich to die,
          To cease upon the midnight with no pain,
          While thou art pouring forth thy soul abroad
                  In such an ecstasy!
          Still wouldst thou sing, and I have ears in vain -
              To thy high requiem become a sod.
          Thou wast not born for death, immortal Bird!

No hungry generations tread thee down;
The voice I hear this passing night was heard
In ancient days by emperor and clown:
Perhaps the self-same song that found a path
Through the sad heart of Ruth, when, sick for home,
She stood in tears amid the alien corn;
The same that oft-times hath
Charm'd magic casements, opening on the foam
Of perilous seas, in faery lands forlorn.
Forlorn! the very word is like a bell
To toll me back from thee to my sole self!
Adieu! the fancy cannot cheat so well
As she is fam'd to do, deceiving elf.
Adieu! adieu! thy plaintive anthem fades
Past the near meadows, over the still stream,
Up the hill-side; and now 'tis buried deep
In the next valley-glades:
Was it a vision, or a waking dream?
Fled is that music: — Do I wake or sleep?

— John Keats

A word about the author . . .

Diana grew up in Virginia where her love of American History began. Living near an abandoned Civil War graveyard as a child sparked her active imagination with tales of honor, romance and things that go bump in the night. She enjoys writing about strong heroines up to the challenge of fighting harsh circumstances while taming the heart of the man she loves.

Diana resides in Nevada. Visit her at www.dianaballew.com.

Also from Diana Ballew

Thorns of Eden — Trifecta Publishing House
Bound by Glory — Coming 2016 — Trifecta Publishing House